I0628983

NOVICES IN LOVE

CAROL ANNE DOUGLAS

SISTER MATTHEW AND SISTER ROSE: NOVICES IN LOVE
Copyright 2021 Carol Anne Douglas

Hermione Books
2701 Connecticut Ave NW #300
Washington, DC 20008

ALL RIGHTS RESERVED
Published in the United States of America

ISBN 978-0-9967722-9-7

Cover Art ©2021 Terry Roy
Cover Design and Interior Layout by Terry Roy
www.TERyvisions.com

No part of this book may be reproduced in any form or by any electronic or mechanical means, including information storage and retrieval systems, without written permission from the author, except for the use of brief quotations in a book review.

This book is a work of fiction. Names, characters, places and incidents are products of the author's imagination. Any resemblance to real people or current events is purely coincidental.

First Paperback Edition

Hermione

REVIEWS FOR

Sister Matthew and Sister Rose
Novices in Love

"Leave your worldly selves behind, all ye who enter here. Can women-loving convent novices Rose and Mattie really do this? Enter with them as they explore themselves and each other. You will likely find it a very interesting and enticing journey."

Camarin Grae, author of *The Secret in the Bird* and *Edgewise*

"A faith-challenged novice and her "particular friend" take cloistered life to new heights. *Sister Matthew and Sister Rose: A Love Story* is a witty, humorous, and deeply thoughtful story about finding one's true passion. There's even a murder mystery."

Becky Bohan, author of *A Light on Altered Land*

"Why does a nice Jewish girl like me love a book about nuns? Because it's written by Carol Anne Douglas, a brilliant author who makes me chuckle, cry, and marvel on alternate pages. And because I've learned from her that some nuns, a mysterious group of women I never understood, never traded their humanity when they donned their habits."

Ellen Levy, author of *Romance at Stonegate*

"An in-depth examination of convent life in the 1960s that is both poignant and insightful."

Elena Graf, author of *Occasions of Sin*

"...Douglas does a fantastic job of building out her fictional world and putting the romance at the center of it. A deeply thoughtful and well- developed love story."

Kirkus Reviews

"Douglas has done a fine job of telling the love story of two novice nuns in a Catholic convent... The detailing of the convent, the appreciation of the little tastes of nature these novices are allowed, and the characters' constant, varied conflicts, all mesh into a captivating story of a little-known way of life that may try to, but cannot quell lesbian passion."

Lee Lynch

Books by Carol Anne Douglas

Novels
Lancelot: Her Story
Lancelot and Guinevere

For Young Adults
The Merlin's Shakespeare Series
Merlin's Shakespeare
The Mercutio Problem

Nonfiction
Love and Politics: Radical Feminist and Lesbian Theories

This book is dedicated to the Carefree Writers' Circle, my friends who have supported me as it developed: Dana Finnegan, Becky Bohan, Sara Fleming, Connie Fried, Cookie Gibbs, Mary Gay Hutcherson, Barbara Lea, Ellen Levy, Lois McGuinness, Harriet Miller, Esther Newton, Barbara Slater, Sara Yager, and Anne Zak.

It is also dedicated to all the Catholic girls who wanted to join the convent—and all the nuns who left the convent. Also to my childhood friend, Brigie O'Brien, who has passed on.

Everything I write is dedicated in my heart to my infinitely dear partner Mandy Doolittle and my loving mother, Joan Flannery Douglas, both of whom have passed on.

Sister Matthew and Sister Rose
NOVICES IN LOVE

Carol Anne Douglas

Chapter 1

Sister Matthew

St. Euphrosnye's Convent, Western Maryland
Summer 1962

S ILENCE WILL KILL ME. I might as well be mute.

I try to enjoy the beauty of the arched, stone cloisters as I mince my way along in tiny steps. I long to shout. I long to run. But novices can't raise their voices or stretch their legs. At least fresh air, not incense, fills my lungs.

I am living in the midst of people, sealed off from each other as if we each had a wall built around her.

I don't believe God wants nuns to live such an isolated life. I don't even believe God is a He, though I didn't dare say so. How could God possibly be male or female?

Instead of saying silent prayers, I recall Robert Browning's *Soliloquy of the Spanish Cloister.*

"G-r-r-r-there go my heart's abhorrence!

Water your damn flowerpots, do!

If hate killed men, Brother Lawrence,

God's blood, would not mine kill you!"

Do the sisters make a mistake when they admit English majors to the convent? Especially English majors who graduated cum laude from secular universities.

Unlike Browning's monk, I don't hate any of my convent sisters, not even the Mistress of Novices, Mean Mother Michael. (The only person I ever hated was one of my high school classmates. I don't want to think about her.) But silently reciting that impious verse makes me feel better. I just want the sisters to shout or jump or do something to break these wretched rules. I want to act as if we were part of the world, not enclosed in cases like relics.

How could I ever run in this long skirt? I once thought these long black habits were elegant, but now my habit feels cumbersome.

My sturdy shoes make up for the long skirt. No more flimsy footwear. If I needed to run, I could tuck up the skirt and make pretty good time in these shoes.

I knew about the silence and the clothes before I entered the convent. I have learned they become more difficult instead of easier to live with.

I hate the fact that Reverend Mother Robert Bellarmine selected the name I must bear for the rest of my life. Matthew, the tax collector, that's me. I wish she had chosen a female saint. There's no way I could have kept my own name, Maureen. Maureen means bitter or beloved. Take your pick.

The nuns allowed us to submit three saints' names we would like to be given, but they weren't obliged to give us any of those names. St. Matthew hadn't been one of my three choices. Reverend Mother said not getting a name we want is an exercise in obedience and humility.

Most of what we "know" about Matthew is legend.

At least he supposedly was a writer, though the apostle almost certainly didn't write the gospel attributed to him. I'm grateful our theology classes here take account of recent scholarship. Still, I like to think of my patron saint as a writer.

His symbol is a man with wings. An angel, or Icarus, bound for a deadly fall? I feel more like Icarus, so full of pride that I try to soar on my own beyond what I'm told to do.

Is my unwritten story the Book of Matthew? Talk about sins of pride. I'm only a novice, but I dare to think for myself.

The beginning of that gospel is bizarre, talking about the genealogy of Jesus traced through Joseph, even though Mary was supposed to be a virgin, so Joseph couldn't have passed on his genes to Jesus. Could the angel Gabriel have miraculously sent Mary some of Joseph's genes? That's not a thought to share with the sisters here.

God forbid we should ever joke. We aren't supposed to laugh much, or even to smile too much.

Living in this convent is damaging my soul instead of helping it grow. How can it grow in such a stifling atmosphere?

Why don't I leave?

Sister Rose de Lima. My answer is always Sister Rose de Lima, my sister novice.

On those rare occasions when I hear her voice, I am transfixed. If only her deep blue eyes would meet my gaze more often. What do I care about my heart's abhorrence if my heart's delight is here?

Cause of my joy, morning star, mystical rose.... I should not use terms from the Litany of the Blessed Virgin Mary to praise Sister Rose de Lima. My mystical Rose. She's not mine, though. I wish she were.

Why on earth call the Blessed Virgin Mary a house of gold, as the litany does? Poor Mary or Miriam or Maryam or whatever her name really was. A simple Jewish girl would have been horrified at all the statues that supposedly depict her and the prayers people have sent to her. Not to mention all the persecution of Jews done in the name of Christianity.

All the statues of Mary should have a yellow star hung on her like the ones the Nazis required the Jews to wear.

"Are your thoughts prayerful, Sister Matthew?" Mean Mother Michael, the Mistress of Novices, frowned at me. She excelled at frowning. I was walking to the chapel for Mass and didn't see her coming. She could tell from the expression on my face that I wasn't praying.

"Yes, Mother Michael," I lied. At least a chance to use my voice. It hasn't atrophied yet.

"Hmmm." The scowling nun wasn't fooled. "See that they are."

"Yes, Mother Michael," I ventured, though not sure she required a reply. Mother Michael must have been a beauty when she was younger. Now that she is probably in her forties, her face has set in hard lines.

She paced on, and I followed her to the chapel. At least I can see Sister Rose at chapel, though she doesn't kneel next to me. Our permanent places were assigned when we entered the order. Two other novices always walked and sat between Rose and me.

Rose isn't unusually pretty, yet her face is so dear. She has the most wonderful thick, black eyebrows. She's Irish American like me, but she looks it, and I don't particularly. When she smiles, oh when she smiles.

She's the only other novice who graduated from college before she entered the order. The others entered right after high school.

We all filed into the chapel, made the sign of the cross with holy water, and genuflected before we entered our assigned pews.

Though I quibble about the blonde and blue-eyed depictions of Mary, I like the sweet-faced women in the images in the chapel. The statue of the Assumption, Mary supposedly being taken to heaven without dying, is my favorite object in the chapel. The peacock blue of her cloak is eye-catching. She stands on the moon, and she is treading on a snake that represents the devil. Pope Pius XII declared a few years ago that Mary never died, and now that's official Church doctrine, though it hadn't been official for two thousand years.

The altar is simple, with a minimum of gold. The crucifix over the altar isn't too gory, for a crucifix. The Stations of the Cross that line the chapel walls are made of unpainted wood. A single stained-glass window over the altar depicts the Annunciation, when the Angel Gabriel told Mary she would bear the son of God, with a vase of lilies beside Mary denoting her purity. We live in a world where the only thing stained is the window.

I pictured yellow stars hanging on all the statues, including of course Jesus on the crucifix.

Matthew or whoever wrote his gospel lied. The gospel claimed that when Pontius Pilot condemned Jesus, the Jewish crowd said, "his blood be upon us and upon our children." No crowd in the world ever said words like that. No crowd ever said that guilt for someone's death should be visited on their children.

At least the nuns who taught me said all the world's sinners, each girl in our class specifically included, not the Jews, were responsible for Christ's death. But the nuns who taught me in grade school and high school—a different order from the one I entered—barely mentioned the Holocaust. I am angry that I didn't learn much about the Holocaust until I left Catholic schools.

I prayed my thanks that Pope John XXIII is removing anti-Jewish words from the liturgy and warmly greeting Jewish delegations.

I gazed at the stained-glass window and tried to let its beauty distract me from anger over the Church's treatment of the Jews.

The colors in the chapel and the flowers in the garden are the only bits of color in the convent. I strive not to feel starved for color. I don't much care about wearing it: I just want to see it. The idea flashed through my mind that being in the convent is like staying with black-and-white television while most people move to color.

I watched Father Nolan officiate in his embroidered green and gold silk vestments, in front of all the black-clad nuns. The Church wants its priests to be elegant like male birds and its nuns to be drab like female birds, though we aren't sitting on nests.

At least here we will be able to lift our voices in prayer and song. I sing like a crow, but I relish the chance to blend in with others who are more talented. Believe me, there are plenty of chances to sing every day. We chant and chant and chant.

No altar boy assists the priest in convent Masses. He seems perfectly able to do everything himself.

I catch a glimpse of Rose. I admire her piety, even though I can't share it. How deep she is.

I hope she doesn't do extreme penances like her saint. Supposedly Rose of Lima sometimes wore a circlet of roses with thorns to suffer like Jesus. Ugh.

In a more appealing legend, she—the saint I mean—brought the sick and poor into her room and cared for them. She had a reputation for kindness as well as piety.

I try to turn my heart toward prayer.

The most difficult part of the Mass for me is the Apostles Creed, which we are required to say aloud. "I believe in God, the Father Almighty, Creator of Heaven and Earth, and in Jesus Christ, His only Son, Our Lord, Who was conceived by the Holy Spirit, born of the Virgin Mary…" (Of course, we pray it in Latin.) How many lies had I told by this point in the prayer? I don't believe in most of those doctrines. Possible God, do you really care whether I believe all that?

Am I a hypocrite? If there is a God, forgive me for my unbelief. I do love the world. I love the earth, the rivers, and the trees. It's difficult to love all the people. I love the Kennedys, Rosa Parks, and Dr. Martin Luther King. I love Eleanor Roosevelt, Pearl Buck, and Marian Anderson. I love Walter Cronkite and President Jawaharlal Nehru of India. And, of course, Pope John.

I don't love any of the public officials of Alabama, Louisiana, and Mississippi. I love the children who are facing a barrage of insults to go to public schools. I pray for the children whose parents are turning them against others because of their race to learn how wrong their parents are. I pray to be forgiven for doing nothing about segregation but praying for it to end.

I love my family, even my uncle who cheated my father in a business deal. Uncle Mark can be sweet and funny. I love the girls who went to St. Agatha's grade school and high school with me, except for Mary Louise McKenna, who used to sneer at me for liking to study and not being a social butterfly. I've asked Possible God to help me forgive her, but my heart isn't big enough. Or perhaps I'm the one who needs to be forgiven. Possible God, what happened to Mary Louise? I didn't kill her, did I?

The Epistle today is from St. Paul, unfortunately not the one to the Corinthians on charity that is my favorite. I don't have enough charity, but probably more than I have faith and hope.

I should be thinking more about Jesus. Jesus, you were truly inspiring. A great man with great thoughts. As fine as Gandhi, who was also murdered.

I'm sorry you had such a terrible death, Jesus, but I think it's sick that so many images of you show you hanging on a cross rather than preaching. I doubt you would have liked being depicted that way all across the world. Even if it's true that you died for our sins, I think you'd have been appalled at being shown more than half-naked in your most terrible moments.

I don't believe I'm your bride. I shouldn't be here.

But I might be able to learn whether God exists if I stay here.

And where else could I be among women who are striving to do good? Where else could I be focused on something other than finding a husband and saving to buy a house?

Where else could I meet someone like Rose?

Possible God, help me to love Rose spiritually and not think of her carnally.

It's time for Holy Communion. While I'm in the convent, I must take it every day or cause a scandal. Possible God, purify my thoughts. Let me be not unworthy to commemorate Jesus and all that is good.

We sing one of my favorite hymns, "*Tantum ergo, Sacramentum, veneremur cernui.*" Therefore, we venerate the great Sacrament with our heads bowed. It's a hymn of adoration to the Host that is supposed to contain the body of Jesus, yet I love the tune and sometimes hum it to myself. It sounds better in Latin.

Ite, missa est. The Mass is finished. The priest blesses us. I need it.

We file out. When I pass Rose in the corridor, she smiles at me.

Now my day is joyous. Filled with delight, I glide to the refectory for a breakfast of scrambled eggs cooked by the sisters who are not considered teacher material. Postulants and novices also are required to do a significant amount of housework.

We cannot talk during meals. A sister reads from a spiritual book while we eat. I find this week's book, which is about the life of St. Francis of Assisi, more interesting than many others. Silent meals can be companionable. I enjoy knowing there will never be arguments during them. My parents didn't argue much, but when they did it always seemed to happen during meals, usually about whether the Kennedys were liberal enough. My mother liked Adlai Stevenson but my father argued that she needed to be more pragmatic.

We see the professed nuns—those who have taken vows—only in the chapel and the refectory. We novices are not allowed to speak with them, except for the superiors who rule us. I try to guess from the nuns' faces who is nice and who isn't.

I REMEMBER THE FIRST day I saw Rose, the day eight months ago, in the beginning of the Year of Our Lord 1962, when we had entered the convent and become postulants.

Saying goodbye to my parents had been harder than I had expected. I had to prevent myself from crying. I kept our goodbyes short. Fortunately, my parents acted cheerful.

When we new postulants left the parlor where we had bid farewell to our old lives, we changed into long black skirts and black blouses with long sleeves that ended at the wrist, unlike the flowing sleeves novices and professed nuns wear.

I scrutinized the other young women and girls. Most of them seemed more like girls. Only one was about my age. Maybe she had already graduated from college too. She had blue eyes that looked upon the world with pleasure as if she believed it was good. The largest birthmark I had ever seen graced her cheek, surrounded by delicious freckles. I wondered whether she had been a tomboy. She had a look about her that made me think she also might have read *The Well of Loneliness*. I hoped so. She smiled at me, and I tried to give her a smile that expressed more than I could possibly say aloud.

The sweet-faced Mistress of Postulants, Mother Gabriel, called the roll. The freckled woman with the Massachusetts accent answered to Rose Clancy. I was next in line as Maureen Collins. I longed to make my often-used joke that I was probably related to the Irish patriot Michael Collins, but fiercer. I was neither related, as far as I knew, nor gun-toting as he had been, though I did have stick-out ears like his. And I didn't want to be cut down in my prime, as he had been. But that was not an intro for the convent.

I studied the faces of the younger postulants. These would be my sisters for the rest of my life. Although they tried to form their faces into suitable, discreet smiles and to keep their hands motionless, most of them had the tiniest of nervous motions in some part of their bodies. I hoped to help them. I chided myself for another arrogant thought. How could someone as iconoclastic as I am help others who were dedicating themselves to God?

Mother Gabriel told us the rules, which were daunting, but the gentle tone in which she relayed them softened her message. Her olive skin and brown eyes suggested a Mediterranean heritage.

"You will join us in a life of prayer," she told us. "The rule of silence enables us to communicate with God more than with other people. That is a privilege people in the world do not have.

"We live in silence, except during recreation, chapter meetings where we confess our faults, and conferences with our spiritual leaders. Otherwise, we speak only when it is necessary as part of our duties. During meals, one of us will read spiritual books while the others listen.

"That may sound intimidating now, but you will find that silence is beautiful. It binds us together rather than keeping us apart.

"When we speak, we speak softly."

I wanted to add "carrying a big stick." Too bad I couldn't make that joke.

"Moving quietly without haste is also part of the rule of silence. We do not swing our arms but keep them folded inside our sleeves when we can." Mother Gabriel held her hands in front of her, tucked into her sleeves. "You will not have long enough sleeves to do that until you enter the novitiate, but you can begin to keep your arms from making unnecessary gestures."

She smiled at us. "You are allowed to smile," she said in a voice that sounded almost teasing.

Her warmth encouraged me to try to follow the rules and see whether serenity followed. I thought I wouldn't mind emulating Mother Gabriel.

"Now that you will be living in a community, you must try to avoid forming particular friendships," the sweet-faced nun cautioned us. "You need to care about all your sisters, not just one or two. During recreation, you should gather in groups of three or more."

That sounded like a difficult way to form friendships. I gathered that the difficulty was intended.

"You have all been given Breviaries with the prayers of the Divine Office, which have been handed down to clergy and religious for centuries," Mother Gabriel continued. "When the bell rings for the prayers of the canonical hours, you must stop whatever you are doing immediately and go to the chapel to pray. No task is as important as the Divine Office. There is no excuse for delaying." After these stern words, she smiled again. "The prayers are beautiful. I am sure they will bring you almost as much joy as the Holy Mass. You will be glad to hear our community does not rise for 2 a.m. Matins though that is part of the tradition. Our prayers begin with Matins and Lauds at 5:30 a.m."

I sighed with relief that we didn't have to get up to pray at 2 a.m.

I wanted to follow all Mother Gabriel's instructions. I tried to walk with baby steps. It felt like walking on ice or sneaking like a child trying to overhear her parents' conversation after she has gone to bed. As soon as I tried to keep my arms from moving while I walked, I felt the urge to swing them. I clasped my hands in front of my waist, which made me feel as if I were pretending to always pray. Oh. That was the point. I am supposed to always be praying. Possible God, you wouldn't care if my arms swing while I pray, would you?

WHEN I FIRST SAW Rose, she shone, even in the plain, black garb.

I looked forward to speaking with her.

The first time we talked at recreation she walked next to me. Even though it's called recreation, there isn't much recreating.

When recreation is indoors, we're often supposed to sew, can you believe it? Sewing. That's not recreation: It's labor. For me, sewing on a button is the equivalent of embroidering a tapestry. Mean Mother

Michael criticizes me for sewing poorly, which apparently demonstrates a lack of spiritual development. I believe it shows a lack of manual dexterity.

To be fair, I knew when I entered that I would have to at least mend my own clothes.

That day recreation was blessedly a walk outdoors on one of the first days that hinted at spring. Yellow and purple crocuses had started to sprout in the garden.

"How did you decide to enter the convent, Maureen?" We were still using our real names then. Rose's Massachusetts accent charmed me. The question pleased me even more. Postulants weren't supposed to ask such personal questions or to say anything about their past lives. Rose's question showed she was curious enough about me to flout the rules.

"I've thought about it since fifth grade." I hoped my voice struck the right tone of detached friendliness, though I've never been the detached type. "Actually, I wanted to be a saint, but I thought being a nun would do as a substitute."

Rose laughed. Her laugh wasn't exactly loud, but more than polite. It was the first real laugh I had heard since we became postulants two months earlier. "Didn't we all want to be saints? I admire you for admitting it."

"I prayed to have a vision of the Blessed Virgin Mary, but a vision of any saint would have been acceptable."

She put her hand over her mouth to muffle her laughter. "I prayed to have a vision too. They fed us too much Bernadette and Fatima. We thought having a vision was normal."

"And being a saint seemed like a difficult but possible career."

Rose held her stomach. "You're too funny, Maureen. I'm afraid I'll burst my seams laughing and have to prostrate myself before the Mistress of Postulants."

"I'm sorry, Rose. I'll try to be sober. Father Nolan gave a fine sermon this morning, didn't he?"

"He gave one of the most boring sermons ever, and you know it."

"Yes, sister. He's so earnest that I feel sorry for him."

"So do I. He must know he doesn't have a gift for public speaking."

"At least he's handsome." Father Nolan was bald and had a face full of wrinkles. The wrinkles probably improved the features he was born with.

Rose giggled.

"I wish I could give sermons." I gave an exaggerated sigh.

"You'd be good at it. You aren't the only one who might have liked to become a priest."

"You too?"

"Mother Gabriel is looking our way." Rose made her features demure. "I should go and walk with someone else to avoid the temptation to favor you particularly. But I'm so glad we had this talk."

"Me too." She felt tempted to favor me particularly! Her words thrilled me. How particularly? I wondered.

She walked away and I decided life in the convent had improved.

I didn't think I could tell her that the real reason I entered, besides wanting to be around women, was that I thought living in the convent might help me believe in God. I also might have committed a terrible sin, worse than anything she could imagine.

I DID HAVE SOME postulant friends besides Rose.

Like a kid at Halloween, my sister postulant Linda sometimes figured out how to get treats. Even better, she liked to share them.

Linda, a pixie-like eighteen-year-old who admitted to a crush on Marlon Brando, knew who would go along. She came to me and announced, "I've got some cookies."

Linda said her family had smuggled them in. I believed her the first time, but when it happened again, I wondered whether they came from the nuns' pantry. Whatever the source, we called it the Motherlode.

"Let's have a party," Linda would say. "Will Toni go along with us?" Toni, a tall, large, perpetually hungry postulant, would have run five miles to get extra food.

"She definitely will. May I ask Rose?"

"Will Rose keep it quiet? She's awfully pious."

"Sure, she will." I asked Rose the first time, but not after I began to doubt the cookies' provenance.

"Don't tell Helen," Linda cautioned me.

"Are you kidding? She'd turn us in before we could eat the cookies." Helen, meek but notoriously strict about the rules, believed reporting another postulant for breaking them constituted helping a sister to mend her ways. I also didn't tell Francine, the shy girl with the alcove next to mine whose overly active nighttime snoring kept me awake, because I thought our impropriety would shock her.

We would gather in the basement for a few minutes during recreation or just before evening prayers.

Then we would tell dumb jokes. I asked Linda what you would call someone who assisted a nun in a duel. She grinned. "Second to nun." Need I add that I liked her for her response?

Toni, who excelled at athletics yet seemed to lack even vestiges of attraction to other girls, giggled with delight at such ventures. The convent's food portions weren't large enough to satisfy her. I enjoyed watching Rose and Toni play intense games of volleyball when we were allowed that much exercise, though I tried to avoid playing the game myself. I feared the ball would hit me in the face and break my glasses, as had happened more than once in high school.

Our illicit feasts took less than ten minutes, but we would have paid dearly for these bacchanals if the nuns had found out our unconventional behavior. I now realize we risked expulsion. When we were postulants, the severity of our breach of the rules hadn't yet sunk in.

I thought these little deviations from the rules made us all the more committed to our vocations.

We were postulants for six months. When we entered the novitiate in the summer and were told our new names, some of us were happy, while others were far from it. I wasn't the only one whose new name didn't delight her.

"Reverend Mother told me I have to become Sister Polycarp!" Linda wailed. "Can you believe it? Polycarp. When I go out to teach, the kids will call me 'Many fish.'"

I tried not to laugh. "It's not a pretty name, but I'm sure your students will call you Sister Poly. That would be a cute nickname."

"I don't want to be Sister Polycarp."

"Who was St. Polycarp?"

"He was bishop of Smyrna, supposedly a disciple of the Apostle John, and a martyr. I don't care what he did. I don't want that name. Don't dare complain to me about being called 'Matthew.' That's not bad at all by comparison."

I preferred the name Sister Matthew to Sister Polycarp, so I didn't complain to her.

Two weeks later, Linda told me she planned to leave.

"Which part of the convent is driving you to leave? Missing your family?"

"No. I'm going to join another order. I refuse to spend the rest of my life as Sister Polycarp."

"The name? Really?"

"Really. Well, the fact that Mother Michael is Mistress of Novices also has something to do with it."

"We won't be novices forever."

"I won't. I'm going tomorrow."

"I'll miss you." I thought she probably had more reasons to leave than she let on. I didn't expect her to confide them to me.

"If you're going to stay, be careful," Linda warned. "Mother Michael forbade two novices from the year ahead of us to talk to each other because they'd done it too often. She expelled one of them later. I don't want to have to hide all the time because some old nun thinks I shouldn't have friends."

I gulped. Linda knew gossip I had never heard. "Thanks for the warning." If even a novice who wasn't attracted to women worried about the stricture against particular friendships, I should be doubly cautious.

Toni became Sister Ursula. St. Ursula led a group of holy virgins who were all martyred in Cologne. Little is known about them besides that. I like to think they were rebels who dressed like men.

With Linda gone, Sister Ursula didn't break any more rules, at least not that I could see. The memory of our shared feasts made me feel a little closer to her than to the other novices, except of course Rose. I think poor Ursula is always hungry. After she takes her final vows in about four years, she could put on weight if she wanted to.

After a year and a half in the novitiate, we would take our first vows of poverty, chastity, and obedience, binding for three years. Then we could take the final vows. If we wanted to leave after taking vows and stay in the Church's good graces, we would have to apply to a bishop. I'm not sure I would stay in the Church if I left the convent.

CHAPTER 2
Sister Matthew

MARYLAND, LATER IN THE SUMMER OF 1962

POSSIBLE GOD, ARE YOU laughing with me, or laughing at me? When I call myself a nun, I am speaking loosely, since I am a religious, not, strictly speaking, a nun, because I'll be a teaching sister, not entirely cloistered from the world, and thank goodness am slated to perform other duties besides praying. If "a religious" is a noun meaning a nun, does that mean that people who aren't nuns are the irreligious?

Nuns are not so sympathetically portrayed in literature. Chaucer's Prioress cares more about her dogs than about people, and the tale she tells is a hideous blood libel of Jews. Since Chaucer didn't like the character, did he also find her tale disgusting?

Shakespeare's portrayal of Isabella in *Measure for Measure* is also unsympathetic. She is supposed to be selfish because she considers her bodily integrity more important than her brother's life: Angelo, a creep, tells her he'll refrain from executing her brother only if she has sex with him (Angelo). I feel for Isabella, who is afraid of jeopardizing her immortal soul, not to mention disgusted at the thought of sex with Angelo.

Shakespeare lived in a time when the English government was hostile to Catholicism, so no wonder the clergy in his plays weren't portrayed too favorably.

Gutless Friar Lawrence in *Romeo and Juliet* gave Juliet a dangerous sleeping potion instead of going to her parents and admitting he had married her to Romeo. As a woman who wanted to kiss other women, I sympathized with the young lovers' forbidden love.

I took Hamlet's advice and got me to a nunnery. Ophelia would have been better off as a nun.

Heloise, portrayed as Eloisa by Alexander Pope, is sympathetic because she loved a man, the abbot Abelard. Paugh. Why should that be necessary to make a nun a full character?

Surprisingly, J.D. Salinger had a more favorable attitude toward nuns, or at least Holden Caulfield did. Unlike Chaucer, he thought they weren't phonies.

But I am a phony, or I'm a phony nun. Does that make me a phony human being?

There's *The Nun's Story*. Like almost every other Catholic girl, I read the book and saw the movie. That should have scared me off. The women in it were told they couldn't think for themselves and were subject to their Mother Superior's will in everything.

We were always taught in civics classes that the Communists used mind control. But we weren't warned that nuns use it too.

I knew I could resist being controlled and would still think my own thoughts. That proved to be true. It takes constant effort to hide what I really think and pretend to be a submissive little nunny bunny.

Secretly, I believe the Mistress of Novices, Reverend Mother Robert Bellarmine, and all the others like them in other orders, are the ones who, like me, never gave up their own wills or even tried to. They are the ones who went along, thinking they would get power later, like submissive young Chinese wives in Pearl Buck's stories who believe they will have a chance to be domineering mothers-in-law when they are older.

Pearl Buck is the one who shattered my belief in Christianity. Yes, she was the daughter of missionaries, but her stories tell how annoyed Chinese people were at the idea that there is only one god and one true religion. And that other incarnations in other cultures have had virgin births. That woke me up to comparative religions and I have never gone back to my simple childhood beliefs.

Was I happier then, when I couldn't wait to take Holy Communion and thought I spoke directly with Jesus and Mary every day, and that they listened? They were my imaginary friends. I don't know whether I was happier, or whether people who still believe that are happier than I am now. I only know I can't go back. I can't believe what I don't believe. Do you understand, Possible God? I miss the certain God, the God of the *Baltimore Catechism*.

The theology classes I am taking in the convent haven't changed my mind. If I were a man, I might have tried entering the Jesuit order, but there's no intellectual female religious order equivalent to the Jesuits.

So I'm a nun. Or at least a nun/none of the above. I can't imagine what other world I could join. One that doesn't exist yet.

A world that is full of Roses, or of women who are something like a Rose. Her eyes are nothing like the sun. They are far lovelier than any sun I have ever seen. They are the dawn, just before the sun rises.

Possible God, do you really believe Rose should be your bride, not mine? Do you think you could make her happier than I could?

I am the nuns' nightmare. I am the rebel. Yes, I have read Camus. Simone de Beauvoir as well. No, I have never told the good sisters— that's what my father calls them—that I have read those books. "One is not born, but rather becomes, a woman," Beauvoir wrote. One certainly is not born a nun.

Maybe becoming a nun is a way of avoiding becoming a woman, as society requires. Perhaps Beauvoir would not see that choice as authentic or in good faith. The priests who rule the Church certainly treat nuns as women, and subordinate, but other men don't. They look at nuns and see a sexless blob of black cloth, which can be a relief for us.

I suppose I entered because of Bernadette. No, not that Bernadette. I mean Bernadette O'Hara, the girl I loved all my grade school and high school life at St. Agatha's. I know she just saw me as a friend, so I never dared to confess my love to her.

When we were ten or eleven years old, we would drape scarves over our heads and play nuns together. We would be nuns isolated on a desert island, trying to convert the animals there. Tigers were particularly difficult to convert, likewise crocodiles.

I persuaded Bernadette to play Romeo to my Juliet and run away from my house to my backyard together, but we never kissed. I wrestled a little with her in another game just to touch her.

Bernadette was a tomboy; I wasn't. I simply wanted to read, perhaps because I grew up like an only child (my brother is fourteen years older) and became used to amusing myself. The only interest I took in sports was watching Bernadette play volleyball, softball, and basketball. I have never been the cheerleader type—no one has ever accused me of being cute—but I was her devoted fan. She didn't know I never watched anyone else during the game.

Bernadette sparkled like no one else. All the girls could see it, though I don't think any others were in love with her. The girls almost always voted her class president, and later voted her high school student body president.

She was kind. I never heard her say a mean word about anyone. Though most people wouldn't call her especially pretty, I loved her looks. When we were little, I would pull her frizzy brown ponytail just to touch her.

I wondered whether she was like me, a lover of girls. But by senior year in high school, she was dating a boy.

We graduated from high school in 1958. The hardest part of graduating was knowing I probably wouldn't see much of Bernadette after that. She planned to attend Trinity College in Washington, D.C., and I would be attending the University of Maryland at College Park.

I had to get permission from a priest to attend a secular college. He had granted it without hesitation because he said that when good students went there, they were a credit to the Catholic schools they had attended.

At the high school graduation ceremony, we wore dreadfully long blue gowns and carried bouquets of roses. The worst part was being required to wear medium high heels, which I never wore otherwise, and having to curtsey to the bishop who gave us our diplomas and kiss his ring after we took the diploma. Try doing that in a long skirt and heels. We had practiced many times, but I often wobbled. I hoped I wouldn't disgrace St. Agatha's and mortify my parents by tripping.

I managed the awkward curtsy and vowed I would never wear heels again.

After the ceremony ended, it was time to go to our families and receive their congratulations. It also felt like the last time I would see Bernadette. I wished I could have watched her during the ceremony, but I couldn't turn my head without standing out. I scurried over to her. No words I could say would be adequate to describe my feelings. Drinking in her friendly face and sweet, frizzy hair, I proclaimed, "I'll miss you. I want you to know how much I've always admired you, especially your kindness to everyone."

She smiled at me. "Thanks. I'll miss you too."

Then I had to go to my parents and get hugged. I didn't dislike the embraces, but my heart was full of my classmates, especially Bernadette.

All the nuns from my high school were present. I hoped to get away before I had to see Sister Veronica, my nemesis.

To my great relief, the only nun who came over to my family was the principal, Sister Thomas the Apostle, whom we always called Sister Doubting Thomas. (Doubting Thomas was the apostle who wasn't with the other apostles when the resurrected Jesus first appeared to them. He refused to believe they had seen Jesus until he saw Jesus. His doubt always seemed sensible to me, though I think that episode had been written to tell us we should believe things we can't see.) The principal smiled at me and said, "You are such a good student, Maureen. I'm sure you will do well in college and show how successfully our school prepares its students for further achievements."

I thanked her and my parents glowed.

In the beginning of college, I did go out with a few guys because they asked me. I harbored a mild curiosity about men. They wanted to kiss me at the end of a date. I saw no reason to do so. I told them going to a movie or a basketball game did not constitute building enough kinship and affection to warrant a kiss. They didn't persist for long. Well, I did kiss a couple of them and didn't find anything particularly pleasant, let alone exciting, about it. I had crushes on some male movie stars—I'm too embarrassed to say which ones—but I found guys up close less attractive.

Of course I heard about *The Well of Loneliness* and read it. It did not offer pleasant prospects.

I heard that some people who preferred those of the same sex went to bars to meet them. At Confirmation, I had taken a pledge not to drink until I reached the age of twenty-one, and I didn't start then. I couldn't imagine going to a bar. I doubted that women in a bar would talk about books.

So the convent was the place for me. I didn't think any woman there would fall in love with me, but at least I might be able to find someone I could love at a distance, as I had Bernadette.

Maybe there is a God because I found Rose.

Pardon me, Possible God, for being so flippant.

I wonder whether any of the other novices, or even the professed nuns, have as many doubts as I do. I'll never know.

Are any of the nuns attracted to women? I couldn't discern any nuns with those tendencies at St. Agatha's, and I can't discern them in the order I belong to now. Maybe there are some. I hope so.

As a novice, I feel so cut off from the world. I can't phone anyone. I can't even write my parents without showing my letters to Mean Mother Michael, the Mistress of Novices, and believe me, she's not someone you'd want to read your intimate thoughts.

I miss going to the movies and watching television, which is mostly verboten here. I miss *Meet the Press*, and all the other news shows. I miss newspapers. I want to know what's happening in the world. I miss *The Twilight Zone*. I feel like I'm living in the Twilight Zone.

What's really intolerable is not being able to choose my own books to read. I graduated from college as an English major, for heaven's sake. I should be able to read anything I want. I can't even keep a copy of Shakespeare's plays in my room. Or Emily Dickinson's poems. What could be more spiritual than those? I want to read the latest books, like *Catch-22*.

I should think of the things I don't miss. I don't miss Elvis. I don't miss *American Bandstand*. I don't miss television cartoons. I don't miss *Gunsmoke* or any of the many TV westerns my father watches. If I wanted to spend time with my parents in the evening after dinner, I had to watch those shows too.

Maybe I miss baths as much as books. Being allowed to shower only twice a week makes me feel perpetually dirty. Using the pitcher of water in my alcove to wash my face is inadequate. I suppose God loves dirt because some saints never bathed, but I don't aspire to that kind of sainthood. My Possible God is fine with bathing.

I also don't like the communal bathrooms. I would like to be able to go to the toilet without everyone knowing I'm there. I would like to change my Kotex without anyone guessing I'm having my period. The women here would not be so gross as to comment on each other's bodily functions, but I still want to keep them to myself.

However, I have no problem with the total lack of mirrors to prevent us from becoming vain. I'm all right looking, but not beautiful, and I've always thought it would be ridiculous to try to be something I'm not. I would worry about not having a mirror if my adolescent acne recurred. I don't think I'd be allowed to use a cover-up. That would be a nightmare.

I don't like not having walls around my bed. We just have floor-length curtains to separate us from others in the dormitory. Some other novices snore. Sister Philomena, a.k.a. Francine, in the alcove next to mine sounds like a buzz saw. Just when I have gone to sleep, her snoring jolts me awake. In my mind, I call her Sister Snorer. I should be more charitable to her because she looks like a scared rabbit and never talks to anyone. I had expected her to quit before becoming a novice.

I'm supposed to pray during minor irritations like her snoring. Instead, I silently recite Browning's poem about the monk who hates the other monk.

Or do other things. If being surrounded only by a curtain is supposed to prevent us from touching ourselves, it doesn't. I have always been silent at such times. I don't believe it's a sin. Whom does it hurt? No one. But I say a prayer of contrition afterwards, just in case.

When I start teaching, I'll leave the Mother House and live in a smaller convent with a room of my own. Surely I'll be able to smuggle books there.

Meanwhile, only the curtains separate us. At 5 a.m., one lucky novice rises first, goes down to the first floor, and pulls a rope to ring the bell that wakes the rest of us for morning prayers at 5:30. The task is rotated, but only among the stronger novices. When it's my turn, I pretend I'm Paul Revere. I long to say, "The British are coming!" I don't want to find out what my punishment for that would be.

I miss all the little things too. I miss snacking on Fig Newtons whenever I want to. I miss Bireley's orange soda. Do the nuns think God objects to Fig Newtons and orange soda?

No, God objects to people being able to eat what they want and do what they want, if those people are living in a convent. Brides of Christ don't lust for orange soda.

The discipline is the point.

How spiritual are these concerns? I knew all I would be giving up before I came here. Well, no, I didn't know about bathing only twice a week. Do I think my inner rebellion is somehow profound? Who do I think I am, Novice in the Rye?

CHAPTER 3
Rose

BROOKLINE, MASSACHUSETTS, 1952

Twelve-year-old Rose Clancy scurried to her bedroom and prayed that her father would stop screaming.

"I told you I didn't want any more damn casseroles for dinner!" Her father yelled at her mother. "I'm fed up with casseroles! Can't you learn to cook anything else?"

Rose heard her mother's tremulous reply, "If you'd give me my household money sooner, I could buy better cuts of meat and make fewer—"

"Don't you pretend it's my fault!"

Tears streamed down Rose's cheeks. Even shutting her door didn't keep out the sound of his shouting. She could escape to another room, but her mother could not.

Gray skies and slush had made the world outside their windows dreary, but gloom spread through their home regardless of the weather.

Rose thought her family used to be happy, or at least happier. What had changed?

She knew that her father made what her mother called "good money" as an accountant. Her mother told Rose privately there was no reason to scrimp on household money: Her father was just stingy. "Old Scrooge," her mother named him, though not to his face.

In her bedroom, Rose grabbed her earmuffs from a drawer and pulled them over her ears. Her father seldom yelled at her, but he shouted at her mother too often. Her mother cooked tasty meals and kept the house immaculate. Why was he so often dissatisfied?

"Please God, calm my father's temper." Rose prayed. *"Please Dear God, I want to live in a house with no yelling when I grow up."*

Maybe, as she hoped, she would be able to enter the convent and live in silence—a holy silence, not the tense kind.

Her parents had told Rose she was a "miracle" child who had come late in their lives. They had no other children. Rose wondered whether they had gotten along better without her.

Rose prayed for her parents. She loved to pray. She still thrilled to the words she had read in the *Baltimore Catechism* when she was six years old. "Why did God make you? God made me to know Him, to love Him, and to serve Him in this world and to be happy with Him forever in heaven."

Now she was old enough to wonder whether heaven existed. Could heaven just be a nebulous state of being with God where you never reconnected with the people you had loved on earth? She hoped she would be able to be with other people. God should be enough, yet it would be thrilling to meet the Blessed Virgin Mary and all the saints.

When she was little, she had believed everything would go well if she just loved God and prayed. But her parents prayed, and still they fought. Mostly her father fought.

She would go to her mother the next day, and her mother would cry about being unhappy. Of course a divorce would have scandalized everyone they knew.

LATER THAT YEAR, HER father had a heart attack at work and never came home.

Rose cried. Was it her fault for praying to live in a house without shouting? She knew God didn't take her father's life because of her prayers, but she felt guilty anyway.

Her mother wept more than Rose did. Her mother's speech often slurred, and she sometimes collapsed onto the sofa after dinner. "Why aren't you crying more over your father's death? Don't you miss him?" she would demand, pushing Rose until tears formed in her eyes, though they weren't tears for her father.

One evening a few months later Uncle Tim, her mother's pious younger brother, came over to their house without calling first. Tim's wife had died before her father had, and Tim showed no more interest in remarrying than her mother did. He was one of those who were sometimes called the "black Irish" because, like her mother, he had dark eyes, and black hair, before it turned gray. Rose knew several widows cast eyes on him, but their efforts to coax him over for dinner were in vain. His four children were in high school and college, and his main social life was visiting her mother.

Rose answered the door. Even before they exchanged hugs, she burst out, "Hello, Uncle Tim. My mother's gone to sleep on the sofa."

"It's only seven o'clock. So she's been drinking again." He roused her mother.

That was how Rose learned that her mother had a drinking problem.

The next morning, Rose went to school, happier than ever to be at St. Euphrosnye's Grammar School in Boston, the best school in the world. She wore the school's blue uniform with pride. She knew she had to be extra careful about her behavior when she wore it outside school, so she wouldn't dishonor St. Euphrosnye's.

The day began when her seventh-grade teacher, Sister Gabriel, always gave her a warm smile. Sister Gabriel spoke in calm, gentle tones.

Rose aspired to be like Sister Gabriel when she grew up. Not all nuns spoke as gently as Sister Gabriel, but Rose vowed that she, like Sister Gabriel, would never warn her students that they risked eternal damnation if they didn't follow the rules precisely.

Rose enjoyed going to Mass at St. Paul's Church, with stained glass windows depicting Jesus, Mary, and many saints. Light streaming through the windows covered the pews in red, green, and blue light, turning the church into a shrine of holy magic. She loved following the Mass in her gilt-edged Missal that had the Latin words on one page and an English translation on the facing page. The mystery of the priest's transformation of bread and wine into the Body and Blood of Christ always thrilled her.

When she had been about eight years old, she had made hosts out of Wonder Bread and pretended to say Mass. That game didn't compare to the splendor of the real Sacrament.

Church and school weren't the only places she loved. The outdoors excited her. Sometimes a rabbit nibbled on plants in her family's yard, and she enjoyed watching that almost as good as going to Mass or reading a good book. She enjoyed the flowers in their garden, but ferns reminded her of a forest. She asked her mother if they could plant more ferns. Her mother shook her head and said their yard didn't have enough shade.

When her mother drank in the daytime, Rose would sit in the garden and watch robins and blue jays. She cawed in response to the crows, though they knew she wasn't one of them.

As she moved on into high school, the girls—of course all the students at St. Euphrosnye's were girls—talked about which movie stars they liked best. Rose thought Elizabeth Taylor was the most beautiful woman in the world. But Audrey Hepburn looked so much more approachable. Rose imagined being close to Audrey, maybe even kissing her. When Rose's classmates asked about her favorite movie star and she said Audrey Hepburn, they laughed and told her they were asking about her favorite male star. She didn't have one, so she decided to say Jimmy Stewart. They laughed at her again and told her he was too old. So she said Montgomery Clift, and they laughed and said he was a pansy. A pansy? What was that? They explained. A man who was attracted to other men.

Rose thought about that. Was she attracted to other girls in a way they would find funny? She had known not to tell any of them how she liked them better than any boy. Or that she wanted to kiss them. Maybe she was a pansy.

Rose's mother was the first person who mentioned the word "lesbian."

"You stay away from Roberta Herlihy," her mother warned Rose during her freshman year in high school. Her mother slurred her words, which made them doubly painful. "I think she's a lesbian."

"What does that mean?" Rose winced at the smell of alcohol on her mother's breath.

"It means doing nasty things with other girls."

Rose realized what that must mean and leapt to Bobbie's defense. "That's not true! Bobbie's a tomboy, but she wouldn't do anything like that." Rose hoped Bobbie was a lesbian, but that was nobody's business.

"You're naïve. I was a tomboy. Roberta isn't just a tomboy." Her mother took another sip of sherry. Rose had discovered a bottle of Seagram's Seven Crown in the broom closet and realized that her mother probably drank one sip publicly to one or two she took privately in the kitchen. "Listen to me. I know more than you do."

Rose longed to say her mother certainly didn't know more about being attracted to girls than she did.

"I need to study for my algebra test," Rose said, hiding in her homework as usual.

Her mother sighed. "I guess it's too much to expect you to keep me company. When I was a girl, I would have been happy to have my mother alive and wanting to spend time with me."

"I am glad to be with you, but I have to study too." Rose felt sorry that her mother's mother had died when her mother was eight years old. She would infinitely prefer to have a mother who loved her and drank to a mother who loved her and died young.

Rose often went to bed early to escape her mother. Then Rose prayed to be able to go somewhere instead of lying on her bed when she wasn't sleepy. She locked her door so she could be alone. Sometimes her mother knocked on the door and demanded that Rose come out and talk to her. Rose would reply she was tired and trying to sleep.

Deliverance had come one night in a form that astonished Rose.

She found herself on a mountain, higher than she had ever been. Was this a dream? She must have fallen asleep. But everything looked so vivid. Nothing wavered, as images often did in her dreams. Rose often flew in her dreams, so she spread her arms but remained on solid ground.

Fir and spruce trees surrounded the mountain top, their scents permeating the air. She didn't remember ever smelling things in her dreams. Tiny flowers with almost no stems carpeted the ground. A chicken-sized bird followed by chicks pecked among the flowers. It saw her and froze. Some of the chicks also stood still, while others hadn't learned that lesson yet and continued to peck. Rose's heart expanded with joy.

Breathing cool mountain air, Rose walked along a trail. She didn't remember taking deep breaths in a dream before. A stream flowed among the rocks. Fish shimmied through it.

She crossed the stream on mossy rocks and almost fell in. In dreams, she usually almost floated along and didn't feel her steps. She bent over and put her hand in the water, which chilled her fingers. Tiny fish darted away from her hand. She saw a little gray bird bounce on a rock, then fly straight into a small waterfall.

Everything looked so clear. She wondered whether she could possibly be time traveling, not dreaming. She had just appeared in this place without any whirring noises or dizziness.

If this weren't a dream, she must be traveling in time as well as in place, because when she had been in her room, deep snow lay in piles on their street. If snow covered the suburbs of Boston, mountains wouldn't be flowering unless she were in the Southern Hemisphere.

Could this be real life, life at its most splendid? Had God granted her wish to travel to mountains? Hosannas and hallelujahs pumped through her.

She never wanted to leave.

Rose found herself back in her bed in her darkened room. Her hand dripped with cold water.

She stared at her hand. Her experience had been clearer than any dream. Could she actually have traveled to that mountain?

She rolled out of bed and dropped on her knees to thank God.

Traveling in time and space was possible. It didn't just happen in stories.

God had allowed her to do something miraculous.

Why had God permitted her to take a journey that seemed to be just for pleasure, with no moral lessons or good deeds? Did God like giving people joy?

The Lord had come to her in the form of nature, and she would go out and find nature in her other life too.

Rose thought of the Sermon on the Mount. The mountain itself was the sermon. Mountains inspired the most profound thoughts, even to Jesus.

She longed for mountains. *Thank you so much, Dear Lord*, she prayed. *Please, God, I know I'm being greedy, but let me travel to the mountains again.*

Rose wondered whether God gave her, and perhaps many other people, the power to time travel without His specific intervention in particular instances. Maybe other people just didn't talk about it.

ROSE'S MOTHER HAD FEW friends. She used to go out for coffee with other mothers after leaving Rose at grammar school, but that stopped when Rose went to high school. When Rose asked her mother whether she might want to marry again for company, her mother always said, "Not that again." Rose understood her mother's reluctance because her father had yelled almost every day. Her mother's spirit had faded more each year.

Rose vowed never to drink and certainly never to marry. She didn't really want a stepfather, so she didn't persist in asking her mother about marrying again. Her mother might be just as well off single. Rose's father had left enough money for her mother to live on if she didn't do anything extravagant.

Even though her mother's marriage had been miserable, she urged Rose to think about dating.

"Why don't you ask your friends if they have brothers or cousins you could meet? You need to learn how to be around boys. You can't keep your nose in a book for your whole life. Don't worry about your birthmark. I'm sure boys will see how pretty you are anyway."

Rose hadn't much worried about the large birthmark on her right cheek and she hadn't known her mother did. "I don't worry about it."

"I'm glad, dear. But you are getting old enough to look for face creams that will make it less noticeable."

"I'm not ready to date yet." And never will be, Rose thought. She decided never to try to hide her birthmark, which she doubted she could hide anyway.

"You don't have to date. Just get to know boys. Play tennis with them or something." Rose's mother had once been good at tennis.

Rose didn't particularly want to play tennis. She would rather play volleyball and basketball. She wished her mother would return to playing tennis if she liked it so much. That would give her something to do. She seldom went out of the house, except with Rose. Her mother cleaned the house again and again, removing every spot or possible spot, drinking when the cleaning began to tire her.

Praying for her mother hadn't helped her cut down on her drinking. Rose hadn't expected it would, but she had hoped.

She didn't want to tell anyone about her mother's drinking, which was fortunately mostly confined to their home. Few people could have guessed. Her mother had a dignified bearing in public. Shouldn't Rose protect her mother's reputation?

After her mother had been drinking for a few years, Rose got up the nerve to speak about it to a priest in the confessional.

After confessing her sins and being given absolution, she had said, "Father, I'm sure my mother is an alcoholic. She gets very intoxicated several nights a week. My father died three years ago, and she's been sad ever since. I wish she had something else to comfort her."

A harsh voice came through the dark screen in the confessional. "What age are you?"

"Fifteen."

"And you can judge whether your mother has a problem with alcohol? You're too young to know. Be loving to your mother. Try to be a good daughter."

Rose bit her lip.

One Saturday afternoon when her mother was in a good mood and they had been playing canasta, one of the few pastimes her mother enjoyed, Rose had ventured, "Pardon me for saying this. I know you have had many things to deal with since my father died, but I think you have a problem with drinking. Have you ever thought of joining Alcoholics Anonymous? That might help you."

Her mother's face contorted. "Why are you spying on me? Why are you judging me? I don't have a problem. I certainly would never go to a group where people talk about their lives in public. That's low class."

"I'm not judging you."

"Yes, you are." Tears formed in her mother's eyes. "I do everything I can for you."

"I know you do. I didn't mean to hurt you."

"You're young. You have many pleasures. I need a little pleasure in life."

Rose did not point out that her mother wept and ranted when she drank and seemed anything but happy. Instead, Rose retreated to her homework.

When she finished her homework, she would go to her room to read, though her mother would beat on her door and demand that Rose keep her company.

The sisters at St. Euphrosnye's were always sober. Rose never had to see them weaving across a room and falling onto a sofa.

Rose now traveled further when she exiled herself to her room in the evening. Mountains and forests were open to her. Deer watched her progress on pine-scented trails, and she watched theirs. All manner of birds sang for her.

Rose looked for summer jobs that would take her outdoors. Perhaps she could be a camp counselor. She had never joined the Girl Scouts. Her teachers discouraged that because it wasn't a Catholic group.

Rose broached the subject with her mother when she was sober and in a good mood. "I'm thinking about applying for a summer job at Camp Assisi in Western Massachusetts."

"You would go away for the whole summer and leave me alone?" Her mother sighed as if she hardly had the strength to move.

"It would just be for a couple of months." Rose had never been away from her mother for more than a few nights visiting relatives.

"That's too long, dear. If you want to be outdoors, I can take you to Maine."

"That would be lovely, thank you." Fear of her mother's drinking dimmed Rose's enthusiasm at the prospect.

Miraculously, her mother didn't drink on the trip. Rose stuck to her every minute to make sure she didn't enter a liquor store. Fortunately, her mother was embarrassed to buy alcohol in front of her. They chatted and enjoyed the scenery though her mother's face sometimes showed tension from not drinking.

The rocky coast filled Rose's heart with delight. Pines grew on the shores and surf crashed on the rocks. Black and white seabirds swam in the waves. Rose's mother had given her binoculars and Roger Tory Peterson's *Field Guide to Eastern Birds*, and Rose learned the birds were guillemots.

She scrutinized every picture in the book over and over, trying to enter the world of the birds.

At Eagle Lake in the park, they heard an eerie sound. Could that be a loon? Rose scanned the water but could not find any birds. Then a long black-and-white bird surfaced from a dive. Far more majestic than a duck, the loon swam in their direction. It wailed like a wolf of the waters, summoning Rose's heart to soar.

When the time came to leave, Rose failed to hide her tears.

She hoped her mother's sobriety would last. However, after they returned home and her mother could buy alcohol when Rose was at school, the drinking resumed. Rose cried in her room.

When she turned seventeen, Rose asked her Uncle Tim to encourage her mother to seek help for her drinking.

Her mother was close to him, though she sometimes laughed at his piety. "Imagine taking his children to 6:30 Mass every morning before school. That's too much to ask of children," she would say, shaking her head. "He's determined that at least one of them will become a priest or a nun, but he's probably making them so sick of religion that they never will."

Even at her most passionately religious, Rose had agreed that getting up for Mass every day sounded tiring, though she knew she would have to do it as a nun.

Tim had seen her mother intoxicated many times. Rose wondered why he had never tried to intervene earlier.

When she asked him to help, he nodded and said, "All right, honey."

The next day her mother had come to her weeping. "How could you tell Tim I have a drinking problem? He said you had complained about me. Don't you have any loyalty? Don't you love me?"

"Of course I love you." Rose gave up her faint hope that anyone could help.

"I love you so much," her mother had sobbed. "You're my whole life."

Rose's stomach sank whenever she heard that. How could she tell her mother that she didn't want to be anyone's whole life?

Her mother drove when she had been drinking.

Rose didn't bring her friends to her house. Once she had, and her mother drove her friend Diana home. Rose rode with them. Her mother wove in and out of traffic, barely missing other cars. Diana said nothing but Rose had been so worried about Diana's safety and so embarrassed that she never asked anyone over again.

Her mother took her to Maine again to celebrate her high school graduation. They went on a whale-watching boat trip. For a long time, they saw no whales, though seabirds circled overhead. At last, a towering fountain burst out of the water, then disappeared, followed by a huge, gray back with one dorsal fin near the tail. The creature dove, flashing its mammoth tail. The tour guide identified the behemoth as a finback, the second largest whale in the world. Rose cried with joy.

Again, her mother did not drink during the vacation, but resumed drinking when they returned home.

Her mother hugged Rose when St. Euphrosnye's College in Massachusetts accepted her. "I knew they'd accept you because you're such a good student. We can make your father's den into a study for you."

"I'm going to move to a dormitory during the school year."

Her mother frowned. "You have a perfectly good home to stay in. It wouldn't be a very long commute."

"It's at least an hour each way. You've always said I should have more friends my own age. I'll see you on the weekends." She broached a subject that had lain dormant in her heart for too long. "After college, I might enter the convent."

Her mother stared at her as if Rose had said she would emigrate to Australia. "How could you even think of doing that to me? You're my whole life."

"I think I have a vocation," Rose ventured.

"A vocation to break your mother's heart?" She began to cry. "I've done everything I could for you. And now you want to abandon me? There's no one else to take care of me when I grow old. How religious is that?"

Rose's heart sank. Now her mother wanted Rose to devote the rest of her life to taking care of her.

"I won't abandon you." Rose begrudged every word, which was probably a sin.

CHAPTER 4

Sister Matthew

LATE SUMMER 1962

CATHOLICISM WAS TAKEN FOR granted when I grew up. Catholic grade school, Catholic high school. I broke the mold by going to the University of Maryland rather than a Catholic college. I wanted to experience the secular academic world.

I didn't know any Protestants or Jews until I went to college. We weren't supposed to enter Protestant churches or date Protestant boys.

I certainly didn't know any Buddhists or Hindus.

Nor did I know any people who weren't white, except for the old Japanese woman who came to our house once a week to help my mother with cleaning. Oshi didn't speak English, so I didn't really know her.

In college, I hoped to make up for some of those deficiencies.

Many of the girls in my dormitory used words like "shit," and even "fuck." I had learned those words from reading novels. I had never heard anyone say them aloud. My relatives' curse words were "darn," "hell," "Jesus Christ," and very occasionally, "Judas Priest" or "damn."

Most of the girls talked about having sex with their boyfriends. They seemed to see virginity as a liability, something one should lose.

I felt so out of place.

I didn't find it as easy to make friends with girls from different backgrounds as I had hoped.

Only one Negro student lived in my dormitory. Bonnie, a business major, kept her head in a book. I tried sitting next to her in the cafeteria and awkwardly told her I admired civil rights workers who tried to integrate the South, but I wasn't brave enough to join them.

"I just concentrate on my studies," Bonnie replied, unsmiling.

She probably had good reason not to unbend with me. But I continued. "My favorite classes are Comparative Literature and Intro to Philosophy. What are yours?"

"Calculus and business management. I don't have time for anything that won't help me advance." She focused on her Salisbury steak and peas.

After a few attempts at conversation in the cafeteria, I gave up. It seemed we didn't have anything in common. Or she simply had no interest in talking to me. There was no reason why she should.

If there was only one Negro student in the dormitory, the chances she would want to be my friend weren't very high. I saw other white girls trying to talk to her. She must have been tired of white girls wanting to have their first Negro friend.

My university wasn't super-integrated. I knew that as recently as 1950 the NAACP had sued it to require it to admit a Negro man named Parren Mitchell to graduate school.

I didn't do much about civil rights except for sending a small contribution to the Southern Christian Leadership Conference, Dr. King's group.

My life hasn't changed in that respect. There aren't any Negro novices or nuns at St. Euphrosnye's. Some orders were established specifically for Negro women who wanted to become nuns. There probably are some other orders with Negro members, but I don't know of any.

Back to my college days at the University of Maryland. I loved the philosophy class, especially Socrates. More than two thousand years ago, he saw that women and men had the same capacity to think. The unexamined life isn't worth living became my motto. His martyrdom angered me. I wished he had chosen to leave Athens.

Aristotle's idea that men should rule women irritated me.

Some of the students had read Kant and Hegel in high school. That amazed me. I wondered whether I could ever catch up. I wasn't sure Thomas Aquinas was the equal of Hegel.

A girl from India lived on my floor of the dorm. She always wore beautiful saris and had a red dot on her forehead that I later learned to call a *bindi*, a symbol of strength, concentration, love, and good fortune. A long black braid hung down her back. She had a sweet smile.

I sat down next to her at dinner. "Hello, I'm Maureen," I ventured.

She smiled back. "I am Prem. I am glad to meet you, Maureen."

"You're from India?"

"Yes, I am from Bangalore. I am doing graduate work in American literature. I already have a master's degree in English literature."

"A graduate student! I'm an English major, but I'm only a freshman."

Prem became friends with me anyway. I felt honored. She became my closest friend.

Some of the girls laughed behind her back at the statue of Ganesha, an elephant-headed god, on her desk. That irritated me. Why was the statue any stranger than the Incarnation or transubstantiation? The other girls thought the *bindi* was odd. Why was it any odder than the Miraculous Medal, symbol of Our Lady of Grace, that I had worn in my adolescence to enable me to receive grace, or the red cloth scapular of the Precious Blood of Jesus that was supposed to keep me from going to hell when I died?

Prem, like me, talked about books, not guys. She told me to read Virginia Woolf, Ralph Ellison, and Dostoyevsky. We would discuss the books. I saw Prem as the sweet yet elusive Mrs. Ramsey in *To the*

Lighthouse, and I was the painter who felt drawn to her. Prem was like the saintly Karamazov brother Alyosha, who tried to love everyone, no matter how bad they were.

Invisibility pained the hero of *The Invisible Man*. His invisibility wasn't chosen. I wondered whether I would choose the invisibility of becoming a nun.

"I couldn't get through *Crime and Punishment*," I told Prem. "The murder disturbed me." (I didn't tell her about the murder in my high school or why the memory made me feel guilty.) "I loved *The Brothers Karamazov*. Though I found Alyosha was very likeable, I felt more drawn to Ivan."

"I love that book too," Prem said. "What do you think of Ivan's story about The Grand Inquisitor?"

"I think Ivan told the truth when he said if someone like Jesus lived now, he would be killed. Someone murdered Gandhi. Maybe people really do resent great goodness."

"Yes, that seems true, isn't?" Prem smiled even when delivering this sad statement. I loved the way she often ended sentences with "isn't?"

Prem didn't date. "My parents will choose a husband for me," she told me one evening as we sat in her dorm room.

I tried not to gasp, though I'm sure my face registered shock. "Why do you accept their choosing a husband for you?" I asked.

"They love me. They will choose a good man."

"But you've had so much education. Will you be able to teach if you're married?"

"My parents know I want to teach, and they will consider that when they choose." She smiled. "I am not so submissive. They wanted me to marry when I was sixteen, so I refused to eat until they promised I could go to college and graduate school. They were afraid I would die, so they promised."

I stared at her. My heart lurched at the thought of her dying at age sixteen. "You did that? That's amazing."

As Holden Caulfield would say, Prem wasn't a phony.

I couldn't even presume to have a crush on her because she was so clearly out of my reach, but when she returned to India just before my junior year, my chest hurt. Her future with a husband chosen by her parents bothered me so much that I couldn't let myself think about it. I couldn't imagine having someone else choose a man I would have to sleep with for the rest of my life.

I feared I would never see Prem again.

I mailed her a book as a gift. She wrote back asking me to please not send any more gifts because she had to pay a high customs duty. Her reproach cemented my feeling that Prem was unreachable, though I still wrote letters to her.

I began to think that only in the convent could I meet women who were as wholesome and sweet as Prem, but who did not have to make the same compromise she had. Women who would not get married to men.

Surely I would have more freedom as a nun than I had had as a student at St. Agatha's high school. I would have more respect. Everyone I knew respected nuns. They seemed to live on a higher plane than other women.

I admired my university professors. Unfortunately, none of them were women. My chances of teaching English literature in a college probably would be greater if I were a nun belonging to an order that ran its own colleges.

I didn't want to enter the convent until after I finished college. That way, I could study what I wanted instead of what a religious order dictated. I finished as an English major and prayed the nuns would let me go to graduate school and teach English.

I had another reason for entering the convent. Perhaps becoming a nun could absolve me of guilt. I don't want to say for what. Not sex. If only it were just that.

I studied the different orders to decide on one. Not the order that had taught me, the Congregation of St. Agatha, but another teaching order. I had hoped to join a convent in which the nuns were, to be frank, gentler. Not that the nuns ever hit us. I was shocked to hear that happened to some children who went to parochial schools. The sisters at my expensive private school, St. Agatha's, called after the order, were merely verbally harsh, and that was only about half of them.

We called them the Agatha Christies. That also happened to be the name of our volleyball team.

When I was twelve or thirteen, I had thought of joining a missionary order. Years later, when I pondered which order to join, I realized I didn't want to go that far from home. I also lacked enough faith to proselytize. I didn't want to try to convert people who were fine being Buddhists, Muslims, Hindus, or Animists. I never thought of trying to convert Prem.

I found information about the Congregation of St. Euphrosnye, which delighted me when I learned that saint from ancient Alexandria, whose wealthy father pressured her to marry, disguised herself as a man and became a monk. She didn't reveal she was a woman until she was dying.

St. Agatha was also a worthy saint, having refused to marry a pagan man, who then demonstrated his love by having her whipped and burned and having her breasts cut off, then throwing her in prison. He planned to burn her at the stake, as a further punishment for refusing to marry him, but she died in prison. The nuns often praised her for her fortitude and warned that we should use equal zeal in protecting our virginity.

I had no desire to marry a man, but I think I might have preferred that to having my breasts cut off. However, if that were the kind of man he was, maybe the marriage wouldn't have been much better.

I much preferred seeing Agatha Christie as the school's patron.

I learned the Euphrosnyes put all their sisters (at least the ones who were academically inclined) through college and many of them obtained master's degrees. A few even obtained doctorates. The order ran many high schools and two colleges, one in Maryland and one in Massachusetts. That was the order for me. The Mother House, where the postulants and novices were trained, was conveniently located in western Maryland, not impossibly far from my parents' home.

I admit that the photos of the Mother House, with its lovely traditional cloisters and blooming garden, influenced me. If I were going to be a nun, I might as well be one in an inspiring setting, though I knew the setting would change when the order sent me out to teach.

CHAPTER 5

Sister Matthew

AFTER I SENT IN an application, had an interview with the Euphrosnyes, said nothing about my doctrinal insubordination, and was accepted, I announced my decision to my mother during spring break.

My mother and father felt like my only real family. My brother, John, went off to college when I was little and never came home much after that. I liked him, but he seemed more like a cousin than a brother. He became a lawyer like my father, except that Dad works in a mostly Democratic law firm immersed in Washington politics while John works for General Motors, much to Dad's displeasure. John's wife, Mimi, is obsessed with clothes and home furnishings. She and I have nothing in common except John. Their three children are cute, but I saw them only once a year when they traveled from Michigan to Maryland to visit us. I enjoyed shopping for birthday and Christmas presents for them with my mother. Buying presents for children was all I wanted to do with them.

My mother and I had just finished eating dinner at the mahogany table in our home in the fancy suburb of Chevy Chase, in Maryland just past the Washington border. We had eaten lamb chops, which my mother often cooked because they were my favorite. For dessert, we ate pineapple upside-down cake she had made, left over from Sunday dinner. We saved some for when Dad came home. My father was working late, a normal habit for a Washington lawyer, so it seemed to be a good time to tell her my news. I didn't want to face my parents as a united front.

Mom looked good as usual. She went to the hairdresser's every week, but she drew the line at dyeing her hair to hide the gray. She considered dyed hair unladylike. So was working outside the home, except for Eleanor Roosevelt. Mom cultivated her garden, volunteered at the parish bake sales and fairs, and belonged to a bridge club. She grew everything from pansies to delphiniums, from peonies to lilies-of-the-valley. Her irises were her pride and joy. She grew them in every color, and some were fringed, so-called bearded irises. Her iris bed won first prize from the Chevy Chase Garden Club two years in a row. She wouldn't call herself an artist, but she saw the garden as her palette. Unfortunately, she often expected me to work in the garden, though I disliked putting my hands in dirt. There be worms there.

Although I would rather die than live a life like hers, I shouldn't judge her because I had enjoyed her driving me to and from school and being home with me after school.

I stared at the walls with subtle light green wallpaper and the cabinet where my mother kept special cups and saucers she collected. A small crystal chandelier hung over the table.

"Let me do the dishes," I said, carrying out the plates. I probably should have washed them every night. I didn't when I had a lot of schoolwork to do. Although we could have afforded a dishwasher, my mother had never bought one. She liked to use good china and silverware at every meal, and she claimed a dishwasher would damage them. I believed she just thought washing dishes was good for building one's character. Considering how clumsy I was, my washing the dishes probably risked them more than a dishwasher would have.

"Thank you, dear," she replied innocently, not knowing I planned to shock her.

After I washed, dried, and put away every dish without injuring any, I went into the living room, where she had just finished watching the news.

"I need to tell you something important. May I turn off the television?" Many Catholic homes had a religious statue on the television set, but we did not. When I was twelve, I had thought my parents weren't religious enough. They never went to church except on Sundays, Good Friday, Christmas, and other Holy Days of Obligation like the Feast of the Immaculate Conception. At that time my only quarrel with the Church was the ban on eating meat on Fridays.

My parents had never once said they hoped I would enter the convent. I preferred that to pushing me to do it, like the parents of some girls I knew. One of my high school classmates' parents constantly told her they prayed for her to become a nun. She eloped with the first guy she dated.

When I turned off the television, my mother squared her shoulders since she didn't know whether my news would be good or bad.

I sat next to her on the sofa. "I want to enter the convent."

She gaped at me. "You can't mean that. This is so sudden. Have you really thought about it?"

"I've been thinking about it for years. I just wanted to wait until I graduate from college. I'm going to take classes all summer so I can graduate at the end of the year because the order I want to enter takes in new postulants in January."

She leaned forward to debate. "You don't know anything about life. You've never had a serious boyfriend. The boys in college may have disappointed you, but you will have many other opportunities to meet a man you could love and marry."

"That's not the life I want." She had no idea how much I didn't want it. "I want to devote my life to God."

"You haven't said anything like that since you were twelve years old. Are you really that pious? When you're home, you just go to Mass on Sundays."

"It's been on my mind. Maybe I should have told you sooner. I think I have a vocation."

"Do you? You always do just what you want. I can't see you as a nun."

She had hit on my sore point. It was true that I generally did what I wanted. "I can learn to change."

"You're fine as you are." She frowned. "I don't understand why you haven't talked to me about this, why you're just springing it on me now."

"I'm sorry about that. Maybe I should have told you."

"How many people have you told?" Her tone sharpened. "Am I the last person to find out?"

"I haven't told many people. I've talked to a priest."

She raised her eyebrows. "That's an objective source. Don't tell me you haven't talked to your friends."

"A few friends."

"But not to your own mother."

"I'm sorry," I repeated.

My mother sat up straight in her battle posture. "Why would you want to spend your whole life shut up in a convent? I don't think you were that fond of the nuns who taught you. You didn't even want to go to a Catholic college. Maybe you should have done that."

"I went to the university to have a broader experience and learn whether I still wanted to enter the convent. I do."

"Have you ever been in love?"

"No." She wouldn't want to hear about Bernadette.

She sighed as if I had said the world was flat and shook her head. "You don't even know what you're giving up."

"Please, mother. I know what the world is like. I know I'm giving up marriage and children. Those are great things, but not for me. You already have grandchildren."

"That's not the point. Do you have any idea how much this will hurt your father?"

"I don't want to hurt him."

"You don't understand how parents love their children. You can't possibly know what it's like to be a mother."

"I just know I have a wonderful mother."

"Oh, Maureen. I love you so much." She gave me a pitiful look as if I had said I had cancer. "I just want you to be happy."

"I will be happy. I can see why you're surprised. I have so many faults. I don't exactly radiate love of God. But I do want to spend my life trying to learn to be a better person."

"You think you can only do that in the convent?"

"I think I have a vocation to be there."

"You've made up your mind. I know how stubborn you are."

"At least I can try the convent. I can leave before my final vows if it isn't the life for me. I couldn't do that with a marriage."

She rolled her eyes. "Of course not. That's what engagements are for."

"I want to become engaged to Jesus." That line was shameless.

My mother snorted at my ridiculous statement. "You think lay Catholics like me don't love God enough?"

"Mother! I know you lead a good life. I just want a different one."

She sighed again. "I hope you'll be happy." Her tone implied I would be miserable.

"I will. Very happy." I couldn't admit I felt completely uncertain about that. "I've already picked out the order I want to join."

"Which order?"

"The Congregation of St. Euphrosnye."

Her eyes widened. "What? I never heard of that order. Where are they? Across the country?"

"No, just across the state. The Mother House is in Western Maryland. You can get there and back to Chevy Chase on visiting days. Let me show you their prospectus. I won't leave you out of this part of my life any longer, Mom. I promise."

"I'll hardly ever be able to see you." She managed an even deeper sigh.

"That would also be true if I went to another city for graduate school or if I married a man who needed to take a job elsewhere."

"But at least you could come home for Thanksgiving and Christmas."

She had found the most painful aspect for me. "I know. That will be the hardest thing to give up." The thought almost brought me to tears. I tried to hug her.

"Oh, Maureen, I need to have time to absorb this. You'll have to be the one to tell your father." She broke away and went to her bedroom.

I felt like a heel, which she probably intended. I wished I could tell her my real reasons. I didn't think I'd be able to keep on attending Mass if I were in the world. I needed to immerse myself in religion to feel love for Possible God. And I longed to be around women. I couldn't bear to think of years of people, her most of all, urging me to date men.

My father spent the next evening at home. He brought his briefcase with him though he didn't always dig into his work. He was proud of his six-foot height but sighed over his thinning hair. Like me, he needed to wear glasses.

He went to the living room and turned on the television.

I brought him a beer as my mother usually encouraged me to do. She stayed in the kitchen, forcing me to tell him alone.

"Dad, could we talk for a minute?"

"Sure we can, honey." He turned down the sound on the TV. "What's the occasion? Do you have a boyfriend?"

"Just the opposite. I feel I have a vocation to enter the convent."

He smiled. "I thought maybe you would. You've always been such an extra good girl. I'm proud of you. You'd better pray for me. Lawyers need all the prayers we can get."

I was the one whose jaw dropped. "You don't mind?"

"No. I saw some of the mail you were getting during the Christmas holidays. Stuff from half a dozen orders of nuns. Honey, no father likes to think of his daughter belonging to another man. He worries about how a husband will treat her. If Jesus is the lucky man, I'm not too worried."

I hugged him, which hid my amazed face.

"Since John immersed himself in materialism, I guess I shouldn't be surprised that you've gone completely in the other direction."

I giggled. "Oh Dad, you're being too harsh. Just because John bought a million-dollar house."

My father groaned and shook his head. Then he smiled at me. "Will the nuns let you go to graduate school?" he asked.

"I hope so." I kept my face hidden. His question worried me more than any of my mother's.

I CALLED MY HIGH school friends to tell them I planned to enter the convent. They all wished me well in voices that sounded as if they thought I was slightly nuts. More than one said, "I never knew you were that religious." Bernadette said she planned to go to graduate school in social work. I wondered whether she chose a better path than I did.

I wrote Prem, and she wrote back that she had just been married to a cousin and believed she had a good life. She said I would no doubt lead a holy life as a consecrated nun. She suggested I must have been very good in a previous life.

If I had been, I must be slipping now, I thought. Goodness eluded me.

THE MOTHER HOUSE WAS all that I expected it to be. I can't say the same of the nuns. They were much the same as those at St. Agatha's, a mixture of more and less pleasant women.

A statue of St. Euphrosnye in her monk's habit stood in the chapel, but the sisters scarcely mentioned how remarkable she was to have lived concealed all those years. I suppose they saw her as something like Shakespeare's women disguised as men who acted like proper women by the end of the plays.

I feared I might become just like the nuns I had disliked. Crabby because I couldn't do everything I wanted. I prayed I would never take out any irritations on my students, or on the other sisters.

Would I ever be able to endure the silence?

I'M LYING TO MYSELF. I love silence, except when I'm near someone I have a burning urge to talk to. I never liked small talk. I have little desire to discuss the weather. Conversations in the world turned too readily to television shows. And I don't miss the talk about clothes. Wouldn't it be awful if any of the sisters asked if the habit was becoming, and wouldn't she look better in a Dominican habit?

Being among women who were silent because they were meditating, or trying to, often feels like a privilege.

Public confession does not feel like a privilege.

Today I knocked over my glass of water at lunch. The glass fell to the floor and broke. That was a fault I would have to confess. Clumsiness is not a welcome trait in the convent. Breaking anything constitutes a violation of the vow of poverty because it will cost the convent money, not that I've taken vows. Those come after the novitiate, which will be in the beginning of 1964.

It's Friday afternoon, time for chapter meeting. My least favorite time of the week.

We filed into the dark room on the upper floor. All the shades have been pulled down. Are we supposed to be afraid of the dark? Worse, the windows are shut even though it's a hot day and we're sweltering. Our taste of purgatory, perhaps?

Reverend Mother Robert Bellarmine and Mean Mother Michael, the Mistress of Novices, are seated in a higher row and look down on us. The rest of us are novices. It would be improper for us to hear the faults of professed sisters, who are above us. They have a separate chapter meeting. When we were postulants, we had our own chapter meeting so we couldn't hear the faults of the novices.

Reverend Mother looks benign, though she has the kind of dignity you would expect a mother superior to have. She is probably in her early fifties, tall and thin. Like most of the nuns, she wears glasses. (I wish we didn't have to wear wire rims.) If she were a movie star, she could have played the parts of queens.

Mean Mother Michael, the Mistress of Novices, would play the parts of unhappy wives, or maybe unhappy career women.

We took turns confessing our faults and saying, "*mea culpa.*" Sister Agnes, a.k.a. Helen, a nervous girl of eighteen or nineteen, is in line ahead of me. She would play the part of the girl who is afraid of boys. Or the snitch, which she is in real life. When she went to the center of the room, she slumped as if weighed down by her little faults. She knelt. She believes in the rules even more than she did as a postulant, when we all knew never to trust her with our secrets. Her humility drives me nuts.

"Dear Reverend Mother and Mistress of Novices, and my dear sisters, I am guilty of eating extra jam when I had kitchen duty." Agnes always confesses in a tone of utter submission. "I also spilled milk when I poured it into the pitcher this morning. I felt annoyance when

Mother Michael criticized me properly for spilling the milk. I am also guilty of being inattentive at early prayers last Saturday morning. I cried out when I fell on the stairs during the time when I was supposed to be silent. *Mea culpa, mea culpa, mea maxima culpa.*"

Reverend Mother gave Agnes her penance. "You shall say an extra full rosary in chapel."

The full rosary, fifteen decades dedicated to the Joyous, Sorrowful, and Glorious Mysteries in Mary's life, is a pain. The five-decade rosary, with its fifty Hail Marys, plus some Our Fathers and Glory Bes (Glory Be to the Father, and to the Son, and to the Holy Spirit, as it was in the beginning is now, and ever shall be. Amen), is boring enough. It takes about 15 minutes, so doing it three times is enough to wear down all but the most pious. The Joyous Mysteries are the Annunciation, when the Angel Gabriel told Mary she would bear the child of God; the Visitation, when she told her cousin Elizabeth about her pregnancy, causing the unborn John the Baptist to leap with joy in Elizabeth's womb; the Nativity of Jesus; the Presentation of the child Jesus in the Temple; and the Finding of Jesus in the Temple, when the boy slipped away from his parents and was talking to the rabbis in a learned manner. The Sorrowful Mysteries are Jesus's Agony in the Garden, when he knew he would be betrayed and killed; the Scourging at the Pillar after his capture; the Crowning with Thorns; the Carrying of the Cross; and the Crucifixion and Death. The Glorious Mysteries are Jesus's Resurrection from the dead; his Ascension into heaven; the Descent of the Holy Spirit on the Apostles, commemorated at Pentecost; the Assumption of Mary to heaven without dying; and the Coronation of Mary as Queen of heaven.

We wear long rosaries with large black beads hanging from our waists. That's my least favorite part of the costume—I mean habit.

Agnes bowed and kissed the floor. She returned to her seat. I'm sure she thought she was quite the sinner.

My turn came next. I tried to refrain from tripping. Being congenitally clumsy is one of my crosses to bear. I knelt.

I would never confess the faults that would really upset my superiors, like the fact that I mind being called Sister Matthew instead of Maureen.

"Dear Reverend Mother and Mistress of Novices and my dear sisters, I ate more than my share of chicken last night. I am often greedy about food. I broke one of the convent's glasses when I washed the dishes on Monday and another one today at lunch. I spent too much time thinking about my mother and father instead of concentrating on prayer. *Mea culpa, mea culpa, mea maxima culpa.*"

Reverend Mother told me to say a full rosary and refrain from eating meat on Saturday night.

Hiding my disgust, I kissed the floor. I knew I would have to give up a meal of meat, but I had to confess at least one real fault because they would be sure I had committed one. If I were lucky, the meat I miss would be liver, though probably on Saturday night it would be something better.

Every time I confessed in chapter meetings, I could hear my father laughing over the minor faults and my mother saying, "I told you so," meaning she knew part of my convent life would be annoying.

I saved my real sins for the confessional, where they were private. The chapter meetings were the place to address rule-breaking, not sins. In the confessional I could confess my dislike of Mother Michael, but not my skepticism about a deity.

When Rose's turn came, I watched her out of the corner of my eye so I wouldn't show what I felt. She moved with grace, in both senses of the word.

Her dear voice told of what she thought were her faults.

"I sometimes wish to spend more time in exercise than we are allowed to do. I am reluctant to get up in the morning. My mind sometimes wanders during the holy rosary. *Mea culpa, mea culpa, mea maxima culpa.*"

My most grievous fault, ha. Rose could never have a grievous fault.

Thank goodness she didn't say anything about wanting to talk to me. She never confesses that.

"You shall say two extra full rosaries and be attentive to your prayers," Reverend Mother told her.

I hated to see Rose's dear lips kiss the floor.

CHAPTER 6
Rose

1958, MASSACHUSETTS

AFTER GETTING AWAY FROM her mother, Rose immersed herself in St. Euphrosnye's College, a girls' college run by the same order of nuns who had taught her in grade school and high school. She joined the college drama club and the swim team. In the drama club, she saw one girl who stood out from the rest.

In her first audition, Rose tried out for the part of Hermia in *A Midsummer Night's Dream*. She laughed to herself at Hermia's decision to run away with the man she loved rather than being forced to become a celibate priestess because she refused to marry the man her father chose. Celibacy. What a terrible fate!

All the parts were to be played by girls from the college, but more girls tried out for the female parts than the male parts. A girl named Nancy O'Shea tried out for the part of Bottom. She made herself so ridiculously obnoxious and obnoxiously ridiculous that everyone who watched her burst out laughing. Rose laughed until the tears ran down her cheeks.

After the auditions, she walked with Nancy to the cafeteria for lunch. "You were great as Bottom. You could be a professional actress."

Nancy blushed. "I tried out for that part because I know I'm too heavy to be chosen for any of the female parts."

"It's the best part in the play, and you're perfect for it. You're very attractive, too," Rose protested. She realized Nancy probably guessed correctly about the drama teacher's casting choices. That angered Rose. Nancy's curly brown hair and big brown eyes were lovely. So was her plump body.

They ate lunch together every day after that, and sometimes dinner too. Rose could hardly wait for the next time they could be together.

The next semester, they asked to be made roommates and were granted that privilege.

One night when they were getting ready for bed, Nancy started reminiscing. "Playing Bottom last semester was the most fun thing I've ever done." She began to sing in a grotesque voice. "The finch, the plain-song cuckoo gray…"

Delighted, Rose tried to remember Titania's lines. "I pray thee, gentle mortal, sing again."

"Good hay, sweet hay. Hee haw, hee haw!" Nancy pretended to chew hay.

They choked with laughter.

"You were so funny," Rose said. "You're the most delightful person I've ever met."

"You really think so? I think you are."

"I care about you so much."

Nancy blushed a deep red. "I care so much about you, too. You don't know how much you mean to me." Nancy's gaze was just as inviting as her words.

"I can't even begin to tell you how much you mean to me." Rose put her arms around Nancy and hugged her.

Nancy hugged Rose in return and didn't move out of her arms.

Rose kissed Nancy's lips, which felt better than anything else ever had. Nancy's breath smelled sweet. Rose paused.

Nancy didn't pull away. She returned the kiss.

Rose felt her whole body tingle. This was love, she thought. If she found true love, that meant God wanted her to stay in the world instead of joining the convent.

They tumbled into Rose's bed, still kissing. Soon Rose wrapped her legs around Nancy. Nancy clung to her. Rose wanted their embrace to go on forever.

She thought her heart would burst with joy. She loved Nancy and Nancy loved her. All her dreams had come true.

But when she woke in the morning, Nancy had already left.

Nancy didn't come to the cafeteria that day.

Rose worried. Was Nancy sick? Or was she embarrassed?

Nancy didn't return to their dorm room until late that night.

"Where have you been? Are you all right?"

Nancy turned away from her and began to cry. "How could I possibly be all right? We sinned terribly. I went to Confession, and my sin was absolved, but I never want to talk to you again. I've asked to be transferred to another room."

Rose slumped onto her bed. "Oh Nancy, I don't think what we did was a sin. We care about each other."

"It certainly was a sin." Nancy sobbed. "Don't talk to me. I'm not listening to you. Please stay away from me."

Rose gasped. Losing Nancy as a friend sounded unimaginable. "Can't we still be friends? I won't ask you to do anything you don't want to do."

"No, we can't be friends." Nancy shuddered. "If you don't recognize that what we did was a sin, you're a monster. It's just like *A Midsummer Night's Dream*. I thought you were nice, but then I learned you were a beast."

A leaden weight descended on Rose's heart. She knew she would never like *A Midsummer Night's Dream* again.

Another dreadful idea occurred to her. "Did you tell anyone besides the priest what we did?"

"No. I could never bear to tell anyone."

Thank goodness for that, Rose thought. She had no doubt she would be expelled if Nancy told. Having to leave St. Euphrosnye's College would be unbearable.

"Am I safe to go to bed tonight without you trying to take advantage of me?"

Rose felt she had died and gone to hell, though not because of sin. "I won't touch you." She went to bed and pulled the covers over her head. Nancy's scent from the night before still clung to the sheets.

Rose sobbed and heard Nancy also crying.

Rose vowed she must never let herself be hurt that way again. She wanted to join the convent and to desire only the perfect love of God. Dedicating herself to God sounded better than dedicating herself to her mother.

ROSE WISHED SHE COULD study deer or some other animals. She would never have had the chance because she couldn't bear to dissect animals in biology class. Majoring in science had not been a possibility.

She hoped to teach high school, though she would never be able to teach about the glories of the natural world. Instead, she would teach about the imperfections of the human one.

Majoring in history had held her interest. She liked the striving for perfection when countries drafted constitutions.

However, she thought her history classes missed important parts of history.

Professor Anthony Pickering, a balding man in his fifties, taught European history at her college.

One day when she went to his office to discuss a paper, she had ventured, "Why do we study only wars, constitutions, and elections? Isn't there something more to history? I'd like to learn about what ordinary people were doing. Could I write my paper about ordinary people, like housewives, in nineteenth century England?"

Although Professor Pickering sat at his desk and she stood in front of it, he seemed to look down on her. He shook his head. "Historians focus on important deeds for a reason. Studies like the one you suggest would bore readers. No one would read them. Why don't you write a paper about Disraeli or Gladstone?"

Rose held back her sigh. "But everyone writes about Disraeli or Gladstone."

"There's a good reason for that. They did important things. History is not about trivia."

"Could I write a paper on George Eliot? Is her character Daniel Deronda inspired by Disraeli? Didn't she influence history?"

His tone sharpened. "This is a history class, not a literature class. I don't think any novelists except Dickens influenced nineteenth century English history. His writings led to reform efforts, but let me preempt any questions by saying no, you cannot write about him. You could write about the reform laws."

"Yes, Professor Pickering."

She repressed her annoyance at his narrow views. If she ever had the chance to teach history, she planned to include in the curriculum novels from the era she taught about.

ONE EVENING DURING ROSE'S junior year, the phone in her room rang. She picked it up and heard her Uncle Tim's choking voice.

"Hello, Rose." He sounded as if he were crying. "Your mother died in a car accident this afternoon. I'm sorry, honey. We must pray for her soul."

The blow almost knocked her over. She gasped. "Oh no." Another terrible thought hit her. "Was anyone else hurt?"

"No. Her car hit a lamppost."

At least her mother hadn't killed anyone else.

Rose wanted to die. The person she loved most. The person who loved her most. She was no one without her mother.

"You should have stayed home and driven her around instead of going to live in a dormitory," her uncle accused. "She wouldn't have died then."

Rose shook her head, though he couldn't see her. No, her mother's death wasn't her fault. Why didn't he also blame himself for not doing more to intervene?

She choked back her tears. "Where is her body?"

"At the city morgue. They'll need to know where to take it. Our family has always used Halloran's Funeral Home."

"Halloran's it'll be."

Rose went through the motions of making the many arrangements for her mother's funeral. She thought of the mother who had read her stories when she was little, the mother who had always seemed to be in a good mood, until Rose's father started yelling all the time. And the mother who gave Rose a field guide to birds and took her to Maine.

At least she could enter the convent without abandoning her mother. Rose felt ashamed to feel a bit relieved. She still had cherished hopes of entering though she had avoided mentioning it to her mother again.

A few days after her mother's funeral, Rose told her uncle she planned to enter the convent after graduation. He nodded. "I'm glad to hear that. Our family needs someone who will." None of his children had entered religious life. Now at least he could brag that his niece would pray for him, Rose thought.

She discovered that her mother's will left everything to her.

She told Uncle Tim she would sell the house and give all the money to charity. That didn't please him as she had believed it would.

He guffawed. "I didn't think your mother raised any foolish children. Read the will again. Your mother was smarter than you give her credit for. She left everything in trust for you because she worried that you'd give it all away. So, if you leave the convent before you're thirty, you'll have a nest egg."

"I won't ever leave," Rose had insisted. "I'll give the money away when I can."

Life in the convent would likely be much less lonely than her mother's life.

DURING ROSE'S SENIOR YEAR in college, her roommate, Phyllis, begged her to go out with a man. "Please, Rose, he's my boyfriend's cousin. Jack wants us to double date. Greg's a nice guy, very Catholic. He goes to Loyola with Jack. He won't paw you or anything. The worst thing that could happen is that you'd be bored because he's a business major. Please, Rose. *Exodus* should be great. You'll like the movie, even if you aren't crazy about Greg."

Rose let herself be persuaded.

Phyllis was a history major like Rose, so they sometimes had interesting conversations. Phyllis had good taste in movies, but Rose wished they sometimes could go without male dates.

Greg turned out to be nice enough looking, square-jawed with symmetrical features. He asked Rose about her classes as well as telling her about his, which was the most she expected from guys. She found going to movies with him no more interesting than she had thought it would be.

They went out as a foursome several times. Rose saw some good movies and some that weren't so good.

Then Greg asked her out alone. She wanted to see *Spartacus*, so she went.

When he took her back to the dorm, he tried to kiss her in his car. She had imagined he understood she didn't have any romantic feelings about him.

Rose pulled back. "I can't."

"I know you're a good girl. I'm not asking you to do anything more than kiss. I respect you."

"I understand that, but I still can't. Please don't ask me." She started to get out of the car.

He frowned. "Why did you go out with me if you don't like me?" His tone became querulous. "I thought you liked me."

"I like you, but not in that way. We shouldn't go to the movies anymore."

Before he could object any further, she left the car and rushed into the dorm.

She thought how much she would like to kiss a girl again. Maybe she would never have the chance.

A few days later, Phyllis confronted Rose as she was getting ready for bed. "Why did you treat Greg so coldly? He's such a nice guy. He really likes you."

"He is a nice guy. I just didn't want to kiss him." Greg's complaining to others annoyed her.

Phyllis gave an exaggerated sigh. "You don't get it. He's serious about you. He might even propose someday if you'd act a little warmer. He wouldn't expect you to go all the way before you're married. You're lucky he's interested in you?"

Rose frowned. "You mean I'm lucky that a man is interested in me in spite of the birthmark on my face?"

Phyllis colored. "I was trying not to say that, but yes. Not to mention that you're so shy around men. Don't you want to get married someday?"

Rose turned away and took out her pajamas. "You don't understand. I want to enter the convent."

Phyllis shrieked. "You're kidding! You can't really mean to do that. I like having nuns as teachers, but I sure wouldn't want to spend my whole life with them."

"But I do." Rose steeled herself to hear weeks of protests from Phyllis. She regretted agreeing to go out with Greg. The whole dating business felt like something out of a comic book.

Life in the convent gleamed ahead like an illuminated manuscript, a world away from the comic book of ordinary life.

CHAPTER 7
Rose

JANUARY 1962
ST. EUPHROSNYE'S MOTHER HOUSE, WESTERN MARYLAND

ROSE REPENTED EVERY DAY for failing to save her mother. Uncle Tim had probably been right that she had been wrong to leave her mother alone.

The other postulants undoubtedly just had little faults. She was the only one with such a great sin of omission.

She would try to act as sweet as possible to the other women in the convent, but that would never make up for failing her mother.

Rose wondered which other postulants in her entrance year would be her friends, though she knew she wasn't supposed to like any of them more than the others.

She didn't mind leaving Boston to go to the Mother House in Maryland. Boston held too many memories.

Leaving the woods forever felt far more difficult. She tried to bury the thought.

The Mother House looked so much like her image of a convent, like a convent on a hill in Europe. The real cloister delighted her.

On her entrance day, she tried not to watch the other young women, who all had parents there to say goodbye. She had told Uncle Tim that he didn't need to come. She wished he would insist but told herself not to be hurt that he hadn't traveled to Maryland because he had a cold.

After going through the door that separated them from their families, the new postulants all donned long black skirts and long-sleeved black shirts. Rose looked forward to wearing a real habit when she became a novice.

She looked cautiously at the other girls. One postulant had the most beguiling smile. Her name was Maureen Collins.

The first morning in the convent, when Rose awakened at 5 a.m. for early morning prayers, her heart sang. She was truly a postulant, on the path to becoming a nun.

Here, she felt at home. Sister Gabriel, her former seventh-grade teacher, had been sent to Maryland to become Mother Gabriel, the Mistress of Postulants. Yesterday she had spoken to Rose in an aside, so that others wouldn't notice. "Welcome, dear girl. I am so glad you are joining our order." Rose's heart surged with joy.

Reverend Mother Robert Bellarmine had taught Rose's freshman college theology class. At the end of the year, Sister Robert Bellarmine had been elected the order's mother superior and had moved from Boston to Maryland. Reverend Mother also had greeted Rose individually, saying, "I remember you. I believe you are in the right place." Yes, Rose had come home.

As Rose walked to chapel, she glimpsed the sunrise. Back in Massachusetts, she had often risen early to watch birds. The summer before she entered the convent, she had taken a final trip to Maine, to bid farewell to the coast and climb Cadillac Mountain to watch the sun rise over the ocean. Now she heard a mockingbird sing and tried to be content with snatches of its song.

She entered the chapel with the others. The postulants went to the first row, near the altar. The congregation began singing the *Te Deum*. Her life would still be filled with song, with women singing instead of birds, and she could take part in it. "*Te Deum, laudamus,*" she sang with the others. "Oh God, we praise you."

Rose didn't mind the confessions in chapter meetings or the penances. Experiencing her mother's alcoholism had been worse than any penance Reverend Mother could give her. The feeling that she had failed her mother stayed with her.

When spring came, Rose thrilled at the mild air in the convent garden. At any air. She would have been just as happy to feel the blows of a strong wind, but the postulants were not allowed out in inclement weather because they might get sick and neglect their duties.

The convent garden was laid out in sections, one for flowers and the other for vegetables. The nuns grew peas, beans, tomatoes, and squash, as well as rosemary, basil, and parsley.

A willow flowed like a waterfall at one end of the garden, while maples and oaks ringed the edges. A statue of the Blessed Virgin Mary stood not far from the willow.

Rose told herself not to mind that she could sometimes hear cars when she walked in the garden. At least the convent wasn't in a city, so the noise was intermittent.

She prayed to be forgiven for wanting to spend all her time outdoors. Now that she was a postulant, she needed to keep herself on that spiritual path. She must not consider walking in the convent garden a poor substitute for hiking in the mountains and watching animals. She failed to confess in chapter meetings how difficult it was to spend so much time indoors because she didn't want Reverend Mother to tell her she should leave. Rose did recount her desire to Father Nolan, the nuns' chaplain, in Confession. He told her it was good to love God's world but not to excess. The convent was as much a part of that world as the forest, and better because it was filled with prayers, he said.

Should she think of the cloister as a trail and the nuns as a herd of deer? She rebuked herself for that joke, which she vowed would never cross her lips.

ROSE'S NAMESAKE FLOWERS IN all colors graced the convent garden, some of them growing across a trellis. They had just begun to bloom that spring when she was a postulant. Tags with the roses' names indicated what colors they would be. Beds of annuals spread out on either side of a gravel walkway.

Rose told herself that she walked in an enchanted garden, a secret garden. She knew she would love it, yet she wished for wildflowers. Some bluebells represented wildflowers, but they weren't the real thing. She prayed to be content.

Yet she regretted that no stream flowed or water pooled in the garden. No swan, goose, or duck could swim there. No migrating sandpipers would stop by to feed. No warblers would bathe. She would miss wild water.

She walked through the garden with Maureen and another postulant, Helen. They were supposed to walk in threes to discourage particular friendships. Helen was quiet and well-behaved, adjectives that described most of the postulants. Rose tried to find something likeable about each of them, though she already liked some much better than others. Especially Maureen.

Squirrels chased each other up the trees and robins scurried across the grass, but Rose hoped for more exciting birds.

A new song thrilled her.

"A Baltimore oriole! It's early in the year for them." Rose stared at the tree that must hold the gleaming bird.

"I've never seen a Baltimore oriole," Maureen said.

"Neither have I." Helen's glance followed Rose's.

"But you're both from Maryland! They're supposed to be common here. I see it! It's at eleven o'clock on the tree."

"You look at the tree as if it's a clock?" Helen peered into the trees.

"I think I see a glimmer of orange. Lovely." Maureen smiled. She wore glasses, so perhaps her vision wasn't good. At least she could catch a glimpse of the bird.

"Now I see it, too." Helen peered at it. "Thank you."

The oriole flew, its orange flashing like flames. Rose tried not to wish she could have brought her binoculars to the convent.

Maureen smiled. Her smile looked somehow different from the other postulants' smiles. "Emily Dickinson wrote, 'Hope is the thing with feathers.'"

"What a beautiful line," Rose said, enchanted.

"Hope is one of the three theological virtues," Helen announced, as if they didn't all know that.

Rose could see Maureen's eyebrows rising ever so slightly behind her glasses.

"You're a birdwatcher?" Maureen skirted on the edge of asking Rose about her past, which was forbidden.

"Yes." Rose didn't think she could say much more to Maureen with another postulant listening.

"Please point out birds when we're outside and are allowed to talk," Maureen urged her.

"I shall." Rose longed to show her every bird. Might a scarlet tanager visit the convent garden? How many migrating birds would stop in it?

She remembered driving to Cape Cod to watch migrating birds in Wellfleet. She could almost feel the salty ocean breeze. That led her to thoughts of lobsters. She chastised herself for letting her mind drift too far. The convent meals were pretty good. She must not mind that she would probably never taste lobster again.

"That's a mockingbird, isn't it?" Maureen asked.

Rose looked across the garden, where the mockingbird sang its head off. "Yes." Even people who had never studied birds knew mockingbirds and robins. Rose suspected Maureen had asked that just to hear her confirm it.

Perhaps Maureen enjoyed the sound of her voice as much as she enjoyed hearing Maureen's. Rose found it hard not to look into

Maureen's hazel eyes. Maureen's glasses did not detract from their beauty.

When they were alone for a rare moment, Maureen would say something ridiculous, like "They seat the postulants and novices in the front of the chapel so we won't see the old nuns nodding at early morning prayers." Rose tried not to laugh too loudly.

Maureen had such a dear way of talking. Such a dear way of moving, trying to keep her hands from gesturing when she talked, then slapping one hand with the other when she failed. Her hazel eyes held hidden depths.

What might have happened if Rose had met Maureen outside the convent?

Rose tried to stop herself from thinking about that. But she did imagine what it might be like to kiss Maureen. To feel soft lips again. She now thought the lips would have to be Maureen's.

However much she liked Maureen, Rose had to fight her urge to fly away, to follow the birds and watch migration across the country. What would it be like to go to Nebraska and watch the gatherings of sandhill cranes? She both wanted and did not want to be rooted at the convent.

Nevertheless, Rose still went on her time and place travels. She begged God and the Virgin Mary to be allowed to see more of the world.

In her curtain-lined cell, before she went to sleep, she sometimes found her way to distant places.

One night she appeared among tall tropical trees, some festooned with hanging creepers. A large black monkey with white cheeks—or maybe it was a gibbon, so an ape—swung through from tree to tree, giving a call that resounded through the jungle, a high-pitched yet booming ho, ho, ho, ho. Rose stared at it until it disappeared from her view. Then birds drew her attention. She spotted a tiny kingfisher decked in rainbow feathers, with a bright yellow front, blue sides, and a dazzling fuchsia and red back. Its long red bill opened, and the bird flew off with a call almost like a hiss. Then a bird with a large, pale bill, a blue head, and a long green tail let out a piercing shriek.

Gunfire blasted through the jungle. A pair of huge gray birds, maybe cranes, made a loud, creaking bellow and flew up over her head. Rose hid in terror in a bamboo thicket.

When the sound of gunfire had stopped, she snuck out from behind the bamboo, walked in the direction from which the sound had come, and found bodies, several of them children—three Asian boys, and a girl too—as well as an adult man. The man was clothed in a uniform, while the others just wore simple pants and tunics. Rose had never seen murdered people covered with blood, some with their guts spilling out. She gagged, and her heart ached.

Then Rose saw one dead American soldier, also young, though not as young as most of the Vietnamese.

Why were American soldiers killing these people? President Kennedy had said they were in Vietnam just as advisers.

Rose escaped to her cell and wept. She wondered whether her time traveling gift was a blessing or a curse.

She chastised herself for that thought. She must have been sent to Vietnam because she needed to know about the horrors of war. She should not expect to learn only about the beauties of the world.

The next day, she wished she had a way to discover the names of the birds she had seen. She beat her chest to beg God's forgiveness for thinking of the birds despite the horror she had witnessed.

IN SUMMER, WHEN THE time came for Rose to enter the novitiate, Reverend Mother Robert Bellarmine told her she would keep the name of Rose, as she had requested.

"St. Rose de Lima is a good patron for you." Reverend Mother smiled at her.

Everything about becoming a novice was perfect, except that no one from her family would be there for the ceremony. She had hoped her Uncle Tim would come from Boston. However, his oldest son was getting married the same weekend, so of course the wedding had priority.

Before the ceremony, the postulants donned their new clothes. The black habit. The white monastic scapular, a large stiff covering over her habit that spread across her chest. The coif that capped her head and the wimple that covered her cheeks and neck. The white veil. Rose trembled with excitement, fumbling as she pinned on her first veil, a white one because she was becoming a novice.

She lined up with the others in a procession into the chapel. Reverend Mother stood before them and asked each of them if she wished to become a novice.

Rose thrilled even more than she did taking Holy Communion or watching a sunset.

Tears of delight formed in her eyes. She now belonged to the community more than she had before. In less than two years, at the beginning of 1964, when she finished her novitiate, she would be able to put on the order's black veil and take her first vows.

The next day, she had a chance to speak with Maureen, now Sister Matthew, when they were both assigned to clean the parlor full of aging but not faded furniture. Thank goodness Maureen had entered the novitiate too. Rose had prayed she would. Losing Maureen would have been a blow.

"I'm glad you were allowed to keep the name Rose." Sister Matthew smiled as she dusted a lamp with a curved shade. "The name suits you."

They weren't supposed to talk, of course, but Rose's heart skipped a beat when Maureen spoke to her. Surely conversation was only a fault, not a sin. She decided she wouldn't confess it in a chapter meeting.

"Being named after a flower embarrassed me when I was younger. It's so silly." Rose polished an end table and enjoyed the lemony scent of the polish. "I wanted to keep the name because it was also the name of my sixth-grade teacher, Sister Rose de Lima, who was quite old and sometimes would reminisce about her early days in the convent in the middle of English or arithmetic class. I loved her. The order likes it when we pick the name of a nun who has died, but I know they favor me." Rose blushed. "That embarrasses me a little."

"They can see that you'll be a perfect novice and will be a perfect nun."

Did Maureen think she was perfect, or just perfect for the convent?

"Hardly. They favor me because I attended their grade school, high school, and college in Massachusetts, and because they know that my father died when I was in grade school and my mother died when I was in college. Mother Gabriel—she was Sister Gabriel then—taught me in seventh grade before the order transferred her to the Mother House. The nuns were always there for me, and I'm grateful."

"Oh, Rose. Sister Rose, I'm glad they were." Sister Matthew's smile looked warmer than ever.

What a wonderful smile she had.

The bell for Terce, the 9 a.m. prayer, rang, so they put down their cleaning implements and hurried to chapel.

Rose regretted leaving the parlor and their conversation. She felt as if she were floating. The joy of Maureen's—Sister Matthew's—company brightened her day. Sister Matthew's presence was a blessing. Rose felt no shame for telling Sister Matthew about her past.

Rose could refrain from thinking about the wilderness for longer periods because Sister Matthew lived nearby.

How much Sister Matthew would enjoy the idea that the nuns were like a herd of deer.

Rose still wished she had been able to study natural history, but she hoped to please Reverend Mother enough to be sent to study for a master's degree in human history. Perhaps that plan was selfish.

Sister Matthew, who loved literature, would understand her desire to include literature in the study of history.

Rose believed Sister Matthew would understand many of her desires.

She wished she could tell Sister Matthew about her mother's alcoholism. Making such a disclosure would be imposing on Sister Matthew, as well as breaking the convent's rules. It would be wrong to relate the problems of her past life. Rose immersed herself in the sisters' chants in the chapel because she must learn to live entirely in this life.

ROSE STILL LONGED TO live in other worlds besides the convent.

One night, she visited treeless tundra where thousands of caribou marched on their annual pilgrimages from their breeding ground to their winter habitat. Though the bare land looked bleak to her, she watched the animals in wonder. Almost all the adults had antlers, even some of the ones with young caribou sticking close to them, but the males' antlers were larger, more branching. The caribous' legs made a strange clicking sound as they walked. Pale wolves followed them at a distance, apparently hoping to find a lame animal. That too was part of nature.

Not far from her, a large bird sat on the ground. A snowy owl! It had gray and white markings, so it was a female. How did birds that nested on the ground keep their young safe?

Then she saw a village of Alaskan or Canadian Native people, who had small, unpainted wooden houses and traveled on dogsleds. The cold bit into her flesh, and she knew it must bite into theirs as well despite their thick parkas with fur around the hoods. She saw the people shoot at the caribou. At the sound of the shots, the herd ran, but two males were hit. Rose gasped at the sight of the majestic animals falling. She told herself to be happy for the people to have the meat they needed to live.

God wanted her to know more about the world than just the parts that she desired to see. She thanked God for increasing her understanding.

REVEREND MOTHER. ROSE REALLY did revere her.

Reverend Mother's college theology classes had inspired Rose. As Sister Robert Bellarmine, Reverend Mother had asked challenging questions. She had assigned readings from Primo Levi and Elie Wiesel so her students would understand the Holocaust.

Even though she had become the head of the whole order, Mother Robert Bellarmine had taken the time to send a note of condolence when Rose's mother died and enclosed a Mass card, promising to attend Masses to pray for Rose's mother's soul.

Nevertheless, Rose shook a little when she went for a conference in Reverend Mother's office. Rose knew she was not just meeting a mentor but also a judge who would determine her future.

Reverend Mother sat behind her desk.

Rose barely noticed anything about the room that her superior dominated.

"Please be seated, Rose." Reverend Mother was the voice of authority, albeit a gentle authority. "How do you find life in the convent?"

Rose tried not to sound giddy. "It's wonderful. It's the life I always dreamed of."

A slight smile crept onto Reverend Mother's face. Her voice held a warning note. "That is good, but perhaps too good. You are in love with the convent. When people fall in love with anyone, or anything, disillusionment is inevitable. You may always love the convent, though not with the same fervor you feel today. Be prepared for that to happen. This is more a life of work than a life of ecstasy, though that solemn joy is an important part."

Rose gazed at her. "You're so wise, Reverend Mother. Thank you for telling me that. I'll keep your warning in mind."

Reverend Mother nodded. "Even now, there must be some parts of convent life that you find difficult."

"Yes, Reverend Mother." She didn't want to say anything negative, but knew she was supposed to name one difficulty. "Chiefly not going outdoors as much as I would like."

"That is difficult. When we talk about giving up the world, we don't just mean society. Pray to accept that hardship. There are many worse hardships."

"Yes, Reverend Mother."

Rose would never admit she visited mountains at night, mountains so real she feared to trip and break an ankle.

CHAPTER 8

Sister Matthew

LATE SUMMER, 1962

I QUAKED AS I STOOD in the corridor waiting for a conference with Reverend Mother Robert Bellarmine. Did she have conferences with every novice, or just those with many obvious faults? Her patron saint was a Jesuit and a cardinal. That suited her personality to a T. I could picture her wearing a cardinal's red robes and hat. Did she see through me? She must know how unsuitable for the convent I am. I didn't want to be sent away. How ignominious that would be. If I ever leave, I want it to be my own decision, not hers.

I couldn't tell her the truth about my lack of belief. Possible God, forgive me for planning to deceive her.

Reverend Mother opened her door. "You may come in, Sister Matthew." Her voice sounded gentler than usual.

"Thank you, Reverend Mother." I took a long breath and entered her office. It is spartan, except for statues of the Virgin Mary and St. Joseph. The inevitable crucifix hung on the wall behind Reverend Mother's desk as it did in every room in the convent.

I began to kneel in front of her, like nuns in *The Nun's Story* when they went to the office of a mother superior.

"This isn't *The Nun's Story*. You do not have to kneel to me." She sat down behind her desk and said, "You may be seated."

Thank goodness for small blessings like not having to kneel. I rose and sat on a chair with wooden arms and a seat padded in maroon cloth.

"Are you preparing for your first vows next year?" Her voice was still surprisingly gentle, which didn't alleviate my anxiety.

"Yes, Reverend Mother."

"That is a solemn undertaking. What are your thoughts about it?"

I shook inwardly. Probably even nuns with more faith than I have would quake at this point. "I ask myself whether I am worthy, whether I am strong enough."

She did not frown. "That is normal. Are you certain of your vocation?"

I faltered. "Not entirely certain."

"That is also normal. This is the time to ponder that question in your heart. I would be concerned if you had said you were certain. What doubts do you have?"

I had never known she could be so human. I might wind up liking her. "I doubt whether I am good enough."

"In what way, good enough?"

What was a safe answer? "I doubt my ability to live up to the vow of obedience."

A smile passed over her face. "We all struggle with that. Not the vow of poverty?"

"I do not want to spend my life seeking material things." However, I would like to own some books, and perhaps have a kitten. I missed Whiskers, my cat who died a few years ago.

"And the vow of celibacy?"

I paused, seeking for the right answer. How certain should I sound? "I know that giving up having a family is a sacrifice, but I feel I am not called to the married state."

"And can you give up the desires of the flesh?"

I felt myself blush. "Yes, Reverend Mother."

She looked at me as if she were trying to read my soul, and she was. "And the wish to have one person who is dearer to you than anyone else, because the convent is not the place to favor one sister over the others?"

"Yes, Reverend Mother. I understand." I thought I sounded convincing.

"Remember that you cannot form attachments to places, either. The order can send you to any place where you are needed."

I nodded. "Yes, Reverend Mother. That might be difficult, but I understand." I hated the idea.

"You must continue to ponder these vows. Do you have any questions for me?"

"No, Reverend Mother."

"I am not sure you understand how difficult these vows are for all of us. You may go now and pray about these questions. If you want further discussion with me, you may let me know, and of course you can always talk with the Mistress of Novices."

"Thank you, Reverend Mother."

Reverend Mother seemed to know that the novices did not want to confide in their severe guardian angel, Mother Michael. I missed Mother Gabriel, the Mistress of Postulants and the gentler of the two archangels. If Mother Gabriel were an actress, she could have played June Cleaver.

I escaped from Reverend Mother's office unscathed. I drew a sigh of relief. I had fooled her. She had doubts about me but didn't seem to guess how unsuitable I am. Thank goodness she assumed I believed in basic Church doctrines and didn't ask me about them.

I felt sure Rose would take her vows. I wouldn't want to take mine and find out she wasn't taking hers. I couldn't last the three years after that until final vows, much less take final vows, if Rose weren't there. My final vows would be in the beginning of 1967. That sounded unimaginably far away.

FOR ONCE, MY UNRULY mind was calm. We were on retreat, our first week-long retreat as novices. I tried my best to find God, or at least to seek the spiritual realm.

I didn't even mind not talking to Rose. I was happy she and I were living in the community in collective meditation. I couldn't help feeling a little sorry that her thick brown hair was covered by the wimple and the veil. I imagined running my fingers through it. I dismissed that thought.

I walked quietly through the halls. How many sisters have walked here, trying to live a good life? How many prayers have enriched these rooms?

I turned my eyes to my soul. Why had I brooded on petty differences among us? I no longer wanted to notice whether sisters cough or snore or speak in nasal voices. I no longer wanted to be irritated by rules that were written long before I came here.

So much unites us. Not only the Euphrosynes, not only Catholics, but all human beings. Why must we be divided into different nations that war on each other?

What part do I play in that? What am I doing to become more accepting, more loving, to uproot my prejudices?

The Buddhists believe all creatures have souls. I wanted to believe that too. I wanted to care about all creatures, but I didn't want to permanently give up meat. It was even hard to give it up on this retreat, along with everyone else.

"I want." How often I think "I want." How many of my wants are for necessities, and how many are selfish?

What a beautiful world we live in. I should be content. Thank you, Possible God, for this beautiful world. I truly am thankful for sunsets and stars, elephants and cats. I am thankful for being able to read and having had a chance to read so many good books, though I wish I could read more of them now.

If I wanted peace in the world, I should try being peaceful. I feel peaceful now. Why not every day?

ON THE LAST DAY of the retreat, Father Nolan told us to meditate on the life of the Blessed Virgin Mary. That proved to be the downfall for my spirituality.

How could I meditate on a life I knew so little about? I didn't believe an angel had appeared to Mary. What had happened to her?

I envisioned her walking down a Roman-built stone road with a jar on her head, going to get water.

A burly Roman soldier approached her. "*Ave*, pretty girl," he sneered.

She froze.

He lunged at her. She struggled. Far stronger than she, he overpowered her and raped her.

Stunned and in pain, she still forced herself to pick up her fallen jar, go to get water, and bring it home because her family needed it. Then she threw herself on her sleeping mat. Her mind spun. She slept, and when she awakened, she told herself the attack must have been a nightmare sent by Satan.

She shrank from Joseph, the kind carpenter who was her betrothed. She had to marry him.

The night after the wedding, he tried to touch her. She recoiled.

"No," she pleaded.

He rose from their pallet and regarded her sorrowfully. "Has someone hurt you?"

She wept.

He saw she was with child, and he pitied her. He would not do anything to hurt her. He decided he must be a father to the child.

She never let Joseph touch her, no matter how kindly he treated her or how many years they lived together.

Instead, she devoted herself to prayer. Following her example, her son immersed himself in prayer and avoided things of the flesh.

When he went forth to preach, she worried about him.

I longed to write that story. I knew I would never be allowed to write any story, and certainly not such a heretical one. That realization hurt so much that I almost wished I had not thought of the story. Almost.

Oh great. That's how my meditation drifted if I spent too much time in my own thoughts. I believed my story more than the gospel. What do you think about it, Possible God?

A FEW DAYS AFTER the retreat, I saw Rose when we both had kitchen duty. After donning our plain aprons, we rinsed the dishes and glasses and placed them in the convent's industrial-size dishwasher, then turned to the pots and pans. Scrubbing pans had never been so appealing. I insisted on washing while Rose dried.

Our large and utilitarian convent kitchen had no quaint sayings on the walls. No frilly curtains. No colorful objects on display. Bare white walls and white cabinets and drawers with metal handles. The appliances were all white. I had no problem with an undecorated kitchen.

I dared to ask a personal question. "How do you maintain your serenity, Sister Rose?"

She flinched as if I had asked whether she minded wearing the convent's ridiculous long underwear.

"I'm sorry if that question was too personal." I couldn't bear the thought of distressing her. "It's just that I have such a hard time trying to be serene."

"No, don't apologize." Her voice sounded pained. "My secret is so unorthodox. But maybe you would understand. You're the only person I could tell."

I must have glowed. My temperature rose. "I'm honored." I rubbed the saucepan extra vigilantly.

She put down her towel, smiled at me, and blushed. "I time travel."

I blinked and let the pan drop back into the dishwater-filled sink. "You think about different times and places? That does sound like a good strategy to overcome boredom and constant restraint."

Rose shook her head. "No, I actually time travel. You're so imaginative that I think you might be able to travel also."

I had never seen any signs of mental disturbance in Rose, so I tried to dismiss that possibility. She couldn't be claiming to travel in time.

She sighed and resumed drying. "It was too much to hope that you'd believe me. I know it sounds strange."

Rose must be able to confide in me. "I believe you are the most honest person I know."

"I should have told the truth but told it slant, as Emily Dickinson advised. That's the one poem I remember from English class."

"No, I'm ready for the superb surprise. Where do you go when you time travel?"

Rose hesitated. She kept drying the same pan again and again.

"Please tell me."

"I ask the Lord to send me to places that will help me to increase my understanding."

Of course, prayer had to be involved. I would probably never be able to do it because my prayers, if they were prayers at all, were so imperfect. "My faith isn't as strong as yours."

"But your desire to learn is perhaps even greater. I have been to Vietnam."

Rose had told me earlier that she had never traveled outside the United States, so I knew she didn't mean she had gone by airplane.

I slapped the pan I had finished washing into the dish drainer. "Vietnam?"

"Yes, I learned to understand the war there. It's terrible." She closed her eyes. "Our country never should have intervened there. Our soldiers aren't just advising the South Vietnamese. They are doing worse things than most Americans believe they are."

"I'm sure you're right. But Rose," (I forgot to say Sister Rose) "how could that make you serene? Don't you travel to anyplace that's more pleasant?"

Rose opened her eyes and smiled like an angel, if indeed there were angels, which I hadn't believed since I was about age ten. "Oh yes. I have seen caribou migrating across the arctic. I have visited mountains and forests."

I struggled with my unbelief. Belief had never been my strong point. "You have? That's wonderful."

She looked into my eyes and I melted.

"I hope you will be able to do it too, once you think about it. I would like to meet you in another world."

Another world? Where we wouldn't have to obey the rule of silence or worry about whether a senior nun would come around a corner and catch us talking? No matter how innocuous the conversation, we would be reprimanded if we held it outside the brief hour in the day when we were allowed to talk. "I would like that very much. I remember that your patron saint, Rose de Lima, was supposed to be able to be in more than one place at the same time." I had never believed that.

"I wish I could tell you how to do it, but I don't know how to teach the art."

"How do you do it? Do you say a specific formula?"

"Not exactly. I just long for it."

"Do you feel like you are traveling through the universe? Does it hurt? Do you gasp for oxygen?"

She shook her head. "Nothing like that. It's so ordinary. I'm just in one place and then in the next instant, I'm in another. It usually happens when I'm in bed, but it's not a dream."

"Does it frighten you?"

"I felt afraid the first time. It didn't hurt me, so I stopped fearing it."

She smiled her very Rose smile and dried the last pan. "We've finished the dishes. It's almost time for chapel."

"Yes, it is." I wished there were twice as many pans to wash.

"I have to go now. I must get the vestments ready for Father Nolan." Despite those prosaic words, she smiled in a way that made my heart flutter.

"Good day, Sister Rose."

Parting from her reluctantly, I watched her as she walked away. Somehow her veil and habit were more beautiful than any other nun's.

Was the world more magical than I imagined? Or could dear Rose be a little unbalanced? I decided to trust the magic.

CHAPTER 9
Sister Rose

STOMACH CLENCHED, TEETH GRITTING, Rose forced herself to walk to the vestry. Why had she told Sister Matthew about the time travel? Now that dear novice would believe she was crazy.

Time travel never took her where she really wanted to go. Back to the time before her mother became an alcoholic, to try to help her avoid that fate. Back to the time when her father's yelling had led to her mother's drinking, to demand that he stop belittling her mother. Back to the time before his heart attack had cast their home into gloom.

Even while Rose set out silk vestments, the memory of her mother flooded her with pain.

The sad mood pervaded even her thoughts about Sister Matthew. Why had she felt so sure Sister Matthew would be able to understand her, much less to time travel? Rose longed to be with Sister Matthew in places very different from the convent, though of course Rose loved the Mother House.

ONE DAY AT RECREATION, Sister Ursula approached Rose. "Would you like to play volleyball, Sister Rose? None of the other novices are interested, but we could play just the two of us. I don't think that would break the rules."

A net stood in the yard where the convent vehicles were parked.

Rose's arms and legs tingled with anticipation. "That would be great. It's hard to get enough exercise here." Although volleyball didn't compare well with a hike in the woods, at least it provided outdoor exercise.

"Good. I'll get the ball."

Sister Ursula returned soon with a volleyball. "Thank you for agreeing to play with me. When I was in high school, our team won the volleyball championship of Catonsville. I've missed volleyball."

They played for half an hour. Rose didn't mind that Sister Ursula clearly outclassed her as a player.

"Could we take a break and talk a little?" Sister Ursula asked. "Recreation is almost over."

"Yes." Rose didn't worry about engaging in a one-on-one conversation with Sister Ursula.

They sat on a bench near the net.

"May I confide in you?" Sister Ursula stared at the ground. "I hate being named after St. Ursula."

Rose wondered whether every nun except herself hated her name. "What's the matter with St. Ursula?"

Sister Ursula dug her foot into the dirt and overturned a clump of grass. "Whenever people mention her, they say 'St. Ursula, virgin and martyr.' That drives me crazy."

"You don't think that means you have to be a martyr?"

"No." Sister Ursula choked. "I'm not a virgin. I can't tell anyone else here. Whenever they call her a virgin, I'm so ashamed." She sounded as if she were going to cry.

Rose leaned towards her. "Don't be ashamed. You have dedicated your life to God. That's all that matters."

"I didn't want to sin." Sister Ursula's voice broke. "I was twelve years old. My...a man in my family..." She began to cry.

Rose handed Sister Ursula her handkerchief. "That wasn't a sin. Not your sin, I mean." Rose strove to control the anger she felt. "What a terrible thing to do to you. It's nothing for you to be ashamed of."

"You think it's all right for me to stay in the convent? I'm not being a hypocrite when they tell us we are brides of Christ?"

"No, not at all." Rose restrained herself from putting her arms around Sister Ursula, which seemed like the natural thing to do. "That man raped you. In the eyes of God, women who have been raped are still virgins." Rose had never heard anyone say that, but it must be true. "You are a perfect bride of Christ." Rose had never been crazy about the term "bride of Christ." This wasn't the time to discuss her objections.

"Thank you." Sister Ursula took a deep breath in an attempt to stop crying. "I confessed at the time. The priest said I must have been at fault. But I didn't have any idea what was happening or why."

"The priest was mistaken." Rose tried not to show too much anger. "They aren't infallible. I don't think you sinned at all."

"I shouldn't wince when I hear the word 'virgin'?" Sister Ursula asked.

"No. Your heart is pure. If you ever want to talk to one of the older nuns about it, I am sure Mother Gabriel would say the same."

"Maybe I will someday. Thank you so much, Sister Rose." Sister Ursula handed back the handkerchief. "I hope I didn't impose on you. I thought you might not condemn me."

"The Church talks too much about virginity," Rose told her. Especially about the Blessed Mother, she thought but did not say because she didn't want to scandalize Sister Ursula. "Charity is much more important." The bell rang for None, the 3 p.m. prayer, named after the ninth hour. "I'm afraid it's time to go to chapel."

Rose raged privately about the many nuns who emphasized the importance of virginity. She raged much more about the man who had injured Sister Ursula. Rose said a prayer of thanks that nothing as awful had happened to her. She saw that it could happen to any girl.

She would never mention this conversation in a chapter meeting, and she was sure Sister Ursula wouldn't either. Some conversations were sacred.

CHAPTER 10
Sister Matthew

SISTER AGNES'S BLUE EYES had turned red, I didn't know whether because of sorrow or a cold. That night after supper, Reverend Mother announced that Sister Agnes's aunt had died, and we would say a Mass for her soul the next morning.

Sister Agnes, who had once been named Helen, bowed her head. Her shoulders shook.

I wanted to comfort her. How could I do that in the rule-bound convent? I loved my aunts, though they lived so far away that I seldom saw them, so I thought she must have loved hers.

Sister Agnes usually cared so much about the rules. Could one say "I'm sorry about your loss" in the convent?

Later, I saw Rose give Sister Agnes a smile in the hallway. Sister Agnes looked at her as if to say thank you.

When we left the chapel after our final evening prayers, I walked up to Sister Agnes and tried to give her a compassionate semi-smile. I felt pretty sure that if I whispered, "I'm sorry," she would report me for breaking the vow of silence.

I wish I lived in a world where I could be friends with the other sisters. Then we would be real sisters.

Did Sister Agnes wish she could talk more? Did she love the rules, or just obey them scrupulously?

I would like to have real conversations with the other novices and the professed sisters. Even Reverend Mother Robert Bellarmine. She has brains. I'd like to ask her what her favorite books are. She has a degree in theology and teaches it to us. I admire her because she told us in class that evolution was part of God's plan, and the gospels almost certainly could not have been written by the original apostles.

Did she choose to study theology, or had some previous reverend mother ordered her to? I wondered whether she might have preferred studying something else because I couldn't imagine wanting to get a doctorate in theology. Had she ever thought about doing anything other than joining the convent?

And Mean Mother Michael? What had happened in her life to make her harsh to the novices? Perhaps she regretted joining the convent, or maybe her parents had treated her badly.

"You have such a serious expression on your face, Sister Matthew." I looked around to see Mother Gabriel. She smiled at me. "How is the novitiate?"

Mother Gabriel had made postulancy a happy time, despite all the new rules we had to follow. Even when she corrected us, her eyes had said, "I know you're doing your best, dear."

"It is more difficult than being a postulant," I replied. The Mistress of Postulants must know about Mother Michael's lack of warmth.

If mothers Gabriel and Michael were the archangels, anyone could see that Mean Mother Michael was the one with the fiery sword.

Mother Gabriel's face radiated serenity. "Think of the joy when you make your first vows. That will be exceeded only by the joy of making your final vows."

I think that was her way of telling me the eighteen-month novitiate would be over eventually, and life would be better then.

"Yes, Mother Gabriel."

I dared to smile at her in return. Her presence reminded me that Rose was not the only sweet soul in the convent. I walked to our dormitory with a song in my heart. The song was "High Hopes," a tune probably not on the nuns' hit parade, but I loved the part about the ant trying to move the rubber tree plant.

My Possible God likes all kinds of music, not just hymns. Possible God would be glad to be serenaded by "Rock Around the Clock," if the singers' hearts were relatively good.

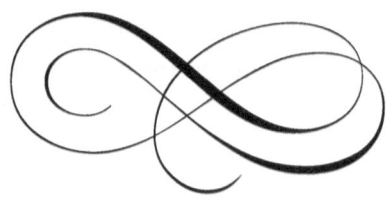

CHAPTER 11

Sister Matthew

POSSIBLE GOD, WOULD YOU help me time travel? There's no reason why you should. I'm not especially good. You don't owe me any favors.

Regardless of my undeserving character, I sat on the bed in my cell and tried to time travel. Sister Philomena the Snorer (a.k.a. Francine) in the next cell serenaded me with her usual noises.

Should I apply to St. Christopher, patron saint of travelers, who supposedly carried a disguised Christ across a river?

No, Christopher didn't travel through time.

The Blessed Mother Mary must be the patron saint of time travelers because she surely has appeared to more people in more countries, at more times, than any other saint.

Again, there's no reason why you should help me, Mother Mary. It would be a kindness if you did.

I probably will have to rely on my own power. Can I think myself into another place so deeply that I travel there? What place? Can I choose?

Concentrate, Sister Matthew, concentrate.

I stood in a forest.

Had I time traveled? Or was this a dream? I didn't feel any whoosh of travel, spinning, or dizziness. Rose said she hadn't felt the traveling either.

I must be nuts. There is no such thing as time travel. I've worked myself up into a delusion.

I had to know whether I had traveled in time, not dreaming. I felt the sharp needles of a tall pine and rubbed my hand along its bark. Resin came off in my hand. I kicked a small rock, not too hard. My toes hurt. I had never felt physical pain in a dream.

If this were time travel, could it be magic? Am I simply able to control my mind to an amazing degree? Or could it be a gift from Possible God? I hoped it wasn't the latter because that would mean I needed to become more devout.

Maybe wanting to time travel was a mistake. I might see things I didn't want to see. If that's what was happening to me, how absolutely amazing!

I still wore a habit. I had hoped to reappear in another guise, perhaps in pants. I used to wear slacks and jeans often before I entered the convent.

I didn't know why a lone nun would be in a forest, but I wasn't going to quibble. The trees were taller than those of the forests I knew. The scent of conifers filled the air. The bird songs were unfamiliar. Maybe I traveled to the Pacific Northwest?

A squirrel darted in front of me and scrambled up a tree. It had a reddish coat and pointed ears. Was I in a western U.S. forest or a European forest?

A large woodpecker with unmistakably green feathers drummed on a tree trunk. A European woodpecker?

If Rose were with me, it would be perfect.

I struggled to walk over the forest's mossy, root-filled floor. My legs were shorter. I was shorter. I put a hand on my stomach. My body felt plumper, and my hands were wrinkled with age. I must be someone else.

I would have preferred to keep my own body and lose the habit rather than vice versa.

Rain began to drizzle on me. I mustn't let that deter me from an adventure.

The rain soaked my habit. I had never before had to experience a waterlogged habit dragging me down. The feeling was not pleasant.

I came to a dirt road and heard a rider approaching on horseback. I prayed that didn't signal danger.

A man in chain mail riding a black mare cantered into view. A woman in a tawdry red gown, incongruous for the forest, clung to his back. Her hair hung in knots. Face paint dripped down her face, which looked young but haggard. She clung so tightly that she could not be a kidnap victim. I could guess what her work had been, and that the man in chain mail probably had not been one of her customers.

The man had a long, handsome face, brown eyes, and dark hair. He looked as if he had never known a happy day.

No, the person in chain mail was a woman, well disguised.

The miserable state of these two travelers prompted me to smile at them as warmly as I could. "May I be of help?"

The disheveled woman lifted her head and regarded me. "I need a place to stay and honest work."

"What good fortune for me!" I told her. I was sure I lived in a convent in this world and that I could speak for what it would allow. Was that certainty instinct? If an old nun could wander through the forest, the convent must be liberal, and I must have some authority there. I must play the part of an old nun. She—I—must be kindly. "Our convent needs a housekeeper, and I have been looking for one. Would you be willing to do that work?"

Her eyes widened. "You'd let me do that?"

"Of course, my dear. Will you come?"

"Yes, thanks."

An old mare grazing nearby walked up to me. I realized she must be mine, or one the convent allowed me to use. I hadn't ridden a horse since my high school years, but the prospect delighted me, especially since this mare didn't look too challenging.

Certainty that the woman in chain mail must be Lancelot flowed through me. Lancelot? I must be delusional.

"What a blessing it is that you will help us," I told the bedraggled woman. "Then come down from Lancelot's horse and join me on mine."

Staring at me in apparent astonishment that I knew her name, the woman warrior helped the other woman down from her horse.

Lancelot's face showed even more pain than the anxious, red-garbed woman's did. I had to comfort Lancelot next.

"And what can I do for you?"

Lancelot's voice sounded like a dying person's. "Nothing. I am beyond help. Today I struck out blindly into a bush, for I imagined that a Saxon fighter lurked behind it, and I killed a girl. Nothing that I can do will ever make up for that."

I thought Lancelot sounded on the brink of suicide. I gazed into her eyes. "No one is beyond help. You must live as well as you can. You have seen that carelessness can be cruel. Do not be careless again, but caring."

I reached up and touch Lancelot's cheek.

Tears mingled with rain poured over my hand.

"Thank you, Holy Lady, I shall do as you tell me," Lancelot replied.

I had the sense that she would not kill herself. I bade her farewell and joined the young woman on my horse. After that, all I had to do was find the convent where I apparently dwelled in this world.

I found myself back in my convent bed and realized that my experience had been far clearer than a dream. It was like time travel, but this must be a story from a book because Lancelot was a fictional character. Meeting Lancelot? I shook my head. I'm crazy.

Maybe I should believe it really happened. I should be glad, but I felt frightened. I pulled my blanket around me.

I couldn't wait to tell Rose about my adventure when we eventually would have time to talk. She would be happy for me.

Although my first time journey was not unpleasant, I hope I don't have to spend much time in that era.

The nun I was in that world seemed happy. How many medieval nuns were?

Thank goodness St. Euphrosnye's order is not too old. Only a few generations of nuns have lived in this convent. That's enough. It lacks the rawness of new block-like buildings, but it's not haunted, as far as I know.

Do I want to know the thoughts of a medieval nun? They didn't all blossom in the convent like St. Hildegard of Bingen or St. Teresa of Avila.

How many were encased against their will? How many longed to flee to men or to bear children? How many sought the convent as a refuge?

I decided not to worry about those long-dead women. I chose this life. To have it imposed, to be shut in—what a nightmare. A woman can be forced to have sex, but how can she be forced to pray? She would pray only for release.

Spirits of nuns past, stay away from me.

I had the strange feeling this hadn't been the first time I had time traveled. I had always had what I thought were daydreams that took me away from my daily life, sometimes to the irritation of other people, but some of those experiences had been so vivid that they might have been more substantial. I remembered being startled at coming back to my real world.

I DIDN'T HAVE A chance to talk to Rose for days after my adventure. I looked out for opportunities and tried to hide my impatience. Rain gushed into the garden, so we spent our recreation time in sewing and dull conversations that anyone in the room could hear.

Finally, Rose and I were both assigned to work in the garden. Despite the muddy ground, being alone with her was paradise.

Her namesake bushes lined the garden. Although many rose blossoms had faded, a pink rosebush still held several blooms, as did a few bushes with yellow roses. Their scent hung in the air.

Much of the garden was devoted to vegetables and herbs, though a few sturdy flowers like nasturtiums, marigolds, and chrysanthemums grew in the inner circle. Thank goodness some generations of the mothers superior had realized beauty nurtures the soul, as well as providing flowers for the altar and the statues of Mary.

The breeze blew my veil. I wished it were blowing through my hair instead.

Rose began weeding. I started weeding a short distance from her and managed to move gradually closer.

The sound of a car driving too fast down the nearby road intruded on the garden's peace.

"How I wish we didn't have to hear the cars!" A tiny wrinkle spread across Rose's forehead. "I wish we lived in a convent in the wilderness."

"The Garden of Eden had no cars or highways. That was what made it Eden."

Rose laughed. "I can always count on you for humor, Sister Matthew."

I refrained from saying the Garden of Eden wouldn't have been Eden for me because Rose wasn't there. Had I been Eve, I guess I would have let Adam lie with me, since I never would have seen another woman. What a shock it would have been to have the first baby! How did anyone think up that silly story?

A mockingbird scolded us, rather like Mean Mother Michael.

Rose continued weeding efficiently and I tried to do the same.

I disliked putting my hands in dirt, damp or dry. I didn't want to touch bugs, or even to see them. I'd never be a Francis of Assisi.

At last I ventured to say what I had been wanting to tell her. "I've time traveled."

She clapped her hands and beamed at me. "Oh, I'm so happy for you. I knew you could."

Delighted to please her, I dug out a weed, being careful not to hurt the marigold next to it.

"I fell into a story, not the real world. Lancelot was a woman in disguise."

"Lancelot! How did you happen upon Lancelot?"

"Probably because the summer before I entered, I went to New York City and saw *Camelot*. I had never seen a Broadway musical before. It thrilled me. Sometimes when I'm doing chores in the convent I silently sing Lancelot's song '*C'est Moi*,' to tell myself I'm astoundingly good, though I know I'm not. '*C'est moi, c'est moi*, the angels have chose…'"

Rose laughed. "Now when I see you doing chores, I'll think of that song."

"I suppose you sing hymns to yourself."

"Sometimes. Did you enjoy your time travel with Lancelot?"

"I did, but I felt sorry for Lancelot. I had never met anyone so full of sorrow. A knight with a woeful countenance."

"I wonder what story she came from."

"I don't think it's been written yet."

"Perhaps you will write it."

"How could I write a novel? No nun would be allowed to do that." The idea that I might have the ability to write, an ability I could never use, drilled through me, leaving me in pain.

Rose gave me a reassuring smile. "I believe nuns will be able to do that in our lifetime."

"Sure, when a nun is elected president of the United States." I rolled my eyes.

"There will be change, since Pope John is calling for a Vatican Council," Rose proclaimed. She radiated excitement. "I can almost see it. Nuns will live in friendlier, less formal convents. Women will become deacons, and someday priests. Oh, Sister Matthew, it will be grand."

I tried to conceal my skepticism in the face of her enthusiasm. Yes, Pope John was a good man, but did he envision all the changes Rose did? And would the council adopt them? Would the Church grant women more power? The Vatican and the cardinals saw us almost as a different species, somewhere between children and men. Would dogs give more power to cats?

After hesitating, I replied, "That would be grand, if it came to pass."

"Let us pray it will."

Rose carefully moved an earthworm so it wouldn't be hurt in the weeding.

Lucky earthworm to be touched by those hands.

"Lancelot was sad because she had killed." For some reason, I didn't want to disclose Lancelot's secret that she had killed a girl by mistake. "It would be horrible to kill someone."

Rose shuddered. "I can't think of anything worse."

Being raped would be worse, I thought. I didn't want to mention that word to Rose. There was something so delicate about her that I wanted to protect her from hearing it.

I once imagined killing my childhood nemesis, Mary Louise McKenna, but I could never bear to tell Rose that, even though I knew I couldn't have killed Mary Louise. I hoped.

CHAPTER 12

Sister Matthew

THAT AFTERNOON I TIME *traveled without trying to, arriving back in my high school. I recognized the classroom, with its blackboard with a crucifix above it on the front wall, wooden desk for the teacher, smaller metal desks for the girls, and large clock on the wall over the door. The anthologies sitting on our desks identified this classroom as the one where our junior year English class was held.*

I knew immediately what day it was. My heart pounded. I could hardly breathe. I had no idea time travel could take me to my own past, to the day I least wanted to visit. I tried to escape to my convent, but I failed.

The girls chattered. Someone said that Sister Veronica, our junior year English teacher at St. Agatha's, was very late.

Finally, Sister Veronica entered our classroom. All talk stopped as it always did at the entry of a nun. Mr. Wilson, our history teacher, irked because girls sometimes whispered to each other during his classes, often said if someone threw a broom with a habit on it into a classroom, everyone would stop talking. He was right.

I loved English class, though Sister Veronica's was not as stimulating as Sister Thomas the Apostle's sophomore English class had been. Sister Doubting Thomas, a middle-aged nun who taught only a few classes because she was busy being principal, encouraged us to write creative essays loosely based on our readings, while Sister Veronica liked to give multiple-choice exams, perhaps because they were easier to grade.

Sister Veronica, probably in her early thirties, clearly knew she was the prettiest nun at St. Agatha's. Girls used to joke that Archie had never guessed he would lose her to the convent instead of to Reggie.

If I had been Archie and she were Veronica, I would have chosen Betty. Without hesitation.

I wasn't one of Sister Veronica's favorites. She was the kind of teacher who liked the pretty and popular girls best.

She had been my second-grade teacher. She hadn't liked me then either, perhaps because I daydreamed. Then she would snap at me. "Maureen, come back from the moon. Pay attention." Maybe I had time traveled then. That happened more in her class than anyplace else.

When I had held up my hand, desperate to go to the bathroom, she had made me wait so long I feared I would wet my underpants. She had let her favorites go as soon as they raised their hands.

I never forgot her meanness.

St. Veronica supposedly approached Jesus on his walk to Calvary and wiped his face with her veil. A veil with the imprint of his face on it was reputed to be one of the Church's holiest relics. No doubt it was a fake.

If Sister Veronica had been in Jerusalem then, she would have wiped Jesus's face because he was famous and she wanted the veil for a souvenir. She never would have wiped the face of some obscure slob carrying a cross. Perhaps I am being uncharitable to her.

In that morning's English class, Sister Veronica's face looked as if she had colored it with chalk. She appeared to be years older than she had been the day before. She shook, and so did her voice. She drew a long breath as if she had to force herself to talk. "Mary Louise McKenna is dead."

Those were the exact words she had said. This was truly the past. I froze. Everything happened word for word like that day. I tried to speak, to say something I had not said then, but no words came out of *my mouth. I tried to get out of my desk, but my limbs resisted. I was powerless to do anything different.*

All of us gasped. Mary Louise's friends began to cry. I felt as if I were falling. Mary Louise, with her silky blonde hair, good soprano voice, and mean disposition, was dead. My fantasy had become horribly true. Was I somehow guilty because I had imagined her death?

"Someone murdered her," Sister Veronica said.

Fran O'Connor fainted. Susan Adams and Bernadette O'Hara shrieked. Cathy Randall burst into hysterical sobs.

Sister Veronica resumed her stiff posture. Her brown eyes regarded us as if we were misbehaving kindergartners. "That wasn't an invitation to hysterics. Focusing on your own reactions robs her death of dignity." She walked over to Fran, felt her pulse, and shook her.

"All of you must remain in your seats and be quiet until after the police have finished examining the crime scene. She was killed in the auditorium." Sister Veronica managed to rouse Fran, who stared blankly. "You can't go to the next class as usual."

I had imagined killing Mary Louise in the auditorium. Could I be insane? Had I killed her rather than just imagining it?

The day before, Mary Louise had shamed me by pointing out my acne to everyone. She had called me "Polka Dot." Two of the girls had tittered. I had shaken with anger.

Susan raised her hand. "I have to go to the bathroom, sister."

The nun frowned. "You may go, but only one at a time. Don't linger or go anyplace else."

Susan scurried out.

"Unfortunately, our class was supposed to discuss Shakespeare's Julius Caesar *today. That is out of the question now." Sister Veronica sighed as if she regretted putting aside the play. "Instead, we'll discuss O. Henry's 'Gift of the Magi.' It's not particularly appropriate, but that is preferable to being overly appropriate."*

I wished Mary Louise, all 110 snide pounds of her, were alive and sitting in the classroom.

Mary Louise, the taunter supreme, had often insulted me in front of Bernadette, the girl I loved. Bernadette, bless her, had turned away instead of laughing.

Earlier that morning, we had celebrated the school's fiftieth anniversary in the auditorium. All the students ate pieces of a yellow sheet cake with the school's emblem, which included a knife, shears, and tongs, symbols of St. Agatha's martyrdom. What a morbid emblem.

A carving knife, large for the purpose, had sat on the empty platter. I had imagined using it on Mary Louise.

At some point, I had blacked out. Not fainted, just drifted off. I didn't remember what happened after that until I sat in the classroom, though quite a few minutes, I didn't know how many must have passed. Such blackouts had happened a few times before, mostly in Sister Veronica's classes.

Had my wishes somehow lifted the knife and moved it with deadly force? Impossible. I hope.

I picked up our anthology and tried to read the story. I felt sure I radiated guilt.

Sister Veronica called on me to read aloud. I attempted to open my mouth.

"One dol…" I choked.

The English teacher scowled at me. "For heaven's sake, Maureen, pull yourself together. I expect better of a good student like you. Anne Fascinato, please read."

"One dollar and eighty-seven…" Anne faltered.

"That's enough." Sister Veronica sighed. "I'll read it." She rattled through the story in a tone different from her usual expressive reading.

I wasn't the only one who failed to read aloud. My shaky voice didn't point directly to my guilt.

When I wished Mary Louise harm, did I cause it, even if I didn't stab her myself? Did my thoughts somehow pulsate to the actual killer?

Or did I linger after the others had left the auditorium on the pretense of cleaning up, after I heard that was what Mary Louise would be doing? She liked to volunteer for extra duties just to show off. She played up to the nuns, but inside she was meaner than a snake.

How could I think of a dead girl that way? God forgive me. I am heartily sorry.

My thoughts were still the same as those of my sixteen-year-old self. I couldn't seem to change them.

Oh no, my younger self thought, I have to confess this sin, or I'll go to hell. Priests are under the seal of Confession, so the priest can't tell the police or the nuns. Which priest should I go to? Who would be the most understanding?

Stop dramatizing yourself, as the nuns would say. I just need to confess wanting Mary Louise to die, not killing her. And I didn't mean it, not really. I won't miss her though.

Her parents will suffer. I don't want her parents to suffer.

I began to cry. I could hear other girls crying too. Did they all like Mary Louise, or were they just crying from shock?

What if one of the other girls killed her? I wasn't the only one she had insulted.

"Concentrate on the story," Sister Veronica demanded. She had apparently finished reading aloud. "What did you learn from it?"

I hadn't heard the story. What had I learned? Not to kill anyone? That probably wasn't O. Henry's moral.

"Sister Matthew, you're daydreaming," Mean Mother Michael, the Mistress of Novices, snapped. "I asked you to read the prayer."

Jerked away from my high school classroom to the refectory, I stammered. "Yes, Mother Michael. I'm sorry, Mother Michael."

I felt so relieved to be pulled from time travel back to the convent that tears formed in my eyes. Reliving that terrible day made me struggle for breath. I certainly hadn't tried to time travel in front of the other sisters. It just happened. That frightened me.

So I could travel to places I didn't want to visit, at times I didn't choose. That must be what had happened in my childhood.

I could barely lift the book to read the prayer.

"Are you sick, Sister Matthew?" The Mistress of Novices' voice sounded softer than usual.

"No, Mother Michael."

"You look unwell. See the infirmarian after lunch."

"Yes, Mother Michael." I appreciated her concern.

This was one time travel episode I would never relate to Rose. I avoided looking at her.

SISTER CATHERINE OF SIENA, the infirmarian, took my temperature. That warm, plump nun of about forty smiled more than most of the other sisters. It always heartened me that another nun did not look abstemious. Too many of them were thin.

"I'm not sick, Sister Catherine. Mother Michael sent me here."

"You're very pale, Sister Matthew. It won't hurt you to rest here for an hour."

"Yes, Sister Catherine."

That good nun turned to working on her record books.

Soon I returned to an unspeakably dull recreation period. Exhausted by my time travel, I welcomed the dullness.

CHAPTER 13
Sister Matthew

A FEW EVENINGS LATER, I summoned up my energy to try time traveling again. I hoped I would not wind up back at my high school.

Trees I had never seen before surrounded me. Palms mingled with unfamiliar deciduous trees, some of them blooming and all of them towering. Sweat poured over me as I steamed in the heat. Sweet scents so powerful they almost smothered me drifted through the air. A bird of many colors flew to a branch over my head. Several different bird songs and several screeches, probably also from birds, filled the jungle—surely it was a jungle.

I hoped no dangerous predators prowled nearby.

Camouflage clothing covered me. I grimaced. I didn't want to be a hunter or a soldier.

A large insect dropped on my shoulder. I stifled a scream and brushed wildly to get it off.

I have always loved nature—except for insects and snakes. Snakes, even venomous ones, probably lurked in this jungle. I would have to scan the path ahead of me and the trees overhead.

I tried to guess what continent I stood in.

It would be wonderful to see a mammal, like a tapir if I were in Asia, an agouti if I were in South America, or an antelope if I were in Africa. No large predators, please.

I crept further and passed into an area where all the trees had lost their leaves. The plants had shriveled. No flowers bloomed and no birds sang. Someone must have poisoned the jungle. I covered my mouth and hurried back over the path I had taken. The poison might still linger in the air.

After I returned to the place where I had first appeared, I stopped. I cried about the devastation I had seen.

The blast of gunfire from many guns almost knocked me over with fear. Too close, it deafened me. I stood paralyzed.

A small plane flew overhead. Friend or foe? But who was friend and who was foe?

I heard an explosion from the place where there had been gunfire. Screams resounded through the jungle. The people in the plane must have dropped a bomb.

I hurried in the direction of the screams, though I believed the people who had been hit would see me as an enemy. Perhaps I could help bandage them or give them water.

Bodies of young Asian men covered the ground, but few of the bodies were whole. Arms and legs lay strewn like logs. The men who were still living screamed.

My head reeled. Where could I find water? What could I do?

I escaped to my dark alcove in the convent. I closed my eyes and took a deep breath. The heat and jungle noises had disappeared.

I felt pleased—and amazed—that my first impulse had been to help instead of to hide.

Terrible as the war in Vietnam was, I had to admit it frightened me less than my own past.

THE NEXT MORNING, I sat mending my habit. Trying not to cry about Vietnam, I sighed.

"A sigh is a complaint," Mean Mother Michael chided me. She seemed to watch me more than she did the others. "You should not mind doing simple chores."

"Yes, Mother Michael. I don't mind," I replied as calmly as I could.

How strange to sit sewing while other people were poisoning jungles and dropping bombs. But what else could I do?

When I finished my mending, I walked through the cloister in the hope of seeing Rose.

The top of the cloisters' gothic stone pillars displayed leaf-like designs. The fine work reminded me of the Cloisters Museum in New York City, though of course the carvings on that cloister's pillars were more elaborate since they had been imported from former monasteries in France. I wondered how my order had obtained donations large enough to pay for its cloister.

A nun walked in front of me. Even though all I could see was the habit and veil, I knew from her walk that it was Rose. I had no childish need for visions: The sight of the woman I loved was all the vision I needed.

"Sister Rose," I said, not loudly. Though it was a time when we were allowed to break silence, personal conversations without a third novice present were still verboten.

She turned and saw me. "Your face is pale, Sister Matthew. What is the matter?"

I said only, "Vietnam."

"Oh! I am so sorry." She made a gesture as if she wanted to hug me. Of course she held back. "I never should have urged you to travel."

"It's good that you did. I need to have more experience of the world." I tried to keep my voice from shaking.

"I'm sorry you saw such a painful part of it."

Her voice warmed me.

I saw Sister Agnes, who though younger than we were seemed so deferential to the rules that she was a threat, approaching from behind Rose. She would be able to hear what we were saying. "I am so grateful for Pope John," I said. "Such a kind man. I want to read his encyclical again."

"Yes, *Pacem in Terris* is beautiful," Rose replied.

"It is better to contemplate the encyclical quietly than to discuss it, except when Reverend Mother or a priest leads a discussion," the younger novice said. "We might misunderstand it without guidance."

"Yes, Sister Agnes," we chorused.

Sister Agnes withdrew as if shocked at her own boldness. Even though we could break silence now, apparently she still feared to speak.

Rose followed Sister Agnes and I moved off to talk with Sister Ursula and Sister Philomena. Perhaps they would like to discuss the encyclical. No one must suspect Rose and I might be particular friends.

THE CONVENT PERMITTED OUR families to visit us once every three months. Those were some of the best days of the year.

Given the ridiculous rules, we couldn't see them in private. Nonetheless, I eagerly awaited my parents' visit, the third since I had entered the convent.

Mother Michael had assigned Sister Jerome, a pasty-faced nun of about forty who at least wasn't mean, to be my chaperon. I entered the parlor, filled with families, supervised by Mean Mother Michael in her role as Mistress of Novices.

I saw my mother and father and walked to them without unseemly haste.

"Hello, darling," my mother said, extending her arms.

"Hello, Mom." I gave her the required quick hug. We weren't supposed to give deep hugs, not even to our parents.

"Hello, Dad." I did the same with him.

"Hello, Maureen, oops, Sister Matthew." He beamed at me. I knew he had used my old name intentionally.

"This is Sister Jerome. Sister Jerome, these are my parents," I added unnecessarily.

"Hello, Sister Jerome," my mother said.

"Glad to meet you, Sister Jerome," said my father.

"I am glad to meet you too, Mr. and Mrs. Collins." Sister Jerome smiled, but not too widely.

"How are you doing?" my mother asked me.

"I'm fine. We are taking theology classes and I'm enjoying them."

"You always did like studying," my father said.

"I think you liked that better than anything else," my mother added.

"Shall I get you some refreshments?" I asked, gesturing towards a table with a pitcher of water and another one of Lipton tea. A plate of cookies, mostly Oreos, also stood on the table. The spread looked embarrassingly poor, but since my parents had visited twice before they must be used to it.

"No thank you, dear," my mother said. "I brought you some Fig Newtons." Each time they came she either brought them or baked oatmeal cookies. I was allowed to have two of the cookies she brought; the rest would go to other sisters.

I delivered the Fig Newtons to the refreshment table, put them on a plate, and ate one.

My father wandered over and took a couple of Oreos.

Mean Mother Michael sauntered over to the table and picked up a Fig Newton, as she always did. A taste for Fig Newtons was the one thing we had in common. I knew she would casually return to the table and get another one a few minutes later. She always did.

The professed nuns ate the same food we did, but some must be allowed to eat larger portions because a few of them, like Sister

Catherine, carried some extra pounds. Mother Michael resembled Shakespeare's lean and hungry Cassius.

"Is everyone in the family in good health?" I asked.

"Yes, dear. Your father just got over a cold."

"No need to mention that. I'm hale and hearty."

"Your nephew Kevin broke his arm at Little League," my mother informed me. "His biggest regret is that he'll have to sit on the bench."

I hadn't seen Kevin in a couple of years, since the last time his family visited Maryland. I scarcely remembered John's children existed. "That's too bad. How is your law firm doing, Dad?"

"Fine, never better. A Democratic firm gets a lot of business when the Democrats are in the White House." He grinned from ear to ear. "I had a chance to see Senator Humphrey at a fund-raising lunch last week. He spoke to me for a few minutes. He's a good man. He's the one who had the idea for a Peace Corps. President Kennedy borrowed it from him."

"I'm glad you got to see Senator Humphrey." My father had mentioned the senator's inspiration to create a Peace Corps every time his name came up. "How is your bridge group, Mom?"

"The same old thing. We're still meeting twice a month. I was given the Garden Club prize again this year."

"For your irises, of course?"

"Yes, for my irises. I planted some new varieties. I wish you could have seen the garden." She made it sound as if I had entered the convent in order to avoid the garden.

After an hour of this excruciating formality, my parents had to leave. I wouldn't see them again for another three months. I wished they had told me more news of the world, but I wasn't supposed to ask about the news. I also wanted to tell them which sisters I liked and didn't like. I knew I wouldn't be allowed to do that.

I relaxed. I had worked so hard to banish negative thoughts they might perceive. It was impossible to say anything real in front of our chaperon. I would be severely chastised if I said anything critical about the convent or told them what secular things I missed.

"You're blessed to have such fine parents," Sister Jerome told me.

"Yes, I am fortunate. My parents really are fine," I said, surprised a nun would make such a personal comment.

Feeling proud of my parents, I went to help the other sisters clear away the refreshments.

THAT NIGHT, I FOUND *myself in another world. Leafy trees looked friendly enough, but can you trust trees? Can trees trust us? Obviously not.*

How did this world smell? Like any wooded park. It felt more like an overgrown park than a forest.

Sounds of music drifted through the park. Perhaps nothing terrible would happen here.

I wore a shirt with long, puffy sleeves, strange pants, and boots much softer than the combat boots I had worn in Vietnam.

Who was I now? I wondered what part I was supposed to play in this world. I still had a woman's body, but I thought I wore men's clothing.

I missed Rose. I wished she were here and would hold my hand. Was this a world where I could hold a woman's hand?

My vision blurred. I had worn glasses in Vietnam, but I wasn't wearing them here. I remembered I hadn't worn them in Lancelot's world either.

I peered between the trees and saw people dressed in Renaissance garb. There were men here, as well as women. One man played a lute.

A strange, crested bird flew out of the next tree. I laughed in surprise.

The people turned in my direction. I prepared to brave this new world.

"Who are you?" A slim young man in brown velvet frowned at me. "Why are you stalking about in the trees like a thief?"

"I'm no thief." I parted the branches and approached the clearing. "I am a writer, looking to find words to describe the beauty of this place." I tried to extend my arm to indicate a sweeping scene but caught it in a branch. I jerked my arm away, causing an avalanche of leaves and twigs to fall on me.

"You're too clumsy to be Robin Hood," said a laughing, dark-haired lady dressed in green velvet. "Don't challenge the poor young man, George. A thief would be stealthier, or bolder."

Mistaken for a guy, not for the first time. That had sometimes happened to me before my breasts swelled up. Here I wore a man's clothes, though unfortunately far less costly than the ones these people wore. My hair was still as short as it was under my veil and wimple at home.

"A writer, are you?" My challenger continued frowning at my unwitting party crashing. "Recite some poetry, if you can."

"I wandered lonely as a cloud," I recited. Judging by their clothes, these people were living at least two hundred years too soon to have read Wordsworth. He wasn't my favorite poet, but the words came readily to mind.

"Why do you say clouds are lonely?" the woman inquired. "They usually fly to us in processions."

"You have corrected me, lovely lady." I bowed to her. I felt so disconcerted that the only other poem I could think of was "tell all the truth but tell it slant," and I didn't think that was a wise choice to recite to this not entirely friendly group.

"How dare you try to flirt with this lady, who is far above your station," George growled.

I bowed. "Yes, very far. My apologies."

"Don't be a bear, George. He's only trying to be polite." She turned back to me. "I am Anne Boleyn and George is my brother."

I sucked in my breath. The brother whom King Henry VIII executed on the charge of committing adultery, not to mention incest, with her. I *did not want to meet this lady, or to like her. All I could think of was the blade that would cut off her head.*

I wished to go to another world, but I remained where I stood.

"Perhaps he's a spy from the king. Henry is always stalking you," George complained.

She laughed again. "That is his way of wooing. It is an honor to be courted by the king."

I gulped. Some honor. "I do not have the privilege of working for the king." Please let me go back to the USA. I wanted to tell her to go ahead and let King Henry have sex with her, so he would forget about her. Stop leading him on to force him to marry her. But I didn't dare.

I willed myself to return to my convent cell, and I succeeded. My small, spartan bed was far safer than Anne Boleyn's.

I tried to block thoughts about pretty Anne's execution.

Instead I thought about my audacity in describing myself as a writer in my visit to Tudor England. What a lie. I would never be allowed to write.

CHAPTER 14
Sister Rose

R OSE TRIED TO BE happy for the other novices on visiting day. She felt like an orphan. It must be wrong to feel that way because one can't be an orphan at twenty-two.

Nevertheless, she wished her Uncle Tim would travel to Maryland sometime to see her. She must be inconsiderate to want him to travel so far just for her.

Her cousins were preoccupied with jobs, engagements, marriages, and children and would never think to travel to see her.

Did she wish she had joined an order that had a novitiate in Massachusetts so her relatives might visit her? Of course not. The Euphrosnyes were perfect, and Rose loved the beauty of the Mother House in Maryland. And Sister Matthew lived there. Never meeting Sister Matthew was unimaginable.

Rose said a prayer of thanks because Mother Michael told her to set up the refreshment table, then allowed her to go for a walk in the garden while the other novices saw their visitors. Rose didn't want to sit in a corner and watch. Mother Michael wasn't so bad after all.

Another novice also paced in the garden. Sister Philomena, the shy girl whose alcove stood next to Sister Matthew's, seemed to walk as far away from Rose as she could. Compared with Sister Philomena, Sister Agnes seemed bold and gregarious.

Not wanting to disturb the shy novice, Rose ambled in a different direction. But all paths in the garden intersected, and she found herself meeting Sister Philomena sooner than expected, near the willow. Tears dripped down Sister Philomena's cheeks.

"What is the matter?" Rose asked. It was a time when they were permitted to talk.

Sister Philomena sank onto a stone bench. "Pardon me, Sister Rose. I thought I had dried my eyes. Pay no attention to me."

"Why shouldn't I pay attention to you? Are you sad because, like me, you didn't have a visitor? That always makes me sad."

"Does it? I didn't have a visitor because my oldest sister just had another baby." Sister Philomena choked.

"At least she's not sick."

"I'm so sinful." Sister Philomena turned her face away from Rose. "I'm jealous. I love little children, but I'll never have any."

"Are you sure you want to stay in the convent? You could have children."

"I'm so plain and timid that no man would marry me."

"That can't be true. Your looks are fine. Women don't have to be beautiful to be married. Thinking finding a husband would be difficult is no reason to live in the convent."

Sister Philomena put her hand over her mouth. "I can't believe I told you that. Please don't tell anyone what I said."

"I'll never tell. But you should think more about whether you want to be here."

"I felt so relieved not to have to worry about dating. I thought I had put all that behind me. But when I think about children.... I try not to, but when my sisters keep having babies, I can't help it."

Rose guessed part of Sister Philomena's secret. "Did your parents think one of their children should enter the convent?"

"Yes. And that it should be me, maybe because I'm the plainest."

Rose strove not to show anger in her voice. "You don't have to spend your life here because they wanted you to. Do think about children if they matter so much to you."

"You don't want children?"

"I never thought much about the possibility of having them." Rose was not prepared to admit she had assumed they were out of the question because she did not want to be intimate with a man.

"Maybe I will let myself think about whether I might be able to have children." Sister Philomena sighed. "Thank you, Sister Rose. This is the longest conversation I've had with anyone since I came to St. Euphrosnye's."

Rose wasn't surprised to hear that. Though the rules severely limited novices' conversation, the others managed to say more at recreation than Philomena ever had. "Thank you for honoring me with your thoughts, Sister Philomena." She walked away marveling at how many problems everyone had. She hoped that Sister Philomena would become bold enough to follow her heart's desire.

SISTER MATTHEW ALWAYS LOOKED radiant after she had seen her parents. Rose smiled at her happiness.

She longed to touch Sister Matthew. To stroke her cheek. To run her fingers through Sister Matthew's hair, with no veil in the way. To hold Sister Matthew's hand. To kiss her and hold her close.

Would that ever be possible? If they managed to time travel to the same place, perhaps Rose would be bold enough to try.

Perhaps. But what if Sister Matthew were horrified? What if Sister Matthew reacted like Nancy, Rose's college roommate? What if Sister Matthew never wanted to talk to Rose again? Would she dare to risk her friendship with Sister Matthew?

She should start by holding Sister Matthew's hand. Then she might be able to discern whether Sister Matthew enjoyed her touch.

Rose felt certain she would enjoy touching Sister Matthew.

She prayed for them to time travel to the same place. A pretty place, where they could be alone together. And where they weren't wearing habits. Rose wasn't sure she could bring herself to try kissing a novice in a habit. That sounded sacrilegious.

Reverend Mother gave the novices special permission to watch the news one night because she said they should learn about the Civil Rights Movement. The convent had a television set in a room that novices were not usually allowed to enter, but the older nuns also seldom watched television because it was a worldly distraction.

Rose looked forward to the program. They were almost always forbidden newspapers and television, but tonight they would gain a little more knowledge about the outside world.

Reverend Mother left the room to attend to business.

Civil rights marchers appeared on the screen.

"I wish we could join a march," Rose said. "I regret not doing it before I entered."

"I also would like—" Sister Matthew began to say, but Mother Michael cut her off.

"You're just showing off," The Mistress of Novices snapped at Rose. "You're not part of the world anymore, and you don't know much about it."

Aghast, Rose stared at her.

"I do know what has been happening in the South. I have seen photos of some nuns marching," Rose said in her mildest tone.

"Not from our order." The Mistress of Novices frowned. "Mingling with unruly protestors and defying the law is no proper place for a religious."

Rose wondered whether she had joined the right order of nuns. Reverend Mother didn't seem to think the way Mother Michael did. Surely Pope John would make it clear that priests and nuns should join people who march for justice. That must be their duty, showing the spirit of Jesus in the world. Rose longed to meet civil rights activists and looked forward to the day when she could join protests. Perhaps she could march after she had taken her final vows.

CHAPTER 15

Sister Matthew

I LOVED THEOLOGY FOR ONE reason: It was the only class the order allowed me to take as a novice. I attended a class in theology taught by Reverend Mother, at nearby St. Euphrosnye's College.

The whole idea of theology, an academic subject about what people imagined regarding Possible God, astonished me. Nevertheless, it was interesting as a study in the history of thought.

At the college, novices were not supposed to talk to the students who aren't nuns. We were required to leave the classroom silently after each class. We couldn't go to the cafeteria for lunch but had to eat in a small lunchroom designated for novices and sisters only.

None of the other novices were taking this class because most of them were attending a freshman class. Rose already studied theology in college, so she wasn't in my class either. I had no one to sit with or talk to.

I didn't envy the secular young women, who clearly wore curlers at night to shape their hair. Some were trying to look like Jackie Kennedy, while others worked to resemble movie stars. The conversations I overheard at the beginning and end of class failed to inspire me.

"That's a gorgeous sweater!" one young woman chirped. "I love that shade of pink. Is it cashmere?"

"Yes. My mother gave it to me for my birthday."

I winced at the memory of similar gifts I had felt required to praise though I hadn't wanted to wear them.

"My cashmere sweater is two years old. I wish I had a new one."

"Do you think I should wear this on my date with Sean?"

"Yes, it's adorable. It shows off your coloring."

I felt no jealousy about the students' blazers and cashmere sweaters. Instead, I rejoiced that I would never again have to shop for clothes and worry about what might be becoming to me. I wished the habit were easier to move around in, but I felt free from the complications of trying to follow fashion.

Then one of the secular students said to another, "Weren't the pictures of Jackie and Caroline in *LIFE Magazine* wonderful?"

I didn't care about seeing that issue of *LIFE*. However, those words reminded me that the other students could read the newspapers or watch television news. I wished I could ask them about international developments.

I knew these students must also engage in the kind of conversations I had enjoyed at the University of Maryland, discussing the books they were reading. Maybe some of them were English majors, but I couldn't ask them about that.

I saw them as women who lived to find husbands, who would never have a permanent community of women, though they might be passing through dormitories at the present time.

Reverend Mother began to speak. Her voice showed her passion for her subject, so I listened eagerly.

"St. Thomas Aquinas had a deep understanding of the natural world," she informed us. "He said animal life could form from plant life, moving from the 'less perfect' to the 'more perfect.' We do not have to believe plants are less perfect in themselves than animals to see that this is an early form of the theory of evolution. Evolution is compatible with theology. Science is compatible with theology."

I felt proud of her. I couldn't have endured being a nun if we had been required to spout nonsense about Adam and Eve.

Not that I cared what Aquinas had said about matters that concerned my own life. Or about anything else. I'm not sure Possible God cared either.

I LONGED TO SPEAK with Reverend Mother outside class. After class ended, I asked whether I could talk to her about academic matters.

"Certainly, Sister Matthew." She didn't exactly smile, but her expression loosened. "Come to my office this afternoon after lunch."

"Thank you, Reverend Mother."

I had learned not to fear going to her office. I entered, filled with deference but not much apprehension.

She nodded to me. "Please be seated, Sister Matthew. What did you want to say?"

"I enjoy your class, Reverend Mother." That seemed like a good beginning.

"You are doing well in it. Theology is important, but always remember that prayer is more important, and charity is most important."

"Yes, Reverend Mother, I'll remember that." I paused. "Reverend Mother, I love studying. Could I take an English literature class next semester?"

Reverend Mother reentered the world of silence for several minutes. Oh no, I must have said the wrong thing. I steeled myself for her answer.

After a long pause, she spoke. "I understand that you love learning, Sister Matthew. That is a good thing, but not if it distracts you from God. Your time as a novice is dedicated to learning to pray and accept the ways of the convent. You may study theology because that might help your soul.

"You have told me you want to pursue a graduate degree in English literature. I am sympathetic to that request, but I don't think an English literature class would help you now. You already spent much time studying English as an undergraduate. Perhaps you will study it further, but not this year. However, I recognize your aptitude for languages, so you may take a college class in Latin next semester. I believe you have not studied it since high school."

I sat back in the chair. "Latin, Reverend Mother?"

"Yes, Latin. Latin will always be on the curriculum in our high schools, but we don't have enough good teachers. You need to be prepared to teach more than one subject, and you have the makings of a good Latin teacher. You may begin now by getting a Latin textbook and reviewing your high school Latin."

I managed to say, "Thank you, Reverend Mother." I didn't want to study Latin, much less to teach it, but at least she didn't ask me to study math or chemistry.

"Do you have any more questions?"

I didn't want to leave her office yet. "Yes, Reverend Mother. Will our theology class study more contemporary theologians?"

"Yes, we shall do that next semester. We shall read some Protestant theologians as well as Catholics so we can understand them and defend Catholic doctrine."

"I look forward to that, Reverend Mother." Imagine me as a defender of doctrine!

"If we send you to graduate school, are you sure you want to study English literature rather than theology?" She looked at me with more interest.

I restrained my impulse to gulp. "Yes, Reverend Mother, I am sure I would be a better English teacher than a teacher of theology."

She sighed. "So few of our students want to pursue theology on the graduate level. You may go now, Sister Matthew."

"Thank you, Reverend Mother." Hoping I had escaped a future mired in theology I didn't believe in, I left the room.

Latin! I groaned internally. At least that meant more time to study, and more work with words. *Amo, amas, amat, amamus*...but I would not be learning about love, except for love of God. I would revisit the formidable but unlovable Julius Caesar and the political polemicist Cicero. I had bad memories about Shakespeare's *Julius Caesar*. I doubted I would be studying the rather obscene Roman satirists.

Still, I wouldn't mind reading Virgil again. Adventures, a love story, and a trip through hell that inspired Dante. What more could I want?

CHAPTER 16
Sister Matthew

I CRAVED AN OUTDOOR RECREATION, where we could walk in the crisp October air, savoring the glowing red and orange leaves on the maples in the garden. Mean Mother Michael deemed it too chilly and told us to stay inside during what the nuns called recreation. She seldom allowed us to go outdoors during the short recreation time. I wondered why. Is Mother Michael an agoraphobe? The convent is the perfect place for one.

Perhaps she fears a yellow and orange palette could ruin our palates for a diet of black and white.

Several nuns filed into the parlor, not chatting. One carried an altar cloth she had been embroidering.

Reverend Mother entered from another door. She looked as if she had just been notified of a death.

"We must go to the chapel and pray, sisters," she ordered in a voice that shook. Her tone, so different from any I had heard before, unnerved me. "The Russians have brought nuclear weapons to Cuba and President Kennedy has warned them that they must take back the weapons. There is a chance of war."

I turned to ice.

Some sisters gasped. Rose closed her eyes. I knew she was already praying.

Mother Michael stared at Reverend Mother as if telling us news of the outside world were a mortal sin. The convent didn't even subscribe to newspapers.

"We are supposed to be sheltered from news of the world," Reverend Mother said, apparently in response to Mother Michael's amazement, "but I believe there are events so significant that it would almost be a sin for me to keep knowledge of them hidden from you. Pray for peace. Pray for President Kennedy." She led us to the chapel.

Thank goodness we have a leader like Reverend Mother Robert Bellarmine. We might have been led by a nun who would have left us in ignorance.

I never prayed so earnestly in my life. I prayed for President Kennedy. I prayed just as fervently for Premier Nikita Khrushchev.

Some Americans had called Khrushchev a clown, ostensibly because he had pounded a table with his shoe at the United Nations, but most likely because he was fat. People tend to underestimate those who are fat. I had been guilty of that myself. When John XXIII became pope, I thought he would be less spiritual than Pope Pius XII because John was fat, and Pius had been thin. Learning more about Pope John had taught me a lesson.

Now I prayed for everyone. Would we face a world of Hiroshimas? Could this be the end of the world?

If there is a God who intervenes in human affairs, that Being would be highly unlikely to prevent a nuclear war because a handful of nuns were praying, but prayer made us feel as if we could do something.

I longed to talk to Rose. I longed even more to phone my parents and tell them I love them. No matter what the crisis, phoning them would be against the rules. If I broke my leg, the Mistress of Novices would call them on my behalf.

We spent hours in chapel. I did not mind. For the first time, I objected to leaving it when Reverend Mother signaled we should go to the refectory and eat.

I barely tasted the fish sticks, rice, and spinach, and felt irritated at the rice pudding dessert. It seemed to be no time for dessert. On the other hand, what if it were the last dessert we ever ate? I thanked Possible God for the pudding.

When we walked along the hallway and passed framed photos of the order's various schools, I felt someone touch my sleeve. Of course, it was Rose. We looked into each other's eyes and communicated as deeply as we ever had when we talked.

In the evening Reverend Mother allowed us to watch television news to learn what was happening. Even though we just said the rosary—all fifteen mysteries of it—some sisters were holding their rosaries and praying it again while we watched the news.

The fear dragged on for days. President Kennedy ordered a naval blockade of Cuba. We wore out our knees in the chapel. I couldn't sleep at night and got out of my bed to pray on my knees as I had as a child, though my mother would come into my room and demand that I get back in my bed.

The hollow-eyed look on many of my sisters' faces suggested others also spent their nights in prayer.

The Russians shot down an American pilot flying over Cuba. Tears came to my eyes, not for the pilot but for the rest of us.

I stole a moment after chapel to approach Rose. She turned her weary face to me. Her thin smile penetrated the gloom.

"I believe this crisis will be resolved peacefully," she said, not caring that we were supposed to be silent. "We must hope that it will. But I want to say how very much I care for you, Sister Matthew."

Faith, hope, and love. That was Sister Rose.

"I care deeply for you, too, Sister Rose. I pray we will all survive and our friendship will grow."

"It will." She touched my hand, and I felt as warm as a baby held by its mother.

"Thank you," I said.

I wished I had as much faith in Kennedy and Khrushchev as I did in Rose.

On October 28, when we watched the news again, Walter Cronkite announced the crisis had ended. Khrushchev was withdrawing the missiles in exchange for U.S. recognition of Cuba's sovereignty.

I burst into tears of joy, and I was not the only one.

Reverend Mother led us in a prayer of Thanksgiving. I felt great affection for her because she had allowed us to take part in a terrible time for the nation, though Mother Michael and some of the older nuns frowned at our use of the television.

My prayers thanked not only God, who after all allowed wars to happen, but also President Kennedy and Premier Khrushchev. Thank you, Premier Khrushchev, I prayed. May you be safe from purges.

My eyes sought Rose's. She met my gaze and smiled.

ON THE NEXT VISITING day, my mother brought oatmeal cookies. Sister Jerome carried them to the convent kitchen to put them on a plate.

I might as well take this relatively unsupervised moment to give my parents a sample of what my life was like. "Reverend Mother allowed us to watch the news about the Cuban missile crisis. I'm so grateful we were able to know what was happening."

"They *allowed* you to learn about the Cuban missile crisis?" My father stared at me as if I had said I had had a vision of the Blessed Virgin Mary.

"How kind of them," my mother snapped. Then she sighed.

"We are supposed to focus on our spiritual lives, not the temporal world," I reminded them.

"Jesus Christ!" My father reddened. "Sorry. Of course you are. It's good they want your life to be serene."

"Maureen, serene?" My mother shook her head.

"Look, Sister Jerome is putting the cookies out on the table and will come back to us after she finishes," I warned them. "It was so kind of you to bake them, Mom."

"I'm happy to do it, dear. Why don't you go get one?" She forced a smile.

"May I get one for you, Dad?"

"No, thank you, we have some at home." He smiled too widely.

If I confessed to Reverend Mother what I had told my parents, I would have been given a penance for discussing convent policies in a way that complained about them. I had no intention of admitting what I had said.

CHAPTER 17

Sister Matthew

ONE NIGHT, I HEARD rustling instead of snoring in the alcove
next to me.

In the morning, Sister Philomena the Snorer was gone. She
had returned to being Francine. I hoped she left of her own volition,
rather than being told to go. In either case, the Mistress of Novices
would never tell us the reason, and we were supposed never to mention
the missing sister's name again.

I repented my uncharitable thoughts about Francine's snoring. I
didn't think she was happy in the convent. I wondered whether she
could be happy anywhere. I hoped there would come a day when her
snoring kept someone she loved awake.

That evening when we returned to the dormitory, I saw a different
novice enter the alcove next to mine. Rose!

My heart leapt with joy, but I kept myself from gazing at her.

My bed had been as far from the noisy sister as possible. Now I
moved it close to the curtain on that side.

I didn't want to sleep. I listened for the sound of Rose's dear breath.

I heard the slightest of rustles. Though it was dark, I could see a
hand reaching under the curtain. I clasped it.

Rose and I were holding hands. That was a miracle. Her touch
warmed my heart.

Would anyone else be able to see us? No, the curtains surrounding our alcoves were floor-length, so long that no one could.

At least an hour elapsed before we unclasped hands so we could go to sleep.

THE NEXT EVENING AFTER *I retired to my alcove, I found myself among mountains. Snow capped them, but the trail where I stood was clear except for a scattering of small rocks. Wildflowers sprouted nearby.*

I spied a woman in the distance and, though I couldn't make out her features, I recognized Rose.

I scrambled over the rocks. Would she want to see me as much as I wanted not just to see, but to touch her, in a world outside the convent?

We both wore jeans and t-shirts.

Short hair looks good on her, better than it does on me because I have large ears like the MAD Magazine *boy. When I wear my habit, my wimple covers them. I hoped Rose wouldn't mind my ears. She had seen them when we were postulants, but she might have forgotten how much they stick out.*

Hiking had made me sweat. Did my underarms smell?

We approached each other.

I extended my hand to her. She took it in both of hers. "Hello, Mattie. I'm so glad to see you here."

Mattie, not Maureen. I liked that. I liked it very much. A special name just for the two of us. My hand glowed and the glow spread to my chest.

"Rose." I was too flooded with emotion to say anything more.

We strolled together, holding hands. There were too many things to say. I felt unable to say any of them.

Rose spoke to me. "Now that we have a chance to talk, let's give it a try. Really, why did you enter the convent?"

"The wimple hides my ears."

Rose laughed. "I knew you'd say something ridiculous. And did you pick the Euphrosnyes because St. Euphrosnye disguised herself as a man?"

"Why not? I'm disguised as a novice. I think they should allow us to dress like monks on St. Euphrosnye's feast day to honor our patron."

Rose laughed harder than she ever had in the convent. "You're the silliest novice ever to chant in a chapel," she said.

Rose led me behind a clump of firs. She kissed my lips softly. I had never kissed a woman, except my mother's cheeks. The touch of Rose's lips felt softer and sweeter than I could have imagined. I glowed.

We sat on a rock and held hands.

She felt the same way about me that I felt about her.

I don't know how long we sat there.

After many minutes, we stood. This time, I dared to kiss her. Tears of wonder formed in my eyes.

We held each other close, then walked back to the path. I floated. I might not deserve it, but I felt something like religious ecstasy. This was heaven.

It was the best day of my life.

BACK IN THE CONVENT, I wondered how I could treat Rose as I had before.

I had to try. Rose loved the convent. She must have the vocation I lacked. I must do everything I could to protect her from suspicion.

At recreation, I sneaked into a room with a few shelves of books. We weren't supposed to go to those shelves, which housed the books that had been used by the sisters who went to college. I had been allowed to take my theology textbook at the beginning of the semester and a Latin textbook a few weeks ago, but no other books. After looking around to make sure no one saw me, I picked up the *Norton Anthology of English Literature* and read poems by Elizabeth Barret Browning.

Reading without asking permission first broke the rules and reading love poems made it a double infraction. I knew I wouldn't confess it in a chapter meeting. I left the forbidden room and went to the parlor, where some other novices were talking. I didn't see Rose.

Did I desire Rose even more than I desired books? It was a tie. I had never met anyone who excited me as much as books.

How do I love thee? I love thee as if thou wert a printed page covered with the finest poems.

I finally saw Rose in the refectory at dinner. When I passed her, she looked at me just for a second. I saw an instant flash of love. Then she began to eat her salad.

When we were filing out of the refectory, she leaned towards me and whispered, "Remember the mountains."

So she really was there in the mountains with me. She really kissed me and remembers.

It's my feast day, I thought, though it's not St. Matthew's.

TWO DAYS LATER WE had our weekly Confession. I worked on what to say to the priest. Should I just omit mentioning everything that happened with Rose? Or should I admit to having impure thoughts? No, my thoughts about kissing her weren't impure. They were elevated.

Why even think about what to tell the priest? I didn't believe that loving another woman was a sin. A sin? I scarcely even believed in God. Possible God, you wouldn't toss me into hell for kissing Rose, would you? That means you wouldn't care if I skipped mentioning it in Confession.

I wondered what Rose would say in her Confession. Don't be foolish, I told myself. She doesn't believe our kiss was a sin, or she wouldn't have done it.

When I had a chance to talk to her, I whispered, "You don't think our kiss was a sin, do you?"

She rolled her eyes. "No, and I don't believe you do either."

"No, I don't. I just needed to hear you say that."

"It was beautiful."

"Yes, beautiful." Thank goodness she thought so too. She didn't seem to feel guilty.

I prayed, though. I prayed for Rose to be happy and safe. I prayed for her to love me, always. I prayed for us not to be discovered. Maybe Possible God would understand. Possible God must see what a fine person Rose is. Did Possible God think we were a well-matched couple?

NOW ALL RELIGIOUS ART made me think of Rose. (Other art probably would too, but in the convent I see only religious art.) Copies of Raphael Madonnas like the one in our refectory used to remind me of my mother, but now I saw Rose in them too. Pictures of the Annunciation seem like Rose because they have a humbler air than my mother ever had. Is Rose humble? Just a tad. Not Uriah Heep 'umble—moderately humble.

MY LIFE HAD BEEN transformed. I no longer minded other nuns' ways that had irritated me before. Well, I minded them less.

I didn't feel restless about being confined to the convent because Rose lives there. At any moment, I might see her, even if we couldn't talk. Even if I didn't see her, I knew she was not far away.

We were breathing the same air.

We said (mostly) the same prayers. We obeyed (mostly) the same rules. We saw the same sights and ate the same food.

A wish formed in my heart that we were living alone together, but I am trying to smother it. We are where Rose wants to be.

CHAPTER 18
Sister Rose

ROSE FELT HER HEART would burst with joy. Mattie loved her. Mattie had kissed her. Mattie enjoyed their kisses. But perhaps she shouldn't risk trying to meet Mattie in time travel again. They were supposed to be brides of Christ. They were supposed to love God much more than any human being.

Rose told herself their kisses didn't break the vow of celibacy but enriched their life in the convent. Their love of each other was love of the reflection of God in each other.

Or was she fooling herself? She wondered.

She knew only that Mattie made her feel the way sunlight made her feel.

She thanked God for Mattie.

How terrible it would have been if Mattie had spurned her the way Nancy had in college. Too much piety smothered life.

Mattie shone with a light much greater than Nancy ever had. Rose prayed, but her thoughts drifted to Mattie. She let them. She longed to hold Mattie's hand again and again. To kiss Mattie's soft lips until they had to stop to breathe. To hold Mattie close, with no clothes between them. This exaltation, this warmth, delight, and trust must be love.

Was it certain that Mattie would not turn away in horror as Nancy had, if they tried more than kissing? Seeing disgust in Mattie's eyes would be unbearable. Far better not to try than to fail. Rose decided to be happy with what they had instead of trying for more.

She prayed that Mattie would love her always.

They hadn't taken vows yet. Would kissing be a sin after they had taken a vow of chastity? Was that distinction between kissing a novice and a professed nun artificial? Rose didn't believe that women sinned if they embraced. But what about novices or professed nuns embracing? Could she be sure that wasn't a sin? She tried to put aside those concerns.

Rose had always enjoyed her convent duties. Now she enjoyed them doubly because Mattie was nearby. Experiencing human love intoxicated Rose.

ROSE'S HEART-BLOOM MOVED INTO her prayers. Happiness brought God down from the skies and the altar and infused her prayers with joy.

She knelt in chapel and felt the Divine Love of the world. The Love reached her also in the refectory, the garden, and during chores.

Her love for Mattie made the world more beautiful and enveloped her in rapture.

She didn't need to be in Mattie's presence to feel that love.

CHAPTER 19
Sister Matthew

S NOW MADE THE CONVENT purer than ever if one believed white connoted purity. Piles of the stuff pressed against the convent walls. Not respecting the sanctity of the cloister, the snow invaded it also. Icicles menaced anyone standing under a corner of the roof, but I would have been willing to take that chance. Even though I didn't have proper winter boots, I longed to walk out in the garden while snow still brought magic to the tree branches. I wouldn't mind risking catching a cold.

I imagined visiting Russia. I envisioned a city with snow sparkling on its onion-shaped domes, not a forest where wolves prowled.

I saw Rose staring through the window at recreation.

"I miss tobogganing," she confided.

"I've never ridden in a toboggan, but I miss sleds."

"I wish we could throw snowballs. Wouldn't Mother Michael love our doing that?"

"I'll bet she would pack hard ones. It would be great to build a snownun. We could use my veil."

Unfortunately, saying Mother Michael's name seemed to invoke that formidable nun. She appeared and scowled at us. She would never let us walk out in the snow. Mother Gabriel had allowed it once when we were postulants.

We silenced ourselves and moved to talk to other novices.

I thought about how grand it would be to see Rose on Christmas. Of course there would be no presents, but we could see each other and commune silently.

THE CHURCH'S ADVENT COLOR is purple, supposedly a color of mourning though it doesn't signify mourning to me, in preparation for Christ's birth. Why mourn? Why not celebrate ahead of time? Aren't most women happy when they are waiting for the birth of a child?

The idea behind the purple is that the world was steeped in sin until Jesus arrived.

This despite the presence of the Hindu Vedas' authors, Siddhartha Gautama the Buddha, Confucius, and Socrates and Plato, all of whom supposedly were confined to Limbo after they died. They couldn't rise to heaven because they had never been baptized. Neither could babies who died before baptism. Still more bizarre, the Jewish prophets of the Old Testament and Jews living in our century were supposedly excluded. Even in my pious adolescence, I hadn't believed such nonsense for a minute and didn't see how anyone could. Limbo is one of the doctrines that would have made Jesus of Nazareth tear his hair out.

I was looking forward to Christmas though I missed the glowing Christmas trees I had decorated with my parents. They have one string of the most wonderful old Christmas tree lights covered by bells decorated with fairytale scenes.

I missed baking Christmas cookies with Mom. (I'm very particular about how to put the sprinkles on sugar cookies. The Christmas trees must have green sprinkles, with a few colored ones, and Santas must have red sprinkles.) I also missed eating the cookies, a little gingerbread, and fruitcake. Some people don't like fruitcake, but I enjoy all the citrons in it.

I wondered whether Rose likes Christmas cookies and fruitcake. Probably Christmas is hard for her because her parents are dead. Maybe she's glad to be in the convent, where the holiday is completely different.

I missed Mom and Dad.

At least we sisters sang many of the beautiful Christmas songs of my childhood, except for "Away in a Manger" because Martin Luther had written it.

We decorated the chapel with poinsettias and pine swags, but there were no decorations in the rest of the convent.

The chapel has a beautiful creche, but I missed the small one at home. My mother let me set it up. It had Wise Men but no shepherds, so I insisted that we buy shepherds, though they didn't match the other figures. I felt sad one year when I unpacked the donkey and saw that a leg had broken off. Mom glued it back on, but I could always see that the poor donkey had been repaired.

On Christmas morning, Rose's face shone with joy. That was enough happiness for me.

I held back laughter at the sisters' idea of Christmas presents. They gave us each a needle case they had made.

I silently sang "Jingle Bells," "Frosty the Snowman," and "Here Comes Suzy Snowflake" in my heart.

The best thing about Christmas and Easter is that those are the only days when we are allowed to talk to each other at any time we want, except when we are in chapel. Of course we are still required to gather in groups, so the conversation can't be too intimate, but it's fun to be able to talk about things like the Christmas decorations and the food. After months when we were deprived of small talk, it has become more appealing.

I should be a little more spiritual about Christmas, but that's hard when you don't believe Jesus was God. I'm sorry, Jesus. I do admire, and even love, you and your teachings very much.

But all these intelligent women around me believe. Am I so much more intelligent than they are that I have to believe something different? Maybe they are right.

ROSE GAVE ME ONE of her intimate glances when we were working in the kitchen together again a few days later. As usual, my heart pounded like a sledgehammer. The spartan kitchen glowed like a sunrise.

"You believe in the magic of time travel, don't you?" she asked.

"I never thought I'd believe in magic, but now I have to," I admitted, scraping food off a plate.

"Why do you find it so much harder to believe in God?" Her tone sounded gentle. Her words didn't feel like a criticism.

I gulped. I didn't have an answer. Time travel persuaded me that magic, or unusual experiences, are possible, but failed to allay my doubts about a God who intervenes in the world.

"I didn't mean to trap you." Rose shook her head. "I sounded so self-righteous. I have doubts too."

I squirmed and stared into the soapy water in the sink as if it were a magical pool. "I never told you how much trouble I have believing. Are you a mind reader?"

"No, but I do intuit things sometimes." Rose put her hand to her mouth. "I shouldn't have said that about your beliefs. I'm sorry. I didn't mean to intrude."

"I was afraid you wouldn't care about me if you knew."

A smile broke out on her face. "Don't worry."

"Really?" I basked in her warmth.

"Really. I know how intellectual you are, almost too intellectual for the convent." She began putting the dishes I had rinsed into the dishwasher. "It must be so hard for you to have your reading and conversation so circumscribed."

"It is," I admitted. "Isn't it for you?"

"Yes. It is sad that the order doesn't trust us to stretch our brains more. I believe you're going to write someday. I hope you'll be able to write whatever you want."

A snicker escaped from my lips. "There's not much chance of my writing whatever I want here."

She looked into my eyes. "Convents will change. Change is coming. Can't you feel it in the air? I can."

"What air? The incense stifles us."

"Trust Pope John XXIII. I know he'll bring more change than we can imagine."

"I hope you're right." Being allowed to write whatever I want was as likely as my becoming the first nun astronaut.

Rose coughed. She turned away from the dishes.

"Are you sick?" Hearing even one cough from her made me anxious.

"It's nothing. I hope I don't spread any germs." She tried unsuccessfully to smother another cough.

"You should rest. I'll finish the dishes."

She left, which she wouldn't have done unless she were really ill. Her departure turned the room from paradise to a mere kitchen.

I took charge of the dishes and told myself they were magic vessels from a fairy tale. Philosophers had dined on them in centuries past, which would be quite a trick since the dishes were Melmac.

What kind of books could a nun write? Perhaps homilies about how to be a good girl, a good woman, or a good nun. Or a meditation on the life of some saint. Nothing more adventurous. Would I ever be able to use language that roared, shattered, or caressed? Would my words always mince in tiny steps?

Did too much religion kill language? Or just nuns' language? Priests are permitted to speak with force.

Would I ever confess in a chapter meeting that I longed to use wilder language? Only if I harbored a death wish or lusted for punishment.

Thank goodness Emily Dickinson wasn't a Catholic and didn't choose to join a convent.

FOR ONCE, OUR HABITS did not feel too warm. As we trudged through the cold cloister to the chapel, I wished for an extra layer. A gray chill had replaced the snow. The shriveled plants gave the bare garden a look of desolation.

The chapel beckoned. Though draughts seeped through the cracks around its windows, the chapel provided some shelter.

A novice just ahead of me fell. Rose. I moved so swiftly that I caught her before she hit the pavement.

Rose had fainted. I managed not to kiss her or do anything else suspicious. I did feel her forehead, which blazed.

Everything around me blurred. Mean Mother Michael and Sister Catherine of Siena, the infirmarian, urged Sister Ursula, probably the strongest novice, and me to carry Rose to the infirmary.

As soon as we had slipped her onto a bed, Sister Catherine shooed us away. Mother Michael led us back to the chapel.

Too stunned even to cry, I prayed with all my heart. Possible God, I won't insult your intelligence by taking away the word "possible," but please help Rose. Mother Mary, St. Euphrosnye, St. Rose de Lima, St. Matthew, please help Rose. Help me to control myself, too, so I don't give us away.

When the novices met later for recreation—but what recreation could there be when Rose was sick?—Mother Michael told us about Rose.

"The doctor has seen Sister Rose de Lima. She has bronchial pneumonia. Mother Gabriel took her to the hospital. We must pray for her."

I had never heard of a nun being taken to the hospital, except one old nun who had cancer.

Rose is no longer at St. Euphrosnye's. There is no chance I could help her or even see her.

My chest aches, though not from pneumonia.

I now learned what it meant to live in contemplation. I had tried it before, but there had been distractions. Now Rose's condition was so deeply embedded in my mind that nothing else existed.

I performed all my duties, of course. Likely I did a better job of it because my body had become a machine.

The thought of living without Rose made my soul shrivel like the winter garden.

My mind constantly repeated God save Rose, God save Rose, God save Rose, I love Rose, I love Rose, I love Rose. Rose, feel my love, let my love enfold you in healing.

CHAPTER 20

Sister Rose

R OSE'S HEAD SPUN. DIZZINESS felt like a permanent condition. Her coughs shook her body the way a cat shakes a mouse. *Will I die? Please God, not before I have done some good in the world. I deserted my poor mother. I want to make up for that. Mother, did you feel this bad when you were drunk? Forgive me for abandoning you.*

Faces swirled around her. Mother Michael, pale and shaken. Mother Gabriel, whispering prayers. Sister Catherine, putting cool cloths on her head. A man? A doctor in white. Nurses who were not nuns.

Rose longed to see Mattie's face. She knew they wouldn't let Mattie see her.

How worried Mattie must be. Will I die without seeing Mattie again?

Though people hovered around Rose, she felt alone. Was she right to believe in God?

Will I see God? God forgive my doubts.

I want to live. Let me see Yellowstone before I die, please God. Let me see a herd of elk. Let me see a sandhill crane. Let me see a grizzly bear. Am I crazy or delirious, to pray to see a grizzly bear? I don't want to die without seeing a grizzly.

Let me see another scarlet tanager, please. Let me see another pileated woodpecker. Let me see more Baltimore orioles. Please let me hear a loon again. Oh, please.

Let me help people, dear God. I'm ashamed that I keep thinking of birds and animals. Forgive me. I love the world so much.

Mattie. I want to see Mattie again. I want to kiss Mattie and tell her how wonderful she is.

I want to make love to Mattie.

I know I can't bargain with you, God. But I will be a better person if I live. I will. How will I be better? I will care more about the other sisters and be more attentive to their needs. Is that enough? What other good deeds can I do in the convent?

If I die, will I fly like a bird? Will I soar?

Will I hear death come on wings, or will it strangle me in my sleep like a burglar come to steal me?

Will I go to heaven? Will I see other people there, or will I be in formless communication with God?

Will I see my mother, never drinking anymore? Will I know her, and will she know me?

I hope nuns aren't confined in some cloistered space in heaven, removed from other souls. I want to live with many souls, not a chosen few.

There will be a simple cross on my gravestone. I would rather have a bluebird.

Mattie will suffer so much if I die.

Not yet, please God. Not yet.

CHAPTER 21

Sister Matthew

R OSE'S PNEUMONIA HAS GONE on and on. Please save her, Possible God. Nothing is impossible.

Hope. I must hope. The thing with feathers. Let dear Rose see many more things with feathers.

Possible God, see what a good novice I am? I pray when I'm supposed to, I pray all the time. I'm quiet. I never talk when I should be silent. I complete every task meticulously. Even my sewing has improved.

I tried to gain strength from chanting with the other sisters in chapel. I could hear that Rose's alto was missing.

I am alone. I haven't felt this alone since Rose began to smile at me.

But Rose still lives in this world. Rose will keep on living. I love you, Rose. Please God, let Rose live.

As the days passed, my mind became wilder. I thought of drawing Rose's name on the frosty windowpanes, but I dared not.

I felt I couldn't live without her.

I longed to run, run as far as I could, through the winter-barren Maryland countryside.

I tried to time travel to a place where I could see Rose, but my desires failed me. Probably she didn't have the energy for time travel.

I WALKED AMONG STRANGERS *in a darker convent. Literally. The only light came from a few candles that sisters carried along the gloomy corridors. The halls smelled moldy, though the walls and floors were stone. I must be in an earlier time.*

The nuns wore habits I did not recognize, and so did I.

We entered an unfamiliar chapel. The old Latin chants failed to cheer me.

The nuns' faces were paler than those of my Euphrosnye sisters. Some nuns coughed, though they held their sleeves over their mouths.

As we left the chapel, a senior nun gave us a command in German. I did not know what she said, yet I recognized the language.

I let myself drift to the end of the line and break away. Surely I wouldn't stay here long enough to be given a punishment in a chapter meeting.

I found my way to the cloister. Sobbing drew me to a dark winter garden, lined with fir trees.

A nun knelt on the cold ground. She wailed, unlike any nun I have ever known. She prostrated herself on the bare earth.

I hoped she hadn't been told to prostrate herself there as a penance. Surely not.

"Please don't do that, sister," I said in Latin, the only common language we had. The words flowed more easily than I expected.

She did not glance at me.

I knelt beside her and put my hand on her shoulder. "Dear sister, you must not lie on this ground. You will become seriously ill."

She rose to her knees and looked at me. Grief wracked her face. The darkest circles I had ever seen surrounded her eyes. "I care not if I sicken," she choked.

"What pains you so much?"

"Sister Gertrude is dead." Her voice sounded hollow.

The nun's agony convinced me that Sister Gertrude must be her lover, or at least her beloved.

I put an arm around her. "Please rise. She wouldn't have wanted you to die too. I know how you feel. My dear friend Sister Rose is seriously ill." My ability to think and speak so much in Latin amazed me.

I stood and pulled the German nun up beside me. She wept on my shoulder. I hoped her mother superior would not discover us and punish her.

"I am alone," she gasped. "Alone. I can't even love God anymore."

"We are all alone." The words came out of my mouth without my thinking them first. "But we must not die of loneliness. Sister Gertrude would want you to go on."

"I cannot bear to be here without her, yet I have nowhere else to go. I have no faith, no hope."

"Not even in the Blessed Virgin Mary, comforter of the afflicted?" I lied to her.

"Would she hear me? I am sworn to a life of prayer, but my heart is in the grave with Gertrude."

"Losing those we love is the worst suffering in the world," I told her. "Try to find solace in your memories. Do not expect to feel the way you did before she died. Try to find another way to live."

She made an effort to stop crying. "Thank you for not saying we will meet in heaven. I hope so, but I cannot feel sure."

"You are wise. Speak to her, if you cannot speak to the Virgin Mary or any of the saints."

"Yes, Gertrude must be a saint. I do speak to her. I will speak to her. Thank you for your kindness."

She stared at me for the first time. "I have never seen you before." She scrutinized my face. "I think you do not belong to this convent."

"No. I think I have come here to comfort you."

She looked at me as if I were an angel. "Bless you! Sent to me! Perhaps I can believe after all."

No, no, I'm not a vision sent by God, I thought.

I found myself back in my convent bed. Tears ran down my cheeks. That time travel was no diversion. It showed how much I would suffer if Rose died.

Could I stay at St. Euphrosnye's if she died? No! Perhaps for a while, I'd be too stunned to move, but not for long.

I must not think that way. Rose must not die. She's far too young.

One day Mother Michael entered the parlor during recreation. "I brought Sister Rose de Lima home from the hospital today, but she will stay in the infirmary for many more days. No other novice is permitted to see her until she fully recovers."

My heart beat like a revving up engine. Rose would live.

Thank you, Possible God. Hosanna!

It takes all my self-control to keep from walking down the corridor to the infirmary and seeing Rose. I know I mustn't. If I did, Mother Michael might forbid me to talk with Rose when she returns to regular convent life. I remembered Linda's warning that novices who talked too much had been banned from speaking to each other.

CHAPTER 22
Sister Rose

Rose tried to reach for a glass of water near her bed. The effort felt like climbing a mountain. She couldn't do it.

"Sister Rose! I told you not to try, but to call me," Sister Catherine chided her in a mild tone. She helped Rose sit up enough to drink and gave her the glass with a straw.

"Thank you, Sis..." How feeble her voice sounded.

"Don't waste your breath trying to talk. Father Nolan will bring you the Eucharist in about an hour. Do you have the strength to wait until then to eat? Just nod or shake your head."

Rose nodded.

Sister Catherine walked away.

Rose began to pray. *Dear God, thank you for allowing me to live. How I long to see the sky and the world around me.*

I'm a little ashamed of the thoughts I had when I feared I would die. A grizzly bear! As a member of the Congregation of St. Euphrosnye, I'll never go to Yellowstone. Is my vocation faltering? Or do I want a different life? St. Thomas Aquinas said that studying nature was studying God. Is that a path I should take?

Mattie. I want to see Mattie. I long to kiss her. Why must I be so close to her, yet alone?

I must prepare to receive the Body of Christ. Lord, help me focus on You. Am I wrong to love Your world more than contemplation?

That afternoon, Rose stirred restlessly in the bed. Her life had shrunk to such small dimensions. Lying in bed, being fed by Sister Catherine, praying. She should not see a life of prayer as a small life. She should be glad to think about God every minute, to offer up her suffering. But she wasn't glad.

She wanted Mattie.

Now that Rose had escaped death, she wanted to live more than ever. She wanted to be bold enough to kiss Mattie again.

She contemplated Mattie's lips.

She loved Mattie. She should be brave enough to try to make love to Mattie and hope for the best.

CHAPTER 23

Sister Matthew

T HE DAYS ARE ENDLESS. A week has passed since Rose returned
to the convent, and I still haven't seen her.
I dragged myself to chapel.

Rose sat in her usual place. I trembled with joy.

After chapel, she walked to the refectory for breakfast, assisted by
Sister Catherine. Rose's face looked pale and her steps were shaky, but
her eyes were clear. She smiled at me.

Not even kissing her had given me so much joy.

That night, we held hands under the curtain.

A FEW NIGHTS LATER, *I traveled to a bedroom. The only light shone
from a small lamp on a bedside table. An old-fashioned quilt of many
colors covered the double bed. Braided rugs lay on the floor. White curtains hung over the windows. The walls displayed paintings of a field of
red and yellow tulips and an autumn hillside, also with blazing colors.
The only other furnishings were a straight-backed chair and a bureau*

with the usual objects on it, like a brush and comb and a statue of the Blessed Virgin Mary. A bookcase was filled with books. My books. I stood in my old bedroom at home.

The room welcomed me, or so it seemed. But did I come here to relive more of my horrible experiences after Mary Louise's murder? I tried to banish the thought of Mary Louise.

The door opened. Rose entered, dressed in slacks and a long-sleeved shirt. I wore similar clothes. Joy, not terror, visited me.

My heart beat as fast as Poe's tell-tale heart.

"I wanted to see your room." Rose blushed. "It's beautiful."

Apparently Rose had more control over planning time travels than I did. Could that be because of years of practice, or because of her piety? I hoped she would plan them for us often.

"You're beautiful. Are you comfortable here?"

"More than comfortable. Happy." She took both my hands in hers.

"Darling." I could hardly speak. She had chosen such a perfect place for us to be together.

She put her arms around me, and we kissed deeply. Her lips parted. Our tongues tasted each other. We continued tasting. I worried about whether I was doing it correctly, then stopped worrying because Rose pressed so close to me.

"I love you," I whispered.

"I love you, too." She guided me to the bed and pulled down the quilt. I recognized my sheets' rosebud pattern. How prophetic.

I clumsily unbuttoned her shirt, and she unbuttoned mine. We took off our bras.

She wrapped her arms and legs around me. We interlaced and clasped each other. She rolled on top of me. Her weight felt like a cloak spun by angels. Then I rolled on top of her and felt that her warm body under mine was the only reality in the world.

Tears of joy dripped down my cheeks as I stroked her breasts and she stroked mine. Rose liked my body! I had never been so glad to live in it. I had always thought my breasts were incidental parts like my appendix, but now Rose's touch gave them a life of their own. I ventured to suck her nipples, and she moaned.

We pulled off our slacks and underpants. Her soft lower hair looked darker than the hair on her head.

She placed her hand on my lower parts and began to rub gently.

"Rose, Rose, I love you so much," I murmured. Thrills beyond anything I had ever felt illuminated my body.

They built and built, and then I flowed.

I kissed her dear lips and felt her sweet body. "Here is Rose's rose," I whispered. I felt her body move, thrash, and flow.

Nothing had ever been this good. I moved on top of her.

We both fell asleep.

I found myself wide awake in my narrow convent bed. Had everything between us been a dream? No, it had been much more vivid than any dream. I still felt moist.

It was nearly time for the morning bell, but her hand appeared from under the curtain. I touched it and she slid it over mine in a sensuous move that almost made me come again. Then she withdrew her hand.

A few minutes later a novice rang the bell.

How could life ever be the same?

I rose from my bed. How wonderful that Rose could be a verb. Did Gertrude Stein see rose as a verb? I would rose and rose and rose.

I washed my face with the water from my basin. My face was different because Rose loved it. I didn't brush my teeth because I wanted to keep the taste of her kisses in my mouth.

I would see Rose that day, even if we couldn't talk.

I parted my curtain and walked into the aisle between the rows of beds.

Rose had just left her alcove. All I could see of her was her back walking towards the door, but it was now the back of my lover.

I had no idea that the "desires of the flesh" could be so beautiful, so all-encompassing.

I worried I would be unable to hide my ecstasy. Fortunately we were going to the chapel for prayers and hymns of praise. If my voice showed joy, anyone who noticed would think it was religious joy. Perhaps it was.

"COULD WE VISIT YOUR bedroom next?" I whispered to Rose when I saw her alone in the hallway.

She flinched. "No. The thought of my bedroom saddens me. I went there much too early in the evening to get away from my mother's intoxicated rants."

"Oh Rose." I wanted to fling my arms around her but had to leave my hands tucked in my sleeves.

"I'm all right now." Her tone failed to convince me.

"Please tell me about it, dear."

"Let's meet in the communal bathroom during the next recreation. I can tell you then."

Annoyed at the need for subterfuge, I agreed.

We met as planned and stood in front of the row of sinks. I hoped no other sister would have to visit the bathroom.

Rose bit her lip. "I don't want to be unfair to my mother. She loved me and tried to be a good mother."

"You couldn't be unfair to anyone if you tried."

"I don't know about that." Her eyes swelled with unshed tears. "My father always bullied my mother, though he treated me gently.

He yelled at her all the time. Then he died of a heart attack. Even though he had made her unhappy, she seemed lost without him. She had inherited enough money to live on, and she withdrew into the house. She cleaned and cleaned and cleaned. She always had, but then she did so even more. She and my father used to have a drink in the evening, but after he died, she took two drinks in the evening in front of me, and I found that she kept more bottles in the broom closet and started drinking earlier in the day.

"She was lonely. She wanted me to talk to her—or listen to her—almost all evening, every evening. She would drink until she fell onto the sofa and went to sleep. I used to long for her to fall asleep. Then I would go to my room and lock the door. After a while, she usually woke up and banged on my door, demanding that I keep talking to her. I told her I had homework, though I had finished it and was reading novels. Sometimes I pretended to be asleep and didn't answer."

"Dear Rose, what a terrible time you had." I longed to take her in my arms but didn't dare in case someone saw us.

"She could be sweet and funny when she wasn't drinking. When she took me on vacations, she didn't drink, and we had a wonderful time. But when we came home, I never knew whether she would be drunk or sober."

"How awful. I'm so sorry you had such a sad life."

"No, no, I had a good life. She loved me and I loved her. When I was a junior in college she drove into a lamppost and died. I missed her. I miss her still."

"Of course you do." I squeezed her hand. How much I longed to hold her.

She looked around. "We need to go off separately now."

I sighed. "Yes, we do. Thank you for telling me about your life."

Reluctantly, I walked to the parlor to find other novices. Not that I wanted to talk to them. We both pushed ourselves to speak with the others so no one would suspect how close we were. Trying not to glance or smile at each other felt more difficult as we became closer.

I vowed to make Rose's life as happy as I could.

THE NEXT TIME WE were alone together we were working in the convent laundry. Washing the heavy serge habits and putting them through the wringer was no easy task. Not my favorite job, even if performed with Rose. Wet habit after habit, each labeled with a sister's name. What drudgery. I wished fewer sisters lived in our convent. Since we lived in the Mother House, there were seventy of us. Seventy habits to clean.

At least the laundry didn't smell too bad, if you liked the smell of soap and wet serge.

We put the habits in the agitator—I loved that name—and used a pole to push them down. Then I turned off the agitator and began to pull a habit through the wringer. The habits dropped into the sink to rinse, then had to go through the wringer again.

"Watch your fingers!" Rose exclaimed. Not wanting to get my fingers caught in the wringer, I jumped back.

"I'm worried about you. Let me put the habits through the wringer," she told me. "You can put them in the drier."

"You mean I'm too clumsy," I grumbled, though her taking that task made me breathe easier.

"Yes, dear sister, you're too clumsy." She gave me a loving smile. My clumsiness didn't lessen her love.

"Thank you for relieving me of that task, Sister Rose." My voice filled with gratitude, and other emotions.

I lifted a basket of clothes to deposit in the huge drier.

"You so kindly listened to my teenage troubles," Rose said. "Is there some pain in your past that you would like to tell me? I want to know."

I turned away to hide my face. "Nothing." I would rather wash seventy habits every day of my life than tell Rose about my fear that I might, just possibly, have murdered one of my high school classmates.

The bell for terce rang, so we had to rush away from the laundry and proceed to the chapel. The rest of the habits would have to wait. For once I was glad for a conversation with Rose to be interrupted.

CHAPTER 24
Sister Rose

PASSION TURNED ROSE INSIDE out. She flew like a bird into the higher reaches of the air. Mattie's wings had borne her over the valleys and far into the mountains of love.

Rose was no longer just Rose. She had fused with Mattie and become Rose-Mattie. That transcendence frightened Rose.

She had sought transcendent communion with God. But should she have such transcendent communion with another human being?

Perhaps such love, minimized by the term "particular friendships," needed to be taken in small doses if she were to continue in her spiritual path as a member of the Congregation of St. Euphrosnye.

She would embrace Mattie again, but she needed to come down for air. The convent's air.

I have to stop thinking about Mattie all day, every day, Rose told herself. *Her body is a world of joy. Her kind listening is a comfort. She means more to me than anyone else ever has.*

The thought frightened Rose. She must find other things to care about.

Where did the Euphrosnyes come from? She hoped to time travel to the founding of the order.

"I HAVE A VISION," *said a middle-aged woman with shining eyes. She wore a long brown skirt and a white blouse with a cameo brooch at the collar.*

Three other women sat around a table with her, and one of them was Rose.

The clothes indicated the women were living in the nineteenth century. Rose wore similar garments. They sat in a parlor with dark green walls, heavy drapes, and a great deal of furniture made of dark wood. A jar of rose petals added a faint, sweet scent to the room.

"Tell us what your vision is, Nora," urged another fortyish woman with hair slipping out of the bun on the back of her head. She leaned towards Nora in anticipation.

"Who is the woman who just came in?" The third woman, whose hair seemed short for the period, stared at Rose.

Rose blushed.

"Who are you?" Nora asked, her voice a tentative welcome.

"My name is Rose Clancy." This did not seem to be a place for lies. "I don't want to disturb you." She longed to beg them to accept her.

"You are Irish," Nora said approvingly, "but you have no accent. I suppose you did not come on the boat yourself."

"No, I was born in Massachusetts."

"You were lucky," said the third woman. "So are we. Our parents fled the famine."

"More important than being Irish, I think you are one of us," said the second woman, she of the slipping hair. She winked. "I am Mary, and this is Brigid."

"I'm grateful to you for welcoming me." Rose wondered what "one of us" meant, but considering the wink, she had ideas.

"We want to work and live with other women," Nora explained, "and I have just thought of a way to do that."

"Please tell us." Mary looked at Nora as if Nora were a prophet, and indeed Nora seemed like one.

"We should become nuns." A beatific smile spread on Nora's face.

"Sure, what order would take us at our age?" Brigid shook her head.

"And with our dispositions," Mary added.

"I am not suggesting that we join an existing order. We should start our own." The excitement in Nora's voice grew.

The other two women gasped.

Rose hung onto her chair.

"We would need the archbishop's permission." Mary rolled her eyes heavenward.

"Yes, but my cousin Tom is the archbishop's secretary. I think he will help us." Nora smiled. *"I paid his way through the seminary."*

"Father Tom is a good man," Mary agreed, *"but does he have that much influence?"*

"I believe he does." Nora's eyes shone. *"I have been thinking a great deal about this."*

"What name do you propose for the order?" Brigid asked.

"The Congregation of St. Euphrosnye." Nora beamed.

"Saint who?" Brigid's eyes widened.

"Euphrosnye," Nora proclaimed in a tone of triumph. *"She was a woman of the great city of Alexandria in Egypt who refused to marry the wealthy man her parents wanted. She ran away, dressed as a man, and became a monk. She did not reveal her sex until she was dying."*

"Truly!" Mary looked as if she wanted to float to the ceiling.

"Perfect." Brigid sighed with satisfaction.

"I knew you would think so, Brigid." Nora's tone became teasing. *"You look so handsome in trousers. But of course our habits must have skirts."*

Rose stared in wonderment. Here was Nora Shaughnessy, the founder of her order. She now recognized her from a photo of a much older Mother Shaughnessy in the convent's parlor.

Nora and her friends were lesbians. That was why they chose St. Euphrosnye. Certainly that part of the order's history had been buried.

What a shame that Rose could never tell this history to the nuns who ran the order today. What if some of them knew, or suspected?

"Euphrosnye is also the name of a Greek goddess, the goddess of merriment." Nora chuckled. "As a goddess of joy, she accompanied Aphrodite."

Brigid laughed.

"Would they really let us use that name?" Mary asked.

"Why not? There is a saint by that name. I would not mention the goddess." Nora beamed at her happy vision.

"Would we take the three vows? Could we never kiss again?" Brigid asked.

"Indeed we would take the vows." Nora smiled like the Mona Lisa. "How else could we be nuns? But we would each interpret them her own way. When I take a vow of poverty, I would not be giving up the photographs of my mother and father. But do not be causing any scandals, Brigid."

"Would we get up in the middle of the night and pray?" Mary bit her lip.

"Maybe we would. We have to discuss all aspects of our order's life." Nora's face showed no concern about the prospect. "Think what we could do. We could open schools and colleges. Irish girls would have a chance to go to college."

"There are a few colleges for women now," Mary said.

"Ah, but how many Irish girls do they admit?" Nora sighed. "These would be Catholic colleges, for Irish, Italian, and Portuguese girls, and any other girls who want to attend them."

"Good." Brigid wrinkled her brow. "Those hoity-toity college women with their Mayflower ancestors, real or pretended, care nothing about the likes of us. They think we all should be maids in their houses. They don't believe we have the brains for their colleges."

When she returned to her convent bed, Rose decided she wouldn't tell Mattie about the founders of their order. Rose admitted that she liked having a great secret all her own.

The next time she entered the parlor, Rose looked at the photo of the founder, Reverend Mother Nora Shaughnessy, and the other founding nuns, Mother Mary Doyle and Mother Brigid O'Brien. The sight of them filled her heart with delight. She winked at them.

Reverend Mother Nora Shaughnessy had known the love of another woman. Rose sensed it had been Mother Mary Doyle. That love seemed to have helped Mother Nora found a religious order rather than deterring her. Perhaps deep love for another woman aided her spirituality. Meeting Mother Nora calmed some of Rose's fears.

CHAPTER 25

Sister Matthew

IRST CAME THE SNOWDROPS, then the crocuses, yellow and purple bits of cheer in the convent garden. Reborn in Rose's love, I rejoiced that the world joined me in rebirth.

Then daffodils filled the world with yellow, the color of joy, though it had no place in the Church's liturgical color scheme. How peculiar that in this thrilling time the priests wore purple, the Lenten color of mourning.

How strange that we commemorated the death of Jesus for a long period of mourning before Good Friday, rather than after it. The gospels for Lent all spoke of him still being alive.

If we recognized that "lent" is part of the word "silent," we lived in Lent all the time in the convent.

When the novices walked out in the garden, I tried to stay away from Rose, which felt even harder than giving up meat. I'm sorry to admit that the latter was no easy task. Fish scarcely seemed like proper food to me. Am I worldly about food? Oh, yes.

I walked closer to Sister Ursula, who had lost too much weight for her height and build. The food wasn't too bad, except during Lent, but the portions were small. I remembered the snacks provided by Linda and wondered whether she had joined another order. I liked to think Linda had chosen a more adventurous life.

I felt fond of Sister Ursula because she had shared those forbidden snacks and had helped me carry Rose to the infirmary. We also strolled with Sister Agnes. I couldn't get into trouble with these two novices, who were both beyond reproach.

We were not allowed to take Communion on Good Friday, the day reserved for deep mourning. Was doing that on the day commemorating Jesus's death considered too close to cannibalism? Or were we not supposed to feel any joy on that day? A difficult task in April, when tulips of many colors bloomed in the garden and birds sang happy choruses to the dawn.

Father Nolan walked around the chapel, stopping at each one of the Stations of the Cross that depicted different episodes on Jesus's journey, like the scourging at the pillar and the crowning with thorns. We chanted the hymn for the stations, which emphasized Mary's suffering. "At the cross her station keeping, stood the mournful Mother weeping, close to Jesus to the last…" Angered that no one ever mentioned the Holocaust on Good Friday, I silently prayed, "At the crematorium her station keeping…"

I could almost hear the Jesus who drove the merchants out of the temple thundering, "Remember the Holocaust! Whatever you have done to the Jews, you have done to me." He wouldn't have capitalized "me."

At dawn on Easter, we sang Handel's "Messiah." Though the music sounded beautiful, I doubted the Resurrection. I didn't like the implication that the Jews were living in darkness until the birth of Jesus. "He shall purify the sons of Levi." Did the sons of Levi need to be purified?

I glanced at the other sisters. All of them looked transported by the music.

If I ever gain a position of power in the order, I will make sure that we speak about the Holocaust during Lent, and at other times too.

I failed to observe Lent properly, because I concentrated on other people's faults, especially the Church's, rather than my own.

I am a hypocrite, always judging other people. I assume I am more intelligent than they are and therefore the rules don't apply to me.

Nonetheless, like most people, I put aside my concern about my own faults so I could enjoy the spring.

Easter dawn revealed tulips, sunshine yellow, Christmas red, and Lenten purple, weaving a tapestry of beauty in the garden. Rose and I permitted ourselves to saunter together in the company of other novices.

Two small azaleas, one pale pink and the other white, had begun to bloom. I suppose the garden has so few azaleas because Reverend Mother fears they are too lush and might render the nuns too sensual. There are no gardenias.

If I ever became Reverend Mother Matthew, I would hide Easter eggs in the garden and invite the postulants and novices to hunt for them. However, my chances of being elected to be a mother superior are less than nun. I smiled at my pun.

I HADN'T EXPECTED ROSE to come to another world for lovemaking during Lent, but I had hoped I might meet her in time travel after Easter. When that didn't happen, disappointment settled in my heart. I wished I could book flights to my bedroom for both of us.

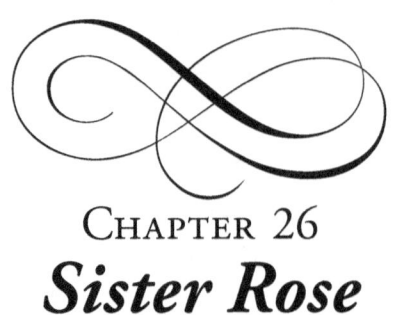

CHAPTER 26

Sister Rose

T HIS SPRING BIRDSONG DID not simply bring joy to Rose. Robins, cardinals, Carolina wrens, and mockingbirds sang in the convent garden. A few times, a Baltimore oriole and its brick-red cousin the orchard oriole visited the garden, and once the northern parula warbler's high notes sounded from the top of the willow. Their voices hurt her. Longing to go out into the woods and fields, to hear and see more birds, pierced her heart.

Lent did not end with Easter. It began then, with wild music taunting her. The spring breezes called her away from the convent.

She learned that planned meditation, with hours set aside for it every day, did not always bring the same joy as spontaneous meditation.

Perhaps it might have been better to enter the convent after high school, when the prayers and meditation might have seemed fresher.

Rose prayed more, but she did not always want to pray. That meant she needed to pray more than ever, to resist temptation, to give herself a soul of steel. She wondered how Mattie could seem to enjoy the brief moments of nature they were allowed.

Rose wanted to return to Mattie's bedroom, but even more she wanted to make love in a meadow. To be in a meadow, even without Mattie.

Perhaps she indulged herself too much in doing what she wanted, and that made her desire it even more. She must be contented with moments of joy, and not expect a life of it.

Was her love helping Mattie, or encouraging Mattie's rebellious streak?

Was Mattie's love helping her or encouraging her to imagine being in places far from the convent?

Rose prayed, not the rosary that bored her, but psalms and St. Paul's Epistle to the Corinthians on love, words whose beauty might soothe her soul.

But when a Baltimore oriole sang, tears formed in her eyes.

CHAPTER 27

Sister Matthew

"NOW WE SHALL CONSIDER the opposition to Hitler," Reverend Mother told our college theology class. When she uttered the name "Hitler," she almost spat.

I listened so eagerly that I could hardly take notes. At last she would talk about the Holocaust.

"The Vatican did not do enough to oppose Hitler." Reverend Mother spoke in an expressionless tone, but she bit her lips. "A Catholic political party opposed the Nazis in the election that brought Hitler to power, but its leaders nonetheless signed the act giving him dictatorial powers. The Vatican signed a treaty with Hitler that was supposed to protect the religious freedom of German Catholics, but the Nazis closed Catholic schools and presses anyway. Hundreds of priests and nuns were put on trial for 'immorality.'

"Some convents hid Jews, especially in occupied countries. Many priests in those countries joined the resistance and were sent to concentration camps. More than a thousand priests died in Dachau."

My eyes widened. I had never heard that the Nazis killed so many priests. In a weird way I felt relieved that many priests had been that brave, hadn't gone along with the Nazis.

"But the leading German theologian opposing the Nazis was the Lutheran Dietrich Bonhoeffer," she explained. "He understood that in the face of Nazism, he had to work in politics as well as teach. In the last relatively free election in Germany, he worked for candidates who opposed the Nazis. Once the Nazis were in power, Bonhoeffer said the church should impose a moratorium on all pastoral services, including baptisms and marriages, until Hitler was out of office, to shock people into understanding what a terrible course their country had taken. But other church officials rejected that radical position.

"Ministers who sympathized with the Nazis gained power in the Lutheran Church. Bonhoeffer drafted a statement affirming God's continuing love of his chosen people, the Jews, but the church authorities watered down the statement so much that Bonhoeffer refused to sign it.

"The Lutheran Church passed a resolution requiring the firing of clergy with Jewish backgrounds, so Bonhoeffer left the church and founded an alternative Lutheran church. He started underground seminaries. He traveled to England and the United States to work against Hitler. He knew about the German generals' plot to kill Hitler. Bonhoeffer returned to Germany, where he was arrested in early 1943 and executed in April 1945 with some of the generals, just before the Allies defeated Hitler's Reich." Reverend Mother sighed.

"That is true Christianity. Please read selections from his work before the next class."

Tears streaked down my cheeks. I was not the only student who cried. Would I ever be as truly good as Bonhoeffer and the nuns, priests, and lay people who resisted the Nazis? My doubts about God seemed like a childish obsession in the face of such goodness and courage.

I appreciated Reverend Mother's willingness to teach us that a Protestant took a leading role.

"Our own Pope John XXIII worked to save Jews when he was the Vatican's Apostolic Delegate to Greece and Turkey during the years Hitler was in power," Reverend Mother told us. "But the Church could have done more than it did. Popes Pius XI and Pius XII feared jeopardizing the lives of Catholics in Germany. Though they wrote encyclicals opposing racism and war, and Pope Pius XII warned the Allies of imminent German invasions of Belgium, the Netherlands, and France, he could have openly condemned the extermination of Jews." She stopped but looked as if she wanted to say more. Even Reverend Mother seemed to think she had to be careful about what she taught us. I felt proud of her for being bold though I wished she had gone further. Could the Church punish someone as elevated as Reverend Mother?

I rejoiced that Pope John now led the Church. Nevertheless, his actions didn't erase the shame that Pius XII did less than he could have.

After a pause, Reverend Mother moved on. "In our next class, we shall hear from a priest working in Central America who is witnessing for social justice today. I won't be able to be present because I have other duties, but I assure you that the class will be meaningful."

I couldn't wait.

FATHER ANTONIO PEREZ, A Jesuit, gave his guest lecture in our next class. Though he looked to be in his thirties, the expression on his suntanned face was so stern that he seemed decades away from youth. I listened eagerly, hoping he would enlighten me.

"Greed is the greatest sin," Father Perez warned. He sounded impatient with the class as if he believed, perhaps correctly, that none of us would ever work among the poor. "Greed leads to impoverishing people and enslaving them. I have spent several years in El Salvador, where plantation owners treat their workers as less than human. Why? Greed. The owners will not recognize the humanity of the peasants because that would mean treating them like human beings with rights, with legitimate needs for education, adequate salaries, and adequate homes.

"Greed is not limited to the owners of haciendas in El Salvador." He looked beyond the class, as if he were seeing workers in sugar cane and banana plantations. "This nation is also full of greed and under-paid workers. And American investment in Central America leads to many abuses. We not only exploit our own people but also export our exploitation."

I tried to take in every word. Possible God, Father Perez was so right. Even in my supposed life of poverty, I am still greedy, still wishing I had more material goods, like tastier meals and more books.

Gratitude toward Reverend Mother for bringing this speaker filled me.

"My own order participated in exploitation in this very state." Father Perez scowled. "The Jesuits enslaved hundreds of people who worked on the order's Maryland tobacco plantations. Jesuits claimed they were better than Protestant slaveholders because they always baptized their slaves and allowed them to receive the Holy Eucharist at Mass. Yet in 1838, when the Jesuits wanted to raise more money for Georgetown College, they sold their workers to even worse conditions in Louisiana."

His words struck a blow to my chest. Jesuits had enslaved people here in Maryland? My stomach churned.

Father Perez went further. "Even some orders of nuns founded in this country enslaved people."

I almost fell over. Nuns owning people? I could scarcely imagine that horror. I remembered that the Euphrosnyes weren't founded until after the Civil War, so they couldn't have enslaved anyone. Thanks be to God.

We needed to learn from Father Perez. We needed many more Father Perezes.

"The Jesuits are not the only order that has done wrong. The Dominicans were the most active order in the Inquisition. Other orders participated, my own among them. Even the Franciscans, whom we think of as the gentle followers of St. Francis of Assisi, participated in the Inquisition. Then, when they came to this country, they used the force of the Spanish military against the people they found here, destroying their communities, and enslaving them in order to convert them.

"If any of us think our hands are clean, we should think again. As a missionary, I have sinned by assuming I knew everything and the people I worked among were ignorant and needed to be enlightened. I gradually came to understand that working to help them obtain social justice was more important than praying for them or worrying about whether they went to Mass."

Tears dripped down my cheeks. I had never heard that the Franciscan missionaries in the American West had been brutal.

I felt sorry when his lecture ended. I wanted to hear more. What he said should change my life, but I wasn't sure it would.

As I left the classroom, one of the young secular students approached me. A pale girl with an earnest face, she looked as if she lived in the library.

"Please speak with me, sister," she urged me.

"I'm sorry, but we novices are not supposed to talk to the other students." I felt like a fool.

"Please," she repeated. "I need to talk to someone." Her voice broke.

"But why me?"

"You have such an open face, sister. Please."

I didn't need any more encouragement.

"All right, just for a few minutes. The classroom across the hall looks empty." So what if I had to say a few extra rosaries for talking to her?

We entered the empty classroom.

"Thank you so much." She looked into my eyes as if I could save her from something.

An alarm went off in my head. Why was I letting her imagine I could help her? I had never studied counseling. I must be indulging in a sin of pride. What kind of problem could I solve? She wasn't wearing a wedding ring. I hoped she wasn't pregnant.

"My name is Sharon. Father Perez's words moved me so much. I want to give up everything and help the poor. I want to join the convent and become a missionary."

I collected my thoughts. "He stirred my conscience too. But I'm not a missionary. The Maryknoll sisters work in missions. I'm just preparing to be a teacher in this country."

"But you gave up everything to follow Christ's example, just like your patron saint, Sister Matthew." Her voice ached with earnestness.

I flushed. "I didn't give up everything. I live in a comfortable convent. I take college classes."

"I admire nuns so much. I don't know whether I can give up all I would have to give up to become one."

"I'm not the person you should speak with. There are many sisters and priests who are better suited to advising you. I'm only a novice, and I have to get back to the convent." I felt in over my head. I moved towards the door.

"Thank you, Sister Matthew, thank you." Sharon sounded incongruously grateful for the minimal words I had spoken, perhaps because she had been so moved by Father Perez.

"We mustn't speak again," I said, feeling foolish for saying those words that sounded like I was sending off a former lover.

"I understand." She beamed at me.

Would she join a convent? I would never know. Nor would I know whether she would be satisfied after she joined one.

I could just imagine Reverend Mother's scolding, not to mention Mean Mother Michael's, at my hubris in presuming to speak to Sharon. They would frown and assign me more rosaries. I hurried back to the convent.

Did I feel annoyed at having to sneak around to have such an innocent conversation? Yes. The serious nature of Father Perez's talk made it even more ludicrous that I was supposed to worry about talking with a young woman just because she isn't in a convent.

FATHER PEREZ'S TALK MADE me think more about my vow of poverty. Did taking a vow of poverty assume I already had enough money to give it up? Did it assume I could easily earn money if I didn't choose to give up the chance to do so?

Would it make sense for someone who is already poor to take a vow of poverty? Most of the poor people in the world don't have as much comfort and security as I have in the convent. They would find the idea of taking a vow of poverty absurd.

Would anyone who had children take a vow of poverty? Very few. That may be why the Church requires celibacy of its clergy.

THE FOLLOWING SUNDAY, FATHER Nolan's sermon reminded us to be grateful for all our blessings.

What is a blessing? Having kind parents? Having all the food we need? Enjoying good health?

If we thank God for those things, does that mean God chooses who will receive them and who won't? That's blessing? If so, He sounds like a Republican God, giving to those He decides are deserving.

Wouldn't it be better to call our good fortune simply good luck, instead of suggesting that a Supreme Being decides which people will have what they need and who will starve?

But I didn't think unequal distribution of wealth was simply a matter of good luck.

AFTER HEARING FATHER PEREZ, I tried to study theology more eagerly.

I listened to Reverend Mother explain the Catholic theologian Hans Kung's argument that some of the differences between Catholics and Protestants were imaginary. The prospect of smoothing over antagonisms sounded good, but the arguments were so abstruse.

I wanted to keep learning about Bonhoeffer and the resistance against Hitler.

I approached Reverend Mother after class. "Reverend Mother, will you approve my topic for the paper we have to write for your class?"

"What is your topic, Sister Matthew?"

"I would like to compare Bonhoeffer and Gandhi and discuss whether nonviolence would have been an adequate response to Hitler."

Reverend Mother's eyes widened, then narrowed. She peered into my face. "Gandhi was not a theologian. He was not even a Christian. How could you write about a Hindu for a theology class?"

"Isn't it possible that a Hindu could have insights about God and ethics, Reverend Mother?" I made bold to say. Reverend Mother could deal with this challenge.

"Yes, Sister Matthew. It is possible. However, that is too far outside the purview of our class. But Judaism is not. I shall permit you to compare a Jewish writer's response to Bonhoeffer's."

"Thank you, Reverend Mother." I admired her more than ever, though I thought Gandhi should not be outside the purview of our class.

As I walked back to the convent, I thought that learning about the Holocaust was good, but would I ever have a chance to meet Jews while I lived in the convent? Or those Negro ministers who took their inspiration from Gandhi?

I had squandered my college years, not trying hard enough to make friends with people different from me. Now that I am in the convent, I can't.

Do I want to spend my entire life surrounded by mostly Irish Catholics?

Will I ever have a chance to learn directly from people who aren't Catholic? Will I ever be able to work with them on trying to change the world?

CHAPTER 28
Sister Matthew

T HAT NIGHT, TIME TRAVEL *took me to the time and place I most dreaded. I tried to escape but could not.*

A uniformed police officer strode into our English classroom at St. Agatha's.

If a nun's entrance silenced our high school classes, the officer's entrance stunned us. At least it stunned me. I saw frozen looks on other girls' faces, too.

A short man in plain clothes followed the tall, young officer. The man in the suit must be a detective.

Sister Veronica flinched. "Welcome, gentlemen. Please pay attention to the officers, girls." She enunciated each syllable as if she were a television news announcer. She might be an Agatha Christie, but she didn't sound like Miss Marple. The detective looked more like Raymond Burr than Hercule Poirot.

"I'm Detective Johnson, and this is Officer Moriarty." He sounded like the actor who played the district attorney, not like Perry Mason.

Some of the girls couldn't help giggling at a police officer having the same name as Sherlock Holmes' nemesis.

Detective Johnson frowned. "There's nothing funny about the murder of your classmate. I know it's unlikely that any of you will be able to provide a clue, but we need any information we can get.

"We can't interview each of you individually without getting permission from your parents" (I breathed a sigh of relief) "but I'm going to ask a series of questions and urge you to think about them, then tell us if you have any information. Your teacher will remain present. If you think you need to speak with us privately, send me a note through Sister Veronica." He nodded to her. She sank into her desk chair.

"Did any of you see Mary Louise today?" He used a tone that sounded milder than the police in television shows generally used when questioning possible witnesses, but the beginning notes of the television series Dragnet sounded in my head.

Everyone either said "yes" or nodded.

"Did she look different from the way she looked any other day?"

Fran put up her hand. "She'd just had a haircut."

Sister Veronica raised her eyebrows.

"Very good," Detective Johnson said without a trace of a smile. "I encourage you to speak up. I mean, did Mary Louise look worried or distracted?"

"We were supposed to have a Latin test this afternoon. Almost all of us were worried about that," Cathy told him.

"But did she look especially worried?"

"No," Cathy admitted. None of us contradicted her.

"Did she tell any of you in recent days or weeks that she was worried about something or someone in her life, or she was afraid of someone?"

No one responded.

She hadn't been afraid of me. She despised me. But I didn't kill her, really I didn't. I couldn't get the Dragnet theme out of my head.

"Did she confide in you about anything unusual, anything at all?"

Fran raised her hand. "A boy on the Loyola football team had asked her to go to a movie next Saturday. She was excited."

"Was there something unusual about that? Was she already dating another boy?"

"No," Fran told him.

"Had she broken up with another boy recently?"

"No."

"Did any of you notice Mary Louise at the party in the auditorium?"

"We all noticed her," Bernadette said. *"She led us in singing Happy Birthday to St. Agatha's."*

I flinched when I heard Bernadette's voice. I hoped she would never guess how I had hated Mary Louise.

"Did anyone notice that Mary Louise lingered in the auditorium while the rest of you left?"

"No," we chorused. *I did, but there was no way I would admit it. I didn't want to be known as the last person who saw her alive.*

Detective Johnson turned to Sister Veronica. "Did you notice that she lingered, Sister?"

Sister Veronica started, as if she hadn't expected to be questioned. "No, Detective Johnson, I did not. If I had, I would have told her to hurry up."

"I'm sure you would have." He inclined his head to her, then turned back to us. "Did any of you notice anyone in the auditorium or anywhere on your campus who you wouldn't have expected to see there? Anyone who didn't belong at St. Agatha's?"

We shook our collective heads. I had a wild impulse to invent a mysterious stranger, but that would just have subjected me to closer questioning.

The detective bowed his head to our teacher. "That's all for now. If any of you think of anything else you want to tell us, please let us know."

He and the silent Moriarty departed, no doubt on their way to question other classes.

Sister Veronica took a deep breath. "Now, girls, do you think it's ironic that the characters in the O. Henry story bought each other presents that they couldn't use?"

Right. There's nothing ironic like giving the wrong gift. Come on, Sister Veronica. You can do better than that.

I couldn't have killed Mary Louise. It couldn't have been me. It just couldn't.

I was more afraid of the Agatha Christies worming information out of me than of the police.

I found myself back in my convent cell. Why did I have to travel to that dreadful part of my past? When I returned there, I had just the same thoughts as I had at the time, not more mature ones. But how could I be more mature about murder?

I wanted to call one of my high school friends and confirm that no one was ever charged in Mary Louise's death, but of course I'm not allowed to make phone calls or write letters to old friends, or even to my family. I couldn't see my family except on visits. They could call me only in an emergency.

I knew the answer about the murder anyway. If anyone had been charged, it would have been in all the newspapers. And it probably would have happened long before I entered the convent and stopped watching the news.

Was it such a sin to hate—that is, to intensely dislike—another girl?

CHAPTER 29
Sister Rose

R OSE RETURNED TO THE *time of Mother Nora Shaughnessy. Sitting in Mother Shaughnessy's parlor, Rose begged the would-be founding nuns to let her help them in their work.*

"Could I help you in any way?"

Mother Nora—Rose couldn't help thinking of her as Mother Nora, though Nora Shaughnessy wasn't yet a nun—smiled. "Indeed you could. It is a good thing you came today. Mary and I are going to see the archbishop this afternoon, and you could go with us. We were going to take another girl about your age, but she caught a cold. You could say that Catholic girls would be eager to attend our schools and colleges. The archbishop is a little reluctant to approve our plans, but I think that eventually he will agree."

Rose prayed that the archbishop would listen to her. She didn't know what state or diocese they were in, but she couldn't ask. She supposed they were in Baltimore since the Mother House was in Maryland. She would find out.

It turned out that Mother Nora was prosperous enough to own a horse and a small buggy. The buggy barely had room for Mother Nora, Mary Doyle, and Rose. Possibly Mother Nora thought Brigid O'Brien looked too masculine to aid in persuading the archbishop. Mother Nora put on the horse's harness and drove the buggy herself.

They rode past brick row houses. Rose tried not to stare at all the people dressed in nineteenth-century clothes, walking and riding in buggies. Gas lamps stood along the street.

The horses left manure in the streets, but the waste must be cleaned away often because most of it looked and smelled fresh.

A reckless young boy rushed in front of the buggy. Mother Nora avoided him and chided him in a tone probably too moderate for him to hear.

Mother Nora drove up a hill above Baltimore Harbor and passed a massive, neo-classical cathedral. Rose recognized the Basilica of the Assumption of the Virgin Mary because she had seen it a century later. Then they came to a fine-looking brick residence that loomed larger than the town houses.

A priest who resembled Mother Nora led them in. He grinned at her. "You are in luck, Nora. His Excellency is in a good mood."

Mother Nora returned his grin. "Thank you, Tom. I am sure you prepared the way. Come to my house for dinner tomorrow night and bring your pals."

"You can count on that. Can I hope for roast lamb?"

"Roast leg of lamb it is. And chocolate cake."

Rose thought many priests liked to eat well as compensation for celibacy. Nuns managed without that form of compensation. She wouldn't have minded having a little more of it.

The bishop's office had even more heavy furniture and velvet drapes than Mother Nora's house. Needless to say, a crucifix hung on the wall behind his desk. A painting of Jesus showing his Sacred Heart with a crown of thorns around it and flames and a cross springing from the top of the heart hung on another wall, and a painting of the Blessed Virgin Mary showing her Immaculate Heart with roses around it, a sword through it, and fire burning from it hung beside the picture of Jesus.

The archbishop rose from his desk and approached them. Like many bishops, he carried quite a few extra pounds. His black cassock had fuchsia piping and he wore a sash of the same color around his waist and a similarly colored small cap on his head, showing he was more important than a priest. He extended his hand.

Mother Nora, Mary Doyle, and Rose knelt and kissed his amethyst ring. Rose remembered how to do that because everyone had knelt to kiss the bishop's ring at her Confirmation and her graduations from high school and college.

The archbishop returned to his desk and told them to be seated.

"I see you brought a young lady with you, Miss Shaughnessy," he said in a hearty see-how-jovial-I-am-pretending-that-I-am-not-vastly-your-superior tone. "Did you bring her to address my concern that you would have difficulty finding young Catholic women to attend your college?"

"Yes, Your Excellency." Mother Nora struck just the right note of deference mingled with determination.

"Well, young lady, what do you have to say? Would you want to go to college?"

Rose tried to mix deference with eagerness. "Yes, Your Excellency. I want to attend this college and I know that many other girls like me would want to enroll. This college could serve many young Catholic women over the years."

"Would they all be Irish girls?"

"No indeed," Mother Nora told him. "I am sure there would be Italian girls and other Catholic girls."

"And would many want to join this order if it was established? Is another order of nuns needed?"

Rose hastened to reply. "I would want to join this order, Your Excellency."

He smiled at her ardor. "Ah, what about marriage and children? Don't most Catholic girls want to marry and have children?"

She could tell he believed women were made for that "station in life." "Some of us have vocations, Your Excellency. I am sure I have a vocation."

"Ah yes, vocations." He fingered the large pectoral cross that hung on a chain around his neck. "I see you have at least one budding adherent, Miss Shaughnessy. And what of your finances? How much financial assistance would you expect from the Church?"

Mother Nora laid out her financial plans in meticulous detail.

"Well, I shall consider the matter, Miss Shaughnessy. You seem well-prepared." He asked no questions of Mary Doyle.

He stood to dismiss them, and they knelt to kiss his ring again.

Rose knew the outcome, but she nearly burst with excitement nevertheless.

BACK IN HER CUBICLE, Rose wondered how the order had adopted all its rules. She couldn't imagine Mother Nora Shaughnessy telling nuns to confess all their real or imagined faults. The woman she met would never have required them to kiss the floor.

The next time Rose went to the parlor, she scrutinized the photo of the mother superior who had had been elected after Mother Nora died, Reverend Mother Claire Franklin. While Mother Nora had been plump and cheerful-looking, Mother Claire had been thin, with a pinched look on her face. She probably made the rules so rigid, Rose figured.

Rose loved the order even more than she had before. Perhaps if she ever gained a position of power, she could return the Euphrosnyes to the less constrained ways that Mother Nora Shaughnessy must have preferred.

"YOU HAVE A LETTER, Sister Rose," Mother Michael said, handing it to her at recreation. Of course, the letter had been opened because it was Mother Michael's duty as Mistress of Novices to read their mail.

Rose felt a stirring of excitement. She rarely received letters.

She smiled when she saw her Uncle Tim's address on the upper left corner. He had thought of her. She delayed opening it to prolong the pleasure.

Dear Sister Rose,

I have the sad duty to inform you that your cousin Gerald has left the Church in order to marry a Jewish woman. I never dreamed that a son of mine would do such a thing. I remonstrated with him, but he remained obstinate. They have already gone through a civil ceremony. I am heartbroken.

Of course I have severed any connection with him. I pray daily for him to repent. Please remember him in your prayers.

Yours in sorrow,

Uncle Tim

Rose closed her eyes for a moment. She felt a pang of grief for Gerald, a serious young man whom she had always liked. She wished she had his address and could write to him expressing her support, but even if she had the address, Mother Michael would never have allowed her to send a letter like that. She would pray for Gerald's happiness, not his repentance, and for Uncle Tim to embrace him, though she knew that was a lost cause. She thought the rule that Catholics could marry only people who were baptized and discouraged marrying Protestants was ridiculous. She hoped that Gerald's wife—Uncle Tim had not provided her name—had a more understanding family.

Uncle Tim would condemn her own disposition much more strongly than Gerald's marriage if he ever learned the truth about her.

THAT NIGHT, ROSE STUMBLED *across a field of withered plants bordered by a low stone wall. She wore a long skirt and a blouse. A nauseating smell filled the air. She gagged and covered her mouth with her handkerchief.*

A thatched-roof house stood not far away. As she approached the house, she saw the thatch was falling apart and the door hung open, nearly ready to fall off.

Sickened by the smell, she closed her eyes and opened them. Tears formed in her eyes.

A man hobbled down a dirt road below the field. His bones stood out, covered by pallid skin.

"Are ye lookin' for the O'Malleys?" His voice croaked. "Sure, they're all dead, like most everybody else in the parish. There's been no food."

"I'm so sorry." The man looked halfway to the grave himself. Her sympathy felt ludicrously inadequate.

"How is it you look so well fed?" His eyes narrowed. "You must be some British soldier's harlot. You should be stoned."

Rose wished herself away. She could do nothing about the potato famine.

She sat on her convent bed and wept quietly. The Irish had suffered, but that hadn't made them all tolerant. She hoped Mattie wouldn't travel to Ireland in that era.

Most of the Irish Americans Rose knew didn't visit Ireland when they took their once-in-a-lifetime trips to Europe. They might express some antipathy toward England, but they never talked about the potato famine, except for a few men she had seen collecting money for the Irish Republican Army to oppose British rule in Northern Ireland. If Irish Americans thought more about their own people's past, would they acknowledge the sufferings of other people? Or would they imagine their history was more painful than slavery?

Rose remembered substitute teaching in Boston's public schools a few times when she had graduated from college and was waiting to enter the convent. She had always believed that Irish Americans were loving.

But one morning when she walked on an almost treeless street in Roxbury, a predominantly Negro neighborhood, on her way to a school, white construction workers, who looked Irish American to her, had spat on her. A drop of spit had touched her hand. She had stared at it in disgust and wiped it on her skirt. One of the men had growled, "What are you doing here?" Apparently they had thought a young white woman had no good reason to walk in a Negro neighborhood. Perhaps they imagined she was seeing a Negro man, which was none of their business. She had shrunk away, wondering whether there was something lewd in her looks—she hadn't even worn lipstick—or in her walk.

The next day, she had seen an Irish American woman teacher slam third-grade Negro children against the wall when they didn't walk in a straight line. Rose had gone up to her and demanded, "Why did you do that?" The other teacher had glared at her and snapped, "That's none of your business." Rose had complained to the principal, who was also Irish American. But he had told her she knew nothing about the school and shouldn't come back. She hadn't wanted to. The principal had horrified her even more than the teacher did.

The pity she felt for the starving man who had wanted to stone her didn't extend to the racists she had encountered in Boston. Rose still felt ashamed because she hadn't done more to challenge them. As a nun, she would be able to teach in any neighborhood without being spat on. She wouldn't have to watch helplessly while another teacher hurt children.

CHAPTER 30

Sister Matthew

I SHIVERED WHEN BEES BUZZED near the flower bed I weeded. Why did I have to go out among insects? Rose wasn't assigned to weed with me, so the chore seemed much less pleasant.

Ragged leaves suggested that aphids or some such thing had infested the geraniums. Ugh.

When I stooped, I couldn't keep my habit out of the dirt. I would have to clean it later.

At least I had a chance to be out in the sun. Thank you, Possible God, for the sunlight. Was it better to sweat in my habit on a hot day than not to go outdoors at all? Of course it was.

Sister Agnes tended the flower bed next to mine. I saw tears on her cheeks.

I stood and approached her. "Are you well, Sister Agnes?"

She gazed at me with red-rimmed eyes. "Did I distract you, Sister Matthew? If I did, I'm sorry."

"There must be some reason for your tears. What's the matter?"

"I miss my family. I know my mother is still grieving over her sister's death and I wish I could comfort her. They were very close. I'm afraid my mother isn't well. She didn't come to our last visiting day." Her voice shook. "I am breaking the rule by worrying so much about my family. Talking to you about them is much worse."

If we had already broken the rules, I might as well keep on breaking them. "It's natural to love your family and worry about them. It's a shame you can't phone your mother and ask how she's doing. I think about my family too."

Sister Agnes turned away. "Forgive me for leading you to break the rule."

Anything else I could say would only make her feel worse. I returned to my bug-infested flower bed.

At our Friday afternoon chapter meeting, Sister Agnes knelt before Reverend Mother and said in a faltering voice, "Dear Reverend Mother, Mistress of Novices, and my dear sisters, I like some of our sisters more than others. I am fond of Sister Matthew. I think too much about my family. I even cried about them when we were weeding on Thursday. I led Sister Matthew to break silence. She said some kind words to me, and I was glad she was the sister assigned to weed with me. *Mea culpa, mea culpa, mea maxima culpa.*"

What a ninny! I had known she would confess her crying and my speaking with her, but I had no idea that she would confess to liking me. She probably didn't understand that the rule against particular friendships had been instituted to weed out those of us who fell in love with other women. There certainly wasn't a particle of sexual attraction between us. I hoped her words wouldn't arouse suspicion about me.

Reverend Mother told the scrupulous novice, "You must not dwell on thoughts about your family. Nor should you favor one sister over others. Say two full rosaries alone in the chapel and avoid talking with Sister Matthew. If you are having difficulties, you should talk about them to the Mistress of Novices or the priest in Confession, not to another novice."

When my turn came, I got down on my knees and confessed, "Dear Reverend Mother, Mistress of Novices, and my dear sisters, I drank a glass of lemonade on Thursday without asking permission. I arrived at Mass five minutes late on Tuesday. When Sister Agnes and

I were weeding, I saw she was crying so I went over to her and spoke with her. *Mea culpa, mea culpa, mea maxima culpa.*" I did not confess to any partiality for Sister Agnes because I felt none.

Reverend Mother's voice sounded mild as usual. "You know that you must not break the rule of silence or use your own judgement about how you should react to another sister's distress. Say two full rosaries alone in the chapel and refrain from talking with Sister Agnes or being alone in her company."

I kissed the floor. Avoiding Sister Agnes wouldn't be any problem. My sin, if any, was feeling annoyed at her. What an ungrateful, rule-bound idiot.

Possible God, are you laughing over these silly rules? Out in the world, people are stealing from others, beating them, and even killing them. But we're supposed to be obsessed with keeping silent.

I can't leave, though. Rose is here. I would spend my life bound to even stricter rules so I could be near her.

"Don't frown at poor Sister Agnes," Rose chided me gently a few days later. "You don't have to carry distancing from her that far."

My face heated. No doubt I blushed. "I don't frown at her," I protested.

Rose raised her eyebrows.

"I'll stop frowning." God's chastening hand for sinners couldn't distress me more than displeasing Rose. "I'm sorry for Sister Agnes. It's difficult to know how to act toward people I feel sorry for."

"She is too thin-skinned for this convent. She'll leave sooner or later."

I agreed, but I didn't know whether to feel glad if Sister Agnes left. What would marriage be like for a woman who abased herself over every mistake?

CHAPTER 31

Sister Matthew

Tears shone in Reverend Mother's eyes one afternoon when we came to the parlor for recreation. The rest of us froze. What could have brought her such grief?

"I have the sad duty to tell you that Pope John XXIII has died." Her voice sounded as if she had lost both her father and her mother. "We should go to the chapel and pray for his soul, though he must be with God. We also must pray for the cardinals who will shoulder the burden of choosing a new pope."

Tears dripped down my cheeks. All the other novices had tears in their eyes. Rose wept openly and choked on her tears.

I determined to see her after chapel. I couldn't bear to see her in such pain.

I prayed earnestly, thanking Possible God for Pope John, and asking for another such pope. I didn't believe we'd be that lucky a second time.

When evening came, I visited my old bedroom. Rose sat weeping in my chair. She stood when she saw me.

Seizing the chance to comfort her, I folded her in my arms. She cried on my shoulder.

"His death is so sad, but I hate to see you grieving," I said.

"I weep not for him, but for the Church." Her voice broke. "His death is a tragedy. I'm afraid the reforms he has begun will fade away into minor changes."

"I hope not. I'm counting on change myself." I didn't believe change would come without him, but I didn't want to make Rose any sadder.

I held her for a long time, stroking her hair.

She moved to the bed. We made love softly, with tears.

Ending our communion and going back to the convent felt harder than ever. It was only the second time we had made love. I wished we could do it much more often. Didn't Rose want that too?

THE NEXT EVENING, I stood in a theater without a ceiling. A stage spread into the pit where the audience would stand. Benches were perched only on the walls.

No audience, save a few men, some on stage and some beside it, watched the play. This must be a rehearsal.

"You need more smoke in the cauldron," Shakespeare said.

I recognized him immediately, with his high forehead and short beard. His voice sounded ordinary, though the words he wrote were far from it.

I stood some distance behind the people and hoped I would not be noticed. I wore a shirt and breeches like those I had worn when I had seen Anne Boleyn.

"I will take care of that," a young man said. "But not enough smoke to blind the audience."

"Enough to blind Macbeth and Banquo when they enter," Shakespeare told him. "Much smoke at first, gradually clearing."

"It is blinding me," one of the witches complained.

"You do not have to see." Shakespeare sounded grumpy as a coffee drinker who had just risen from bed and couldn't find his favorite beverage. *"You are almost in a trance. You are supernatural. Perhaps you do not even have eyes. You will sense that Macbeth and Banquo are there. You are seeing the future."*

"We have to see enough not to fall into the cauldron."

"You are witches, not fools. You know where the cauldron is."

"Speaking of fools, I think the Porter should have more lines to say," another man put in.

"You have plenty of lines, Robert. We have discussed this before. You can fool about before and after the play. That is enough. This is not A Midsummer Night's Dream.*"*

"I am tired of hearing all this blabbering," a handsome man said. *"Get on with it."*

"Do not be so impatient, Dick." Shakespeare used a milder tone with Burbage, his star. *"Your hour is coming all too soon. You will have your chance to kill and to die."*

"With all that smoke, I might smite the witches by mischance. I should be able to see how loathsome their aspects are."

"We cannot all be handsome, Burbage," a witch retorted.

"Enough." Shakespeare waved. *"Start the lightning and thunder."*

Booms reverberated.

"Where is the lightning?" Shakespeare demanded.

I am transfixed. Shakespeare. This is the best possible time travel. I hope I can stay here a long time.

"Why work so hard to get the effects right when our first performance will be at Hampton Court for the king? The space there will be completely different," a stagehand complained.

"Why do anything well?" Shakespeare's annoyance grew. *"If we learn how to do the thing correctly here, it will be easier to do it right when we take it there."*

At last the lightning and thunder were produced to Shakespeare's specifications.

"When shall we three meet again?

In thunder, lightning, or in rain?"

"You are not in unison!" Shakespeare groaned. "Witch number two, match your voice to the others or you could be sacked. Dick, where is your gore? You need to be covered with blood when you enter. You have just been engaged in a great battle."

"Will all great Neptune's ocean wash this blood clean from my hand?" Burbage intoned.

"Later, Dick. You are not evil yet." Shakespeare sighed. "So much evil. I hope King James appreciates the strain it takes to produce so much evil as an entertainment."

"Our good king knows nothing of evil." Burbage smirked. "All evil comes from witches."

"Take care with the sarcasm, Dick. You never know who might be listening."

Shakespeare looked around. "Who are you?" he asked me.

"Just an extra stagehand, sir."

"Then go work with the man who is producing the lightning. He could use some help. We need a fierce glare, but not a fire."

"Yes, sir." Shakespeare spoke to me! I hope he doesn't think I'm a spy for the king, or for a rival playwright.

I found myself back in my convent bed and felt both thrilled at the adventure and sorry it hadn't lasted longer.

Please, Possible God, let me go back to Shakespeare's time again! I want to see the play as he produced it.

I can't wait to tell Rose that I've seen Shakespeare.

Could I perhaps see Emily Dickinson? She would be much more difficult to drop in on inconspicuously because she would probably be alone.

I tried to remember Lady Macbeth's "unsex me" speech, but most of the words eluded me. If only I had a copy of the plays!

It occurred to me only later that there might be some significance to my visiting a rehearsal for *Macbeth*. Even when I traveled to

Shakespeare's world, every place I visited was associated with death, or even murder. Except for meeting Rose.

I wish I could control where I went as much as Rose apparently could. Maybe I can't because she is a better person than I am.

"I SAW SHAKESPEARE!" I burst out the words when by a lucky chance we were washing dishes together again. Thank goodness we were still assigned to do chores together sometimes. Apparently Mean Mother Michael didn't guess how often we broke silence. At least she never came bursting into the kitchen to find out whether the novices talked while washing.

Rose smiled. "I'm so happy for you. Did you like him?"

"Like him? He's beyond liking. I was awestruck. He's beyond anything."

She raised her eyebrows. "You sound as if you had seen a saint."

"A saint? He's better than a saint."

Rose chuckled and shook her head. "Not everyone would agree with you. You had better not advance that opinion here."

"I wouldn't, but really, he was one of the world's greatest geniuses."

"And you would rather see a genius than saint?"

"Yes. Maybe you wouldn't?" No, she wouldn't. "Have you ever time traveled to see a saint?"

"I don't feel worthy. I've never tried to see a saint."

"If you aren't worthy, no one is."

"I'd rather see Emily Dickinson."

"So would I! You admit wanting to see a genius."

"I suppose so. Have you ever wanted to see a saint?"

"No. Not a Catholic saint. I would like to see Gandhi."

Rose sighed. "He's a good choice. We have been taught such limited ideas about who is a saint."

Reverend Mother's face looked solemn in a way that always augured bad news. "There is a piece of news that I think you should know," she told us in the refectory after breakfast.

I knew that if she took the trouble to inform us, the news would be bad.

"Troops belonging to the brother of President Diem of Vietnam attacked Buddhist monasteries and killed hundreds of Buddhist monks."

We gasped collectively.

"Let us pray for the souls of the monks and pray that those who killed them will stop the violence."

How could anyone kill a monk? The people who killed them were supposedly our allies, helped by the United States. President Diem and his brother were known as pious Catholics. Was the Church somehow at fault for the murders? Were we beyond the days of the Inquisition?

I turned to Rose. She was praying, as were many other sisters. I joined in.

On the next visiting day, I longed to introduce my parents to Rose, but when I mentioned it to her ahead of time, she rejected the idea. She feared that Mother Michael might discover our secret.

Disappointed, I nonetheless enjoyed the sight of my parents.

My father's eyes shone. "I hope they let you watch part of the March on Washington."

I stared at him. "What march on Washington?"

The sparkle left his eyes. He sputtered. "Jesus Christ! They didn't even tell you about it. You never hear any news."

"I did hear about the slaughter of the Buddhist monks in Vietnam."

"But not about your own coun—"

My mother put a restraining hand on his arm. "Calm down. It seems the novices can hear bad news, but not good news." She turned to me. "There was a march of at least a quarter of a million people who support civil rights. All the major civil rights leaders spoke at the Lincoln Memorial. Dr. King gave a particularly moving speech. He said he had a dream that Black and white Americans could live together in freedom and justice. I'm sorry you couldn't hear it."

"A quarter of a million people!" Stunned, I tried to conceal my resentment at not learning about the march. "I wish I had heard his speech."

"They allow you to vote, don't they?" My father's voice still sizzled with anger.

"Yes, I'm looking forward to voting for President Kennedy next year."

"But they don't let you learn the news, so most of the nuns who vote will be ignorant." He steamed.

"Hush, Pete," my mother chided him. "Sister Jerome is coming over to us. You must calm yourself."

That perpetually placid nun approached. "Hello, Mr. and Mrs. Collins. How are you today?"

"Just fine, Sister Jerome," my mother told her. "How are you? I've brought oatmeal cookies. Would you like some?"

"We always appreciate your cookies, Mrs. Collins. Thank you very much. Please put them on the refreshment table, Sister Matthew."

"Thank you for the cookies, Mom." I carried them to the table, put them on a platter and ate one. Sister Jerome must have seen that my father had been angry, though she didn't know why. I never knew how much of our conversations she reported. I tried to let the cookie's sweetness overcome my own anger at my enforced ignorance.

CHAPTER 32

Sister Rose

OSE TRIED TO CONCENTRATE on the rosary. The nuns around her droned like bees, their words unintelligible. Rose remembered Reverend Mother's warning that she wouldn't always feel spiritual exhalation in the convent.

She hadn't felt the same since her pneumonia. Her life seemed shorter and her time to do something important had shrunk to hours. Every hour that she merely observed the routine might be an hour wasted.

Pope John's death had made everything worse. She could no longer count on him to change the world. She should be doing it herself. Was praying the rosary changing the world? She was supposed to think so, but she didn't. Did God or Mary really want to hear endless Hail Marys? That almost suggested vanity on Mary's part, a fault the Blessed Mother surely did not have. Rose always thought of her as the Blessed Mother, not the Blessed Virgin, because the former title was more certain.

Was Mattie influencing her thinking too much? Rose wondered.

Boredom and restlessness must be sins, though they were not listed among the deadly ones. They probably could be filed under the category of pride. Rose didn't think she deserved endless stimulation, but she wanted to feel she was doing something that mattered.

That night she prayed to do something meaningful in her time travel.

A giant wall of flames bore down on her. She stumbled. The thought that she had been cast into hell horrified her as much as the fire.

"Don't stop! Keep on!" a man in strange gear yelled at her as he chopped away brush and trees. "We have to make a firebreak." This wasn't hell. It was a forest fire.

Rose realized she also wore heavy fire gear that weighed her down. She held a hatchet. She imitated the man's moves, slicing small trees.

The fire's glare blinded her. The heat made her reel. The fire roared like ten thousand lions. A deer plunged past her, almost knocking her over. Birds screamed.

If she loved the forest, she must work to save it.

The fire mesmerized her. She tried to swing her hatchet with force, but she collapsed. I'll be burned to death, she thought in terror.

Rose came to in her convent bed. She couldn't stop shaking. Was this travel a warning that she could go to hell, a hell she scarcely believed in? She had never thought God would really send people to eternal flames. God must be too loving to torture people for eternity.

Or was this travel a warning that trying to do good in the world was difficult, but she must do it anyway? What kind of person was she if she wavered? She tried to pray that she would be able to face terrible challenges like the fire, yet she couldn't force herself to say those words, even in silent prayer. She didn't think she would ever have the courage of people like the Freedom Riders, who had ridden in integrated buses through the South, facing beatings, jail, and possible death to work for integration. She feared dying, especially dying young.

Perhaps being a nun was all she was good for.

CHAPTER 33

Sister Matthew

O H NO. I HAD *traveled back to my high school on the same hideous day. My stomach clenched.*

"Class dismissed," Sister Veronica announced.

I jumped up from my desk, as did most of the other girls. We were ready to move on, to gossip about Mary Louise, to cry over her, or to forget about her. In my case, to try to remember what had happened.

The teacher spoke terrible words I could never forget. "Maureen, you will stay here. I need to talk with you."

I froze. Tell-tale heart time. I tried to compose my face.

When the last girl left and closed the door, Sister Veronica ordered me, "Come stand next to my desk."

I did as she bade me. I felt too frightened even to pray.

I said I was frozen, but it was Sister Veronica's face that looked frostier than a freezer.

"You didn't like Mary Louise, did you?" *Her voice seared through me. She really was an Agatha Christie.*

"She wasn't one of my friends, sister." *I hoped my voice sounded normal.*

"No, she wasn't. In fact, you hated her." *Her eyes pierced through my navy-blue uniform and my chest.*

"No, sister. I don't hate anyone." My voice cracked.

"Mary Louise told me you hated her. She feared you."

"That's impossible! I'm not frightening." Even though Mary Louise was dead, hearing she had said that made me angry at her. Rather than fearing me, she had despised me.

"You can't hide, Maureen." Sister Veronica's eyes bore into me like two drills. "I saw you linger in the auditorium. Don't tell me any more lies. You're just adding sin to sin. You killed her."

"No, I didn't."

I ran out of the room without asking permission to leave.

THE TIME TRAVEL MOVED *to me washing dishes in the kitchen of my parents' home. I heard my parents arguing in the living room.*

"I don't want her to go back to that school." My mother's voice seldom reached that pitch of anger.

"Maureen loves the school," my father responded in his official I-am-the-sanest-person-here tone that always infuriated my mother. "They closed it for the rest of the day and tomorrow. They're hiring security guards. What more can they do?"

"They can catch the killer! I don't want her to go back until they at least do that."

I grabbed one of Mom's flowered dish towels, wiped my hands, and rushed to the living room to join them. "Please don't take me out of school. All my friends are there. I've gone there since kindergarten."

I had forgotten to put down the dish towel. My hands twisted it.

On seeing me, my mother lowered her tone. "But the murderer is still loose, honey. I just want to protect you."

My father tried to placate Mom. "I called Sister Thomas, the principal. They're doing everything they can. She took my recommendation on which security firm to hire to guard the school. But the killer is probably miles away by now."

"How can you be so calm? What if Maureen had been killed? What about the men who work at the school?"

"I asked about them. Sister Thomas told me the maintenance man was attending his mother's funeral and the gardener had gone to an auto dealership to look at a new van for the school."

Thank goodness. I shuddered at the thought of the police arresting Richard Brady or Alfredo Moreno. They were nice guys with families. Their daughters attended St. Agatha's grade school on scholarships, integrating the school for the first time. I had heard that the police sometimes were more suspicious of Negroes like Richard Brady.

I began to cry. "Don't blame the Agatha Christies."

My mother put her arms around me. "You've had a shock. Try to rest, dear. Don't worry, you'll be able to go back to join your friends. I just think you should stay home for a few days."

I pulled away from her. "I have to go to the funeral," I demanded.

My mother gasped. "Oh Maureen, that's not a good idea. I've never seen you in such a state of distress. You've cried so much. You hardly ate any dinner. The funeral would upset you even more."

"I have to go," I insisted. If I didn't go, my absence could suggest I was guilty.

"I didn't think you were so fond of Mary Louise."

"That's not the point." I choked. "She was my classmate."

My father intervened. "Maybe not going would upset Maureen more than going. Funerals can be cathartic."

Mom glared at him. "You go with her then."

The funeral that Saturday was a nightmare. Grim, pale nuns. Crying girls. I couldn't bring myself to look at Mary Louise's family. I stared at the flower-covered coffin that held her body. I tried not to feel faint. Dad's presence steadied me.

I didn't think I had committed the murder. But I wasn't sure, and the uncertainty shook me. I couldn't remember what had happened *between the time I last saw Mary Louise and the time I found myself sitting in the English class. Why not?*

I prayed for Mary Louise. I hoped she had gone to heaven, not Purgatory. Were nasty remarks enough to send a teenager to Purgatory? I forgave her for her trespasses against me. That wasn't enough for God to forgive me if I had killed her.

After the service, Dad had to steer me out of the church. When we were in the car, he said, "Buck up, Maureen. Your Mom is so worried that she's talking about sending you to a priest in our parish who does pastoral counseling. I don't think you'd like that."

I groaned. "Oh, no! You're right. I wouldn't. Thanks for warning me."

The last thing I wanted was someone prying in my psyche. That could get me sent to prison, or at least a mental institution.

When I came to in my convent bed, I had sweated so much that my sheets were damp. I had never before had such a long time travel, visiting several days. I didn't want any more like it.

Though I stayed awake for a long time, eventually I fell asleep.

In my dream, Mary Louise loomed over me. "You killed me!"

I stumbled backwards. "I didn't. Go away."

"You did, evil Polka Dot. Your pimples mark you as evil. I hate you." She lunged at me.

I woke. This time I had been visited by a nightmare. If I hadn't killed her, why would I feel so guilty? Were my feelings of guilt proof that I had committed murder?

THE NEXT MORNING, ROSE followed me out of the communal restroom. "What's the matter? You were groaning and sobbing in your sleep. You've been having nightmares."

"Was it only a nightmare? I thought it was time travel."

"I don't think so. What is disturbing you?"

"We'll be late for chapel."

"Yes, we'll be late for chapel." She stood there, determined to listen to what I didn't want to tell her.

"I keep reliving something I'm fairly sure never happened, some horrible thing I did. I keep asking myself whether it could have happened."

"You're feeling guilty about something else." She paused. "I hope it's not guilt about us."

"No! Definitely not."

"Then it must be about pretending to believe in the doctrines of the Church."

I gasped.

"You have a questioning mind. I understand. But please don't let yourself become mired in guilt. Guilt doesn't help anyone."

Rose shone more than ever in my eyes. I felt incredibly lucky to love her, and to be loved by her.

"Thank you." I took a deep breath.

"Now we can go to chapel. At the chapter meeting, please confess we were detained because I stayed so long in the toilet that you were worried about me."

I blushed. "I couldn't say that."

"Sure, you can."

We moved to the chapel in unseemly haste. Another fault.

I wanted to ask Rose why it had been so long since we had time traveled to make love. I held back because I feared she wasn't trying to travel with me. Did those time travels require both of us to wish for them at the same time? And did she desire me as much as I desired her?

I didn't deserve her love. But maybe, just maybe, I was certain I hadn't killed Mary Louise McKenna. Maybe I wouldn't dream about her again.

I NEEDED MORE THAN prayer to help me recover from the nightmare about Mary Louise. I needed Shakespeare. I tried to remember parts of *Hamlet*, but my memory failed me.

When the other novices were having recreation in the parlor, I snuck to the forbidden room where college books were kept. There must be a volume of Shakespeare's plays—at least, I hoped there was.

I opened the door quietly, stole across the carpet, and aimed for the shelf where I had found *The Norton Anthology of English Literature* some months earlier. Yes! There stood a volume of the complete works of William Shakespeare.

I touched the book reverently, as if I touched a Bible or Missal. I read the table of contents, a list of marvels. I turned the pages with care.

True, Shakespeare's use of ghosts as characters was not particularly consoling to one who wanted to deny their existence, but nonetheless I plunged into *Hamlet*. I couldn't remember all the words of the "To be or not to be" soliloquy, and I wanted to refresh my memory. I cherished the words "the slings and arrows of outrageous fortune."

"Sister Matthew, what are you doing?"

I had not seen Mean Mother Michael enter the room behind me. I jumped, almost dropping the book but catching it in time.

She crossed the room and grabbed the book from my hands.

"Shakespeare? Just why did you break the rules to read Shakespeare? Were you reading some comedy?"

"I was reading *Hamlet*, Mother Michael." My voice squeaked as if I had been caught stealing.

"You think you are so special that you have to read *Hamlet*." Her voice dripped with scorn. "Your intellectual pretensions are disgusting. You are badly in need of humility. I am going to ask Reverend Mother to ban you from taking any classes, even theology, until you finish your novitiate."

I gasped. I longed to cry out, "No, no, not that."

"If you break any more rules, I promise your punishment will be more severe. Go to the chapel and pray the rosary. You will return there at dinnertime and not eat any dinner tonight."

I could hardly speak. "Yes, Mother Michael."

Missing dinner mattered a great deal less than not being allowed to take Reverend Mother's theology class that fall.

I had heard through the grapevine that Mother Michael had never been sent to graduate school. Did she dislike me because I longed for more learning, and would probably get it?

I slunk off to the chapel. What a fool I had been. My slings and arrows could so easily be multiplied.

I longed to tell Mean Mother Michael that spies in *Hamlet* were severely punished. How would you like to face Polonius's fate, Mother Michael? Oh sure, threatening the Mistress of Novices would really help my position.

Was I a monster because I had that thought? Had I killed Mary Louise after all?

Help me not to be a monster, Possible God.

LIKE THE BIBLICAL EVE, I had sinned though a thirst for knowledge. Perhaps Reverend Mother would understand.

Later that day, I knocked on the door of her office.

"Who is there?" she asked.

I opened the door. "May I speak with you, Reverend Mother."

She sighed. "Come in and sit down, Sister Matthew."

I slunk in and sat in the designated chair.

"I am disappointed in you, Sister Matthew." Reverend Mother shook her head. She looked as stern as if I had snuck out of the convent to see a movie the Church condemned. "Are you planning to ask me to remit the punishment from your superior? You are a promising student, but I shall not do that. The decision of the Mistress of Novices stands."

My already sunken spirits sank even lower. I had hoped she would not accept deprivation of knowledge as a punishment. "Yes, Reverend Mother."

"I cannot tell you how appalled I am that you let yourself be ruled by your curiosity rather than accepting the limits set for you. Have you never heard of Pandora's box?" She looked me in the eye. "Your misbehavior was not trivial. It shows that intellectual pride is your governing motivation. We have tried to teach you that learning to love God is more than a matter of the intellect. Understanding theological arguments is nothing if your heart is elsewhere. We are a community, not just a collection of individuals. Our community has adopted a particular way of joining together and witnessing God's presence in the world. If you want to belong to our community, you must learn to live our way. Do you understand?"

"Yes, Reverend Mother." I had to admit her argument was logical.

"'Yes, Reverend Mother.' But what does 'yes, Reverend Mother' mean? That you will try to comply outwardly with my orders, or that your heart is touched?"

I bit my lip. Tears were threatening to form. "I am trying to understand with my heart, Reverend Mother."

She sighed again. "I hope so, Sister Matthew. I, too, was filled with intellectual pride when I was young. I rebelled inwardly against being assigned to study for a doctorate in theology. I would have preferred getting a doctorate in philosophy. But I am glad I submitted to my superiors, who knew that the order needed me to teach theology.

"I am sorry that you will not be able to take any classes this semester. I shall allow you to spend five hours a week studying Latin on your own, but that is the most I can do for you. I hope you will use the time you would have spent studying in self-reflection and prayer."

"I shall try, Reverend Mother. Thank you for allowing me to continue studying Latin." Moved by her unusual reference to her own difficulties when she was young, I struggled to feel gratitude. My suspicious mind wondered whether the previous reverend mother had other reasons for keeping someone with Mother Robert's considerable intelligence from studying philosophy.

"If you have no more questions, you may go now."

There was no point in trying to plead or argue. "Good afternoon, Reverend Mother."

"Good afternoon, Sister Matthew."

Dismissed, I left her office. I felt torn between anger at myself for getting into this situation and rage at Mother Michael for giving me such an extreme punishment, the worst I had ever heard of except for expulsion. Was I really the worst novice in my cohort? Or was she jealous of my brains? I would have preferred saying ten rosaries a day.

EVEN THOUGH I HAD already been given my punishment, I still had to confess my fault in the next chapter meeting. I didn't have a chance to tell Rose ahead of time.

When my turn to confess came, I knelt. "Dear Reverend Mother, Mistress of Novices, and my dear sisters, I snuck into the room where college textbooks are kept and began reading a volume of Shakespeare's plays. I am heartily sorry for my presumption. *Mea culpa, mea culpa, mea maxima culpa.*"

"That is indeed a serious fault," Reverend Mother intoned. "Studying is good, but obeying the rules is more important. You were granted the privilege of taking college classes, but that privilege is now suspended until after your novitiate ends. You will spend the time you would have spent studying in prayer, reflection, and labor for the good of the community."

I kissed the floor. No doubt Mean Mother Michael gloated.

Later Rose passed me in the hall when no one else was there and gave me a look of sympathy. "I can't believe you did anything so foolish, but I'm sorry you won't be allowed to take any classes this semester. By next semester, you will have taken your first vows and can take more classes."

Shame made it difficult for me to face her. "I hope so." Meaning that I hoped I would be allowed to take my vows at the end of my novitiate.

CHAPTER 34

Sister Matthew

I TROD GLOOMILY ALONG THE cloister on my way to pray in the chapel while other sisters had recreation in the parlor. Missing recreation was the least of my worries.

A mourning dove cooing in the twilit garden failed to cheer me. Doves had the right temperament for the convent. I didn't.

A nun came up behind me.

"Good evening, Sister Matthew."

Mother Gabriel's tone sounded so welcoming that I wondered whether she had heard about my disgrace.

I tried to make my voice as warm as hers. "Good evening, Mother Gabriel."

"Would you help me with a project?" Even in the fading light, I could see from her expression that she knew about my punishment and sympathized.

"Certainly, Mother Gabriel."

She extracted a small volume from her sleeve. "I want to understand these poems, but I'm having difficulty. Perhaps you could explain them to me."

She handed me a book of Emily Dickinson's poetry. Too stunned to take it from her, I stared.

Her sweet face smiled even more than usual. "If anyone sees this, you must tell her that I have assigned you to read it, although I have no authority over you. I am sure that Mother Michael will take it away if she finds it."

I accepted the book and hid it in my sleeve. Mother Gabriel was prepared to take the rap for my reading poetry. "I can never thank you enough, Mother Gabriel."

"Just pray for me, Sister Matthew."

"With all my heart, Mother Gabriel. Please pray for me also."

She walked on, leaving me as replete with gifts as I had been on Christmas mornings when I was a child.

When I returned to the dormitory, I hid the book under my mattress and prayed that no one snooped there.

As soon as we retired for the night, I strained my eyes to read the poems in the darkened dormitory.

ON A WARM NIGHT *illuminated by a full moon, I stood next to a house that loomed large and pale, with dark shutters. A grassy expanse with a few trees spread between it and the next house.*

A woman emerged from the house near me. I leaned into the shadows so she wouldn't spot me.

She wore a light-colored, nineteenth-century dress, but her feet were bare.

She scanned to be certain no one else was around, but she didn't see me.

Moonlight illuminated her face. She was Emily Dickinson.

I managed not to make a sound.

She moved towards the other house, the house where her dear friend Susan, now married to Emily's brother Austin, must live. I wondered what Emily had felt about Susan.

Emily stood there for a time, then tiptoed back to the center of the dewy grass.

Bathed in moonlight, she danced.

Her house and her brother's stood on a suburban street in Amherst, Massachusetts, but she must have been dancing late at night because no people were in sight and no lights shone in the windows of nearby houses.

I reassured myself that no one who doubted her sanity would see her.

The words of her moon poems I had just read drifted through my head.

"The moon was but a chin of gold
A night or two ago."

Emily's poem had continued saying something like the moon was now showing its full face and the stars were trinkets at her belt. I wish I had memorized the exact words.

Was Emily thinking those glorious words now?

I waited.

She stretched out on the dewy grass and watched the moon.

At last she rose and slipped back inside the house.

I lingered loving the moon.

I hoped the poet wouldn't have minded my watching her. In one poem, Emily called herself a wayward nun beneath the hill.

Back in my convent cell, this wayward nun longed for dew.

THE NEXT DAY I had a cold. Too much dew, I suppose. Did Emily ever catch a cold from dancing in the moonlight and lying on the grass?

I could cover my sneezes, but not hide them.

"How could you get a cold in September, Sister Matthew?" Mean Mother Michael chided me. "The fall weather hasn't even begun. Take care of your health so you can fulfill your duties. Go to the kitchen and eat an orange. Eat another one tonight."

My superior's stern tone annoyed me as usual, but her prescription pleased me. Oranges are my favorite fruit, something we don't eat every day. Compared with Sister Veronica, Mother Michael is a peach.

That night I traveled *to my least favorite place again. The nun of my nightmares sat at her desk. My heart belly flopped. I tried to look at my classmates, but against my will, my gaze kept traveling to Sister Veronica.*

"We shall read Julius Caesar *aloud today," the teacher announced. Several students murmured.*

So I was not the only one who hoped we would skip that play. But I'm sure my wishes had been the most fervent.

We all had heard in the news that the murderer had stabbed Mary Louise, so Caesar's murder by knifing was much too similar.

Once again, everything happened word for word as it had when I was sixteen, and I was unable to say anything new.

"Bernadette, you will read the part of Julius Caesar. Susan, you will read Cassius. Fran will read Mark Antony. Maureen will be Brutus."

I clutched my desk to keep from falling. Sister Veronica was forcing me to act the part of a murderer. Even worse, I was supposed to kill my dearest friend. I believed Sister Veronica guessed I cared about Bernadette and the casting was part of my punishment.

I wanted to plead that I had a sore throat, but there wasn't a chance in medieval hell that Sister Veronica would let me beg off.

Everyone knew I read aloud well, so I would have to read the part as stirringly as I would have if Mary Louise had not been murdered.

Sister Veronica cut parts of the play, but not those with Brutus's most damning words.

I forced myself to say, "It must be by his death…" Brutus was supposed to sound tortured, and I'm sure I did.

A while later, I read, "I have not slept. Between the acting of a dreadful thing and the first motion, all the interim is like a phantasma or a hideous dream..." Whatever I had done, it wasn't premeditated murder.

I pressed on. "...Let's kill him boldly but not wrathfully. Let's carve him as a dish for the gods..."

I made the mistake of looking up and seeing Sister Veronica's gaze fixed on me, her eyes filled with hatred.

I had to continue. She would not force me to confess a deed I had not done. Probably.

Then came the most terrible moment. Along with the girls who played my fellow conspirators, I had to make stabbing motions.

Bernadette moaned, "Et tu, Brute? Then fall, Caesar."

I tried to remind myself that she wasn't talking to me.

By the time I had to read Brutus's speech to the Roman people, I had talked myself into a trance in which the words seemed to come of themselves. I scarcely knew what I was saying.

"...as he was ambitious, I slew him..." Rage at Sister Veronica for forcing me to say those words fired me up to finish the speech.

By the end of the class, I felt as if my own blood had drained from my body. I hurried through the door before Sister Veronica could demand that I stay. I ran to the biology classroom and threw myself onto a desk there. I pulled out my biology textbook, opened it, and stared unseeing at a page as if the words were a scripture enlightening me on ineffable truths.

When I returned to my convent bed, I jumped up and washed my hands in my bowl. I thought of Hamlet as well as Lady Macbeth. "Conscience doth make cowards of us all." Even if I hadn't been too good to kill Mary Louise, I must have been too cowardly. Hadn't I?

I prayed for Mary Louise, cut down so young. I hope not by me.

I WATCHED ROSE KNEELING in the chapel. How serene she looked.

Were her time travels never terrible since the one to Vietnam? Did good people experience only good time travels?

It had been at least ten days since we had a chance to communicate in private. This wasn't the only time our gap in conversation had been so long, but it was one of the hardest. We hadn't made love in months, not since Pope John died. I longed for a chance to talk with her every day and tell her everything—almost everything. Nothing about Mary Louise and Sister Veronica.

If Rose loved me, didn't she ache to talk to me too? And why didn't she try to go to a place where we could make love?

CHAPTER 35

Sister Rose

R OSE LAY IN HER convent bed remembering how Mattie's caresses had lifted her up, filling her with joy. Were they united in a special way, a kind of marriage, the closest connection any people could have? Was love a sacrament even if it wasn't officially blessed?

Why did Mattie have to defy the rules? Why would she risk punishment just to read *Hamlet*? How could a play matter that much? Was Mattie dangerous to know? No, Rose chided herself, she loved Mattie's passionate mind and almost wished that her own desire for learning matched Mattie's.

Rose remembered being taught in high school that she must be in the world, but not of it. She could live in a secular world but keep firm her Catholic values. She could resist temptations.

Now she wondered whether she was living in the convent world but was not of it. Had she learned her lesson too well? When surrounded by prayer, she longed for wild places. Was she being true to her vocation? Did she even have a vocation?

Would she have been able to live in the convent without Mattie's love? Did she depend on Mattie too much? Rose rationed trips to see Mattie in time travel to keep from becoming too dependent.

CHAPTER 36

Sister Matthew

AFTER A SUNDAY MORNING Mass, we indulged in a late breakfast of crullers as well as scrambled eggs and link sausages. We all smiled more than usual at these pleasures of the flesh.

Father Nolan, who always ate in a separate room reserved for priests, entered the refectory. His normally red face had paled. He gestured to Reverend Mother, who hurried over to him.

He spoke to her, and she sagged as if she were going to faint.

She turned to us.

"We must return to the chapel and pray. Something truly terrible has happened. Father Nolan heard on the radio that someone bombed a Baptist church in Birmingham, Alabama, and four young Negro girls were killed."

I gasped. Tears formed in my eyes. I could hear other sisters exclaiming, but I felt so stunned I didn't even look around to see Rose. My heart plunged. How could anyone be so evil, so full of hate?

Praying was all we could do. Not for the first time, I wished I could do more. I felt too angry at the killers to pray to turn their hearts around. But Reverend King would pray for that, so I should too.

THAT NIGHT, I TRAVELED *again—unfortunately, back to my high school. I hurried down the path to the gym at St. Agatha's. Would Miss Hammond, the gym teacher, let me off if I said my cramps were too*

painful? I didn't want to try to learn basketball, just to watch Bernadette play. Miss Hammond looked extremely unfeminine, so I should have liked her, but her brusque manner put me off.

As I passed the shrine to the Virgin Mary with her statue set in a grotto, I heard a voice behind me.

"Have you been to Confession?"

I turned. Sister Veronica confronted me.

She peered at me as if she could see all my sins. "I don't believe you've been absolved. I see the guilt on your face."

"Yes, sister," I faltered. "I have to go to gym class, sister."

"Hmm. Gym class indeed."

She let me go.

Why did I feel so guilty when I hadn't done anything terrible? Had I? I still trembled as I drew near the gym courts.

The principal, Sister Doubting Thomas, approached me on the path. As usual, she walked purposefully, as if she never had a moment without a task to do.

"Are you well, Maureen?" The principal peered at me through her thick glasses. She must see my trembling.

"Yes, Sister Thomas."

"You don't look well. Tell Miss Hammond I said you may sit on the bench if you want to."

I blushed. It was unheard of for a nun to say something like that without even being asked. Did she want to separate me from the other girls? No, her face held no trace of dislike.

"Thank you, Sister Thomas." I couldn't wait for senior year when she would probably be my English teacher again.

I didn't tell Rose that I had had a guilt episode again. I still felt guilty. Did hearing about the terrible murders in Birmingham trigger a memory that I, too, had killed a girl? Was I hate-filled?

CHAPTER 37
Sister Rose

THE DAY AFTER THE Birmingham bombing, Mattie's face looked so anguished that Rose had to find a way to speak with her.

Mattie and Sister Ursula had been assigned to wash the dishes, while Rose had been charged with dusting the statues in the hallway. She finished her task quickly, then moved with seemly haste to the kitchen.

"Sister Ursula, would you mind if I took over drying for you?" Rose thought Ursula would agree without reporting her.

Sister Ursula's eyebrows shot up, but she merely said, "Thank you, Sister Rose. That's very kind of you," and surrendered her dish towel.

Mattie stared at Rose. As soon as Sister Ursula left the kitchen, Mattie said, "Why did you take that risk? Sister Ursula is trustworthy, but we might be discovered anyway."

"You look so troubled by the murders in Birmingham."

Mattie's gaze shifted to the sink. "Among other things. When we remember slavery, when we remember the Holocaust, how can we believe in a God who responds to prayers? I think the spiritual realm must be less concrete. Maybe, as the Hindu Vedas suggest, we are each part of the divine and we have to create it ourselves-or fail to."

Rose's head spun. She wished Mattie had not spoken those words or she had not heard them. She had sometimes thought of that possible explanation of the world, but it had never struck her so deeply. "Maybe that's true. Do our prayers count for anything?"

"If trying to concentrate on goodness can bring it about, maybe so."

Rose attempted to hide her distress. She internally gasped for breath, but Mattie didn't seem to notice. "There aren't many dishes left," was all Rose could say.

"That's true. Maybe you had better go before someone notices that you're not in your assigned place."

Rose walked to the chapel at her normal pace, but she felt she must be staggering. Perhaps there wasn't a God who listened to them. Did that mean she was a fool to live in the convent?

CHAPTER 38
Sister Thomas

ST. AGATHA'S MOTHER HOUSE IN BALTIMORE
SEPTEMBER 1963

SISTER THOMAS THREW OPEN the window of her new office. She plopped into her chair and sorted through her files. One file compelled her to open it: the file on the murder of Mary Louise McKenna.

Sister Thomas frowned. The unsolved murder haunted her. She had done all she could as the principal of St. Agatha's High School. The police had irritated her by looking obsessively for a Negro man, though there was no reason to think the murderer was Negro. Thank goodness William Brady, the school's friendly and efficient maintenance man, had been attending his mother's funeral that morning, so the police couldn't try to pin the crime on him. But they seemed to look at every Negro man within 30 miles of the school as a suspect.

When they failed to find the murderer, Sister Thomas had asked her superiors in the order to give her permission to investigate the case, but they had ridiculed her for asking. Ancient Reverend Mother Sebastian and her deputy, Sister Therese of Lisieux, had told her in no uncertain terms that she was no detective and had to back off. "You're not Nancy Drew," Sister Therese had said. Sister Thomas had always disliked the appellation for St. Therese, "the Little Flower." She mentally called her order's Sister Therese "the Little Weed."

Now Reverend Mother Sebastian had died, and the new Reverend Mother, the former Sister Cecilia, had appointed Sister Thomas as her deputy. Though she would miss being a high school principal, Sister Thomas was ready for a new job. Like investigations.

She had been glad the order had named her Sister Thomas the Apostle. She always made it clear she was named for him, not for Thomas Aquinas the theologian. She knew the girls called her Sister Doubting Thomas, and she aspired to live up to the name. She liked her nickname so much that two or three times a semester she would say something like, "Jane, I doubt that you have read the assignment." She enjoyed the class's suppressed giggles and the knowledge that her nickname would live on.

She doubted many things, more than she would ever tell her superiors or her confessor. She didn't doubt that Jesus was God, but she found many other aspects of doctrine dubious, with papal infallibility high on her list.

Sister Thomas especially doubted that it would be impossible to find Mary Louise's murderer, even though seven years had passed. There was no statute of limitations for murder.

Mary Louise had been a rather unpleasant girl, who flattered the nuns and, Sister Thomas had made it her business to know, insulted many of her classmates. Mary Louise had tried to be the arbiter of who was popular and who was unpopular, not recognizing that she herself would never win any popularity contest. She might have won a beauty contest, if the school had such a thing and if the girls she had insulted hadn't been allowed to vote.

But unpleasantness was not a criminal offense. Mary Louise did not deserve to be murdered.

Though a number of girls probably disliked Mary Louise, Sister Thomas doubted that any of them could have killed her. In Sister Thomas's experience, high school girls seldom committed murder.

She stared at the file, reading Detective Johnson's reports of his interrogations, which he had given long afterward at her request, and the responses to some questions she had asked the teachers. They were no more illuminating than they had been the first time she had read them seven years earlier.

Though Sister Thomas did not believe that any of Mary Louise's classmates had killed her, she did think they might provide clues. The police detective had balked at interviewing them one by one, which would have required obtaining their parents' consent.

The girls were young women now, and no parental consent would be required.

Who was the patron saint of detectives? Perhaps St. Genesius, the patron saint of lawyers and actors, was close enough. But Sister Doubting Thomas would settle for her own patron. *Dear St. Thomas the Apostle, help me find who killed Mary Louise*, she prayed. *You who didn't even believe the other apostles when they told you they had seen Jesus, help me with my skepticism so I do not prematurely rule out any suspects.*

Sister Thomas decided to start with questioning Mary Louise's parents. She looked up their phone numbers. She had heard they had divorced after the murder.

She phoned Mary Louise's mother.

"Hello, Mrs. McKenna. I am Sister Thomas, who used to be the principal of St. Agatha's—"

"How dare you phone me!" The voice over the telephone shook with rage. "I never want to hear from anyone at your horrible school again. You let my daughter be killed."

Not many people screamed in rage at Sister Thomas. But no other parents' children had been murdered at her school. "I am so sorry. Your grief must be terrible. We are very sad about that—"

"Sad! You should be. I always thought we should sue you for negligence, but my husband said we would never win. Don't you dare ever call me again." The irate mother banged down the receiver.

This was not a promising start. But it didn't discourage Sister Thomas. Perhaps Mary Louise's father would be more forthcoming. She called his architecture firm, but she learned that he had died two years previously.

Probably the parents had known nothing about the killing since it happened at St. Agatha's.

Sister Thomas found the list of the girls who had been Mary Louise's classmates. Then she compiled a list of the teachers who had been at the school that year. Almost all of them were nuns, except for Jonathan Wilson, who had taught there for fifteen years, and Madame Jeanne LaSalle, the French teacher, who had been hired the year before Mary Louise was killed. Madame Lasalle had moved to New York City three years later. Mary Louise had not taken French classes, so Sister Thomas doubted that Madame LaSalle would have had a motive to kill her.

Sister Thomas phoned the remaining lay teacher and asked whether he would be available if she came to the school the next day.

When she arrived at the high school, Sister Thomas smiled fondly at the gray stone buildings where she had taught for so many years. She had chosen a time when there would be no classes, rehearsals, or events in the auditorium. She entered the empty auditorium, housed in its own building. She had visited it many times in the weeks after the crime but scrutinizing it again would do no harm.

The gray metal chairs were folded in the closet, but she remembered how they had been set up, the same way they always had been, in rows with an aisle in between. She took two chairs from the closet and placed them near the stage, with a good view of the murder scene.

She could picture Mary Louise's body lying broken and bloody.

Sister Thomas closed her eyes for a moment, then reopened them. This investigation would be painful, but she must be strong.

Mary Louise had met her death on the left side of the auditorium—stage right—near where the long, Formica-topped table with the cake had stood. The table had been about 25 feet from the stage. A door stood about ten feet closer to the stage. The murderer almost certainly had come through that door. The murder most likely had been planned, though the knife that cut the cake was the murder weapon.

After the killing, Sister Thomas had purchased a softer-edged knife for cutting cakes.

Mr. Wilson walked through the main door of the auditorium because she had told him to meet her there rather than using the principal's office.

The history teacher, who also led the glee club and directed the school plays, was now in his late fifties, a few years older than she. He had put on weight since the year of the murder and his hair had turned gray.

Sister Thomas had hired him because no nuns in her order had backgrounds in theater or music. She added history classes because he had a master's degree in that subject and the additional classes would give him a full-time job. She had never regretted her decision.

"Good morning, Sister Thomas," he said in his usual cheerful voice. He had always been discreetly friendly with everyone at the school, not overfamiliar. "It's good to see you at the school again. We miss you."

"Good morning, Mr. Wilson." She inclined her head to him. "I miss the school too, but like most people, I'm pleased to be promoted. Please take a seat."

She sat in one of the chairs and indicated that he should take the other one. Perhaps the interrogation would be easier because she would be questioning someone she liked. She must keep alert and not let liking him deceive her. However, she didn't want this to sound like the Inquisition.

"How are your students this year?" She knew that interrogators tried to put the interviewee at ease.

"Just fine. A few have the potential to be good scholars." He gave her an inquiring look as if asking whether she had summoned him merely to chat.

"Do they still whisper in your classes?"

"That hasn't changed. I suppose I'm not enough of a disciplinarian." He shrugged.

"You know it's just that they think they can get away with anything with lay teachers. How is your wife doing?"

"She's fine, thank you. Still enjoying teaching at the grammar school."

"I'm glad. We're so fortunate to have you both." She had always liked Jonathan and Ellen Wilson and thought it was good for the girls to see a couple who were in a happy marriage. Their three children were already grown. "I see you still aren't wearing glasses."

He put his hand to his face as if to confirm that he wasn't wearing glasses. "I wear them for reading now."

"You have much better vision than I do. I've been wearing these all the time since I went to college. What play are you directing this year?"

His eyes lit up. *"Arsenic and Old Lace.* One of my favorites. We did it ten years ago. This is the first time we're doing it since…." His voice trailed off.

"Since the murder," she filled in. "I enjoyed it the last time. I'm sure the students will be able to appreciate the play now without thinking about Mary Louise. You've directed many plays in this auditorium."

He smiled. "That has been the best part of my job."

"We are grateful for that. But not everything that has happened in the auditorium has been pleasant."

The history teacher's brow creased. Perhaps he guessed why she had asked to speak with him. "The murder was by far the worst thing that ever happened at this school. For the first few years after it, the auditorium felt haunted."

"You don't think it feels haunted now?" It still gave her the creeps, but perhaps that was because she was reopening the case.

"Either that or we, or at least I, have become desensitized to it." The lay teacher sighed. "I suppose it's awful to come here and not think about poor Mary Louise."

"What was your opinion of her?"

Mr. Wilson stared at Sister Thomas as if she had asked him whether he loved his family. "I'm sorry for the poor girl, of course. Are you reopening the investigation? Have you uncovered new information?"

"I haven't yet, but I hope to. The murder has worried me for years. Now I am in a position where I can look at the evidence again, such as it is. What did you think about her before she died?"

Mr. Wilson drew a deep breath. "Of course, no one wants to say anything critical about a person who has died a tragic death. She was a talented singer, an adequate actress, and an uninterested history student."

Sister Thomas plunged on. Murder investigators couldn't be too sensitive about feelings. "Did she talk in your classes?"

"Yes, but not more than several other students."

"Did you think she was likeable?"

He looked pained. "She wasn't one of my favorite students, but she was an ordinary teenage girl. Pleasant at times and not so pleasant at other times."

"Were you surprised that she was murdered?" She asked though there was only one possible answer.

'Mr. Wilson jerked back in his chair and stared at her. "Of course. I was astonished that a student could be killed at St. Agatha's."

Sister Thomas looked him in the eye. "Did you attend the school's anniversary celebration in the auditorium?" She knew he had, but she thought questions should be asked in that order. She had made a list of them the night before and memorized it.

Mr. Wilson returned her look without flinching. "Yes, I directed the singing. Mary Louise was the lead singer. I hope you find the murderer, though it's been a long time. I would do anything I can to help you."

She cringed inwardly at interrogating a person she had always trusted, but she pushed on. "What did you do after the singing?"

"I picked up a piece of cake, then left for my next class."

"Were you one of the first people to leave the auditorium?"

"I waited until most of the girls had gotten their cake before I took mine. I carried it to the classroom."

"Which classroom?" Sister Thomas asked, though she knew the answer. She was pleased that he seemed to be what the police call a cooperative witness.

"I think it was the third room on the upper floor of the Immaculate Heart building. I was teaching the senior European History class."

"Did you go there immediately? When did you arrive?"

"Yes, I went straight to the classroom. I arrived about ten minutes before the class was due to start. I sat down and ate my cake."

"Were any of the students there?" Even though she didn't think he could be the murderer, she wanted to determine whether his testimony could be corroborated. Fortunately, his memory seemed as acute as her own.

"Three girls came in about two minutes after I did. Charlotte Crane, Margie Panzarella, and another girl whose name I don't remember. A redhead. They also had brought their cake to their desks."

"How did you learn that something had happened?"

"I was teaching about the French Revolution. The class had gone on for about forty minutes when you knocked on the door. I went to the door and saw you. You beckoned me into the hall. Your face looked distraught, and your voice shook. You told me that something awful had happened and that the police were going around from classroom to classroom. You said I should keep my students where they were until the police came to interview them. Then you left."

"What did you do then?" Sister Thomas repressed her own pain at the memory.

The history teacher's face and shoulders sagged. "I was stunned. I wondered what could have happened that was serious enough for you to call the police. One of the girls must have been injured. I tried to hide my concern and told the class we were going to continue learning about the French Revolution beyond the time when the class period usually ended."

"When did the police come to your classroom?"

"About half an hour later. That was when I learned that Mary Louise had been murdered." He paused and put his hand to his forehead. "The girls were upset, naturally. Some of them cried. I told them that crying was normal, that we were all in shock.

"After the police left, I asked the girls whether they would like to pray for Mary Louise. We prayed aloud. That calmed them a little."

"That was a good move. Thank you." Sister Thomas remembered that not all the nuns had said they had led their students in prayers for Mary Louise. How strange. "Please continue."

"About half an hour later, the police questioned me individually. I told them what I had done that day."

"Did you suspect anyone of being the killer?"

He shook his head. "I would have said something if I had. I didn't have any idea. I couldn't imagine anyone at St. Agatha's committing a murder."

"On thinking about it later, have you had any guesses about who might have done it?"

"I could only imagine that it must have been someone from outside the school, though I didn't see how he could have gone to the auditorium and then escaped."

Sister Thomas also puzzled at the mystery. "I have always feared that some of the girls might have been damaged by the horror. Did you notice any girls who might have suffered particularly?"

The history teacher nodded. "Many of them were sad and upset, especially the juniors. They were taking my American history class. But I remember one girl in particular. Maureen Collins was a creative girl who wrote well and cared about history. She had always been rather quiet, but after that I think she seemed depressed and sometimes jumpy. Not an unusual reaction for a sensitive girl."

Sister Thomas returned his nod. "That's the very girl I was thinking about. I should have done more for her. She has entered the convent, but not our order." She wondered whether talking to Maureen might give her a clue. Could Maureen have seen or heard something suspicious? But if she had, why wouldn't she have said anything?

"Thank you, Mr. Wilson." Sister Thomas smiled and rose from her chair. "It was kind of you to agree to be questioned again. I found it difficult to question you without sounding as if I suspected you."

"I want to do anything I can to help, Sister Thomas." He also stood up. "I hope the murderer can finally be brought to justice. As a teacher at the school, I feel responsible, even though I don't know how I could have done anything to prevent it. Should I have patrolled the grounds between classes because I was the only male teacher?"

"We all feel responsible. I most of all. I could have patrolled." She smiled again to lighten the mood. "I am probably more frightening than you are, at least to the girls and the faculty."

"It's good that you're revisiting the crime."

"I'm called Sister Doubting Thomas for a reason. You must have heard that nickname."

He barely suppressed a grin. "Once or twice."

She knew he probably had heard it dozens of times.

Sister Thomas hadn't suspected the history and music teacher, but she had hoped that he might provide a clue.

"I think it's time for your next class."

"Yes, sister. I'm sorry I couldn't be more helpful."

"If you knew anything significant, you would have spoken about it years ago. It was pleasant talking to you again." She extended her hand, and he shook it.

The lay teacher inclined his head. "I hope you'll visit the school again soon, sister, for a happier reason."

Jonathan Wilson left the auditorium.

Now if this were a mystery novel, Sister Thomas thought, she would have found his pleasant manner suspicious. But it wasn't a mystery novel, and she didn't.

Sister Thomas went over her own schedule on the day of the murder.

She had been one of the first people to leave the auditorium so she could get back to work. Like Mr. Wilson, she had carried her cake with her. She had made a mental note to ask the sister who ordered cakes to request chocolate the next time.

When she had returned to her office, she had listened to her phone messages. She had sent Alfredo, the gardener who had been a mechanic and knew something about cars, to look for a new van for the convent. He had called from the car dealership and asked her to return his call.

When she reached him on the dealer's phone line, Alfredo said he had found a couple of suitable vans, one used and one new. She told him she valued his judgement and would meet him at the dealership in an hour to look at the vans he had selected.

She went over her budget to make sure the school could afford a new van.

Sister Luke, the biology and chemistry teacher and the youngest nun at St. Agatha's, burst into her office. The young nun sobbed hysterically.

"Murder! Come quick, Sister Thomas! Call the police! A girl has been murdered."

Sister Thomas remembered freezing for a moment. "Surely not," she had said.

"It's true! In the auditorium! It's horrible!"

Sister Thomas had leapt from her desk and followed the weeping nun to the auditorium.

What she saw there still brought tears to her eyes. The body of a girl in St. Agatha's navy-blue uniform was lying crumpled on the floor, with the knife that had been used to cut the cake stuck in her chest. Blood oozed over her body.

Sister Thomas had stared for a moment and made the sign of the cross over the poor girl's body. Then, after telling Sister Luke to gather up her courage and stay with Mary Louise's body, she ran back to her office and called the police. Immediately afterwards she called a priest to pray over Mary Louise's body. All the while she prayed God to take Mary Louise to heaven right away. After what the girl had been through, she shouldn't have to spend time in Purgatory.

Sister Thomas had braced herself to phone the girl's parents. She could still remember Mrs. McKenna's screams and sobs.

Taking a deep breath, Sister Thomas returned to the present day.

She found it interesting that Jonathan Wilson had prayed with his students but not all the nuns had said they had done so.

She looked back at her old notes from the time of the murder and made a list of the sisters who had told her they prayed with their classes for Mary Louise's soul.

Sister Bartholomew, Sister Jeanne d'Arc, and Sister Anthony of Padua. Neither Sister Veronica nor Sister Ignatius of Loyola had said anything about praying with their classes. How odd. Probably they forgot to mention it in their interviews.

CHAPTER 39

Sister Matthew

ID I DARE TO time travel? I tried because I hoped to meet Rose in a private place.

I found myself sitting on a cushion on the floor of the grubbiest room I had ever seen. Nine other women sat in a circle, most of them also on cushions, and three sat on rickety chairs. They all wore jeans and plaid shirts or t-shirts. I also wore jeans and a t-shirt with a picture of Gertrude Stein on it. I had gained weight. If this were a time travel, did it mean that when I was older I wouldn't still be in the convent?

One woman's t-shirt said, "Lavender Jane." Another proclaimed, "A woman without a man is like a fish without a bicycle."

That slogan thrilled me, but the moldy carpet didn't, and neither did the faded walls or the cracks in the ceiling. Unframed posters were taped to those walls. One showed a woman in a blue shirt with her hair in a kerchief. She raised one of her hands in a fist and the words "We Can Do It!" came out of her mouth. We can do what? Anything we want? Another poster showed a woman with a broom and the words "Fuck Housework." The verb shocked me, but I agreed with the sentiment. What appealing though shabby icons those posters were.

235

The women were all in their 20s or their 30s. Several of them smoked cigarettes. Some held bottles of beer. A bottle of orange soda, not Bireley's but something called Orangina, sat beside me.

"Now it's time for criticism-self-criticism," said a pretty, dark-haired woman with a serious expression. "I criticize myself for arriving late to the meeting."

"I criticize myself for failing to make enough fliers for the demonstration," said a tall, thin woman with a cigarette.

"Your turn, Maureen," she added.

"I don't believe this. This self-abnegation is just like nuns confessing their faults in a chapter meeting in a convent," I complained.

Several women started talking at once in angry tones.

"It's nothing of the kind," the dark-haired woman snapped. "You know we got the practice of criticism-self-criticism from the Chinese Communists."

She wasn't speaking ironically. A perfect model, no doubt, I thought.

"Oh wow," I said.

I returned to my cell. Where on earth had I been? Could this have been the future? "Oh wow?" What sense did that make?

Thank goodness they didn't kiss the disgusting carpet.

If this were my future, where was Rose?

At least this time travel, if it had been that, suggested I had a future. And it wouldn't be in prison, at least not in the time I visited.

Or was this trip just a delusion, or a fiction like the Lancelot travel?

Why were these people trying to imitate Chinese Communists? Were the Chinese Communist meetings that much like a chapter meeting?

What on earth was the place where I had been, and why was I there? Could this be my future, or only a possible future? Did this mean I would leave the convent? Would Rose leave too?

The best part was that there hadn't been a murder.

As I left the refectory after lunch, Mean Mother Michael approached me. "You need to go to the visitors' parlor, Sister Matthew. You have a visitor."

I couldn't have been more astonished if she had said she saw a giraffe running around the garden. We never had visitors except during official visiting days. "A visitor, Mother Michael?"

"Your visitor is a sister from the Congregation of St. Agatha. That is why we are permitting the visit, though I cannot imagine why she says she needs to see you." The Mistress of Novices eyed me suspiciously.

I almost fell over. Possible God, please let it not be Sister Veronica!

"Don't keep her waiting," Mother Michael admonished me.

I staggered to the visitors' parlor. There, to my relief, stood Sister Thomas the Apostle, the principal of my old high school. She looked thinner than ever. She wore thicker glasses than she had during my high school years. By now she must be at least fifty. I still felt anxious, but not petrified.

"Good day, Sister Matthew. I am so pleased that you have entered the religious life," Sister Doubting Thomas said, smiling.

Surely she didn't come to our Mother House to tell me that.

"Thank you, Sister Thomas," I managed to say. "Please be seated."

We both sat in wooden chairs with cloth seats.

"I hope your novitiate is going well."

"Yes, Sister Thomas." Was I lying to her?

"I am surprised and pleased that the Mistress of Novices allowed me to see you alone, as I requested, without the presence of another religious of this congregation. But would you like to have another member of your order present?"

Why did she request that she see me alone? That frightened me even more. I bit my lip. Who knows what she would disclose? "No, thank you, Sister Thomas."

"Do you know yet whether you will be sent to graduate school?" She sounded as if she cared.

"Not yet, Sister Thomas." Did she think I should be in graduate school, or in prison?

"I hope the order will send you. You were one of our best students, especially in English. I still remember your essay on *Romeo and Juliet* saying that the Nurse and Friar Lawrence deserved severe punishment for concealing the marriage."

"Thank you, Sister Thomas." Oh dear, she mentioned punishment. Will she next mention crime? I tried to maintain a calm face.

"I am no longer principal of St. Agatha's. I now am the deputy to our new Mother Superior, Reverend Mother Cecilia, which is a signal honor. I would like to ask you some questions about your time in our high school."

I shivered. Would these questions be about Mary Louise? Had Sister Veronica told the other nuns that I was guilty?

I struggled to make my voice sound normal. "Of course, Sister Thomas."

"I hope that, on the whole, your high school years were pleasant," she said, smiling at me.

"Yes, Sister Thomas." That question I could answer honestly. "I was very fond of St. Agatha's."

"I am glad you were." She paused. "Were there any unpleasant incidents? Other than the terrible death of your classmate, that is."

"No, Sister Thomas." My voice began to falter. The nuns really were Agatha Christies.

"Such a dreadful experience for your whole class." She gave me a sympathetic look. "I worried that all of you would be traumatized for years. I was so glad I had a chance to teach you when you were seniors to see how you were doing and try to give you a good senior year."

"Thank you, Sister Thomas." I had enjoyed her class, but now I wondered whether she had suspected me then. I don't think she had acted as if she did.

"Is there anything you would like to say about Mary Louise's death that you didn't think to tell anyone at the time? Did something about it particularly disturb you?"

I couldn't control my shaking. "No, Sister Thomas." She couldn't possibly believe me. I was acting like Raskolnikov in *Crime and Punishment*. Innocent people should be calmer.

"I am glad to hear that, Sister Matthew. Please don't be overly concerned about my questions. If you think of anything you would like to tell me, please let me know."

Not without a lawyer. Since when did the police send nuns to do their work? "Yes, Sister Thomas." My head spun. I felt as if I would faint.

"Thank you so much for answering my questions, Sister Matthew. I won't detain you any longer." She smiled again, but I didn't trust the smile. "I hope you will become a professed religious. It is a wonderful life."

"Thank you, Sister Thomas."

She rose and left the room.

I could barely stand and accompany her to the front door. Was she suggesting that if I stayed in the convent, they wouldn't refer me to the police?

I went to the chapel. It was time for recreation, but I thought it would be permissible for me to go to the chapel instead.

Please, Possible God, I prayed, burying my head in my hands. I didn't kill Mary Louise, did I? I don't remember doing it, but why can't I remember what happened at that time and why does the memory of that day frighten me so much? Please, dear Possible God, help me to lead a good life. And help me stay out of prison.

I didn't even know whether I was a murderer. Was I insane? If I killed Mary Louise, I would be unworthy to belong to the Euphrosnyes. Worse, I would certainly not be worthy of Rose's love.

Should I ask Reverend Mother Robert Bellarmine to send me to a psychiatrist? What a crazy idea. The Church doesn't believe in psychiatry.

I should tell Rose and risk losing her love, but I can't bring myself to do it.

Were the Agatha Christies closing in on me? Would Detective Johnson be my next visitor?

Should I run away? Nun on the Run. That would make a catchy title for a movie.

I could just walk away from the convent while all the other sisters were in the chapel. I could steal the suit I had worn when I entered because I knew the closet where those old clothes were kept, and put the suit on under my habit. I could walk to the tiny hamlet nearest the convent and beg for a little money. The hamlet's denizens were not accustomed to seeing nuns beg, but some would likely give me a little cash. Then I would walk to a bus station and take a bus to the nearest river. I would stroll along the river, then go behind a tree, strip off my habit, and toss it into the roiling waters. If it washed up, so much the better.

Then I would return to the local bus stop and ride to a Greyhound Station, from which I would travel west and lose myself in Chicago. I know no one there.

My parents would be grieved at my disappearance, but perhaps they would think it no worse than my being arrested for murder. Or perhaps they would send me money if I wrote to them secretly. No, I should ask my brother. John wouldn't want the disgrace of having his sister tried for murder. That might hurt his career. What about Dad's career? Probably he was too well-established to be damaged.

Dad and Mom would miss me, but they already didn't see me very often. Rose? How shocked she would be to learn that she had loved a killer. I didn't want to see her pain if I were charged.

What would I do in Chicago? Get a secretarial job, if I could, and try to save enough money for grad school. But wouldn't applying to grad school be a dead giveaway?

What would I do for identification? Purchase a fake I.D. from a gangster? Weren't there plenty of gangsters in Chicago?

Settle down, Nun on the Run. You aren't really going to run away.

How could I know what to do when I wasn't certain whether I had killed Mary Louise?

I COULDN'T SLEEP THAT night. Did I have blood on my hands? I wanted to wash them again and again like Lady Macbeth. But I didn't remember seeing any blood. My last memory of Mary Louise was of her waiting in the auditorium as if she were going to meet someone. I longed to go back to that time and scream at her, "Come back to the classroom with us, Mary Louise. Don't stay in the auditorium."

Is that why I had time traveled to see Anne Boleyn, whom I was unable to warn?

Could I time travel back to the time before Mary Louise died, and prevent it?

After midnight, I traveled. I stood back in the auditorium. Mary Louise ate the last piece of cake. She had waited for everyone else to finish. Good for her. I had eaten mine as soon as I could and congratulated myself on getting a corner piece with extra frosting. It had tasted delicious, though I preferred chocolate cake to yellow cake.

No one had killed her yet. Could I prevent her possible death, and spare myself fear and guilt?

"I saw you eat an extra piece, Polka Dot Pimples. You're gaining weight." Mary Louise gloated at my flaming cheeks.

"Several other girls ate second pieces too. There was enough left over."
Oh darn, my mouth wouldn't let me add a warning to the words I had
said that day.

"You don't care if you never get a date." She smirked. "I can guess why."

I shook with anger. "You don't know anything about me," was all I
managed to say.

"More than you think, Dot."

Imagining picking up the knife, I turned away from her and joined
the others leaving the auditorium.

But my pace was slow.

I hesitated, then turned back.

I thought I saw a shadow approaching Mary Louise.

I landed back in my alcove, just at the crucial moment. I stifled a
scream unsuited to my convent bed.

Tears of frustration spilled from my eyes.

I tossed and turned. If I couldn't return to the scene of the crime,
I must try to remember every detail. I tried to remember picking up a
knife with the intent to stab. I recoiled. I couldn't imagine doing that.
I remembered only thinking, "I wish I could cut Mary Louise with
that knife." But picking up a knife and threatening her? No. I didn't
even remember visualizing that, just thinking the words.

I must think logically, like a detective. A knife was not like a gun.
I couldn't imagine stabbing anyone with a knife. To kill her, I would
have had to drive it in forcefully while she struggled. Could I have
done that? I shuddered. I couldn't picture such a struggle. I hadn't
been that angry. I had never been that angry with anyone.

If I had done it, wouldn't I have been covered with blood?

Or was I deceiving myself?

CHAPTER 40

Sister Matthew

I LONGED TO RETURN TO my bedroom with Rose. Or indeed anyplace where Rose and I could make love, even though I was unworthy of her. Although the possibility of traveling back to my high school terrified me, I kept trying time travel in the hope that I would find her in another world to do what we could not do in the convent. I was often disappointed. Some time travels disturbed me, others fascinated me, but none held Rose. For weeks, I traveled alone.

One night, after lights out in the convent dormitory, I found myself on a deserted coast. I am not sure whether I should call it a beach, because it looked unlike any I had ever seen. I was used to the sandy beach at Rehoboth, Delaware, where my parents had taken me on vacations. Now I stood on a cliff high above the ocean. Twisted pines sprouted from the rocks. The sun shone, but a wind whipped through my hair. I wished for a sweater, but my clothes were light. I laughed at myself for imagining I was a fragile flower. I spread out my arms and welcomed the wind.

Swallows flew through the wind like, well, swallows. "Bird thou never wert?" No, wert. Wonderfully birdy. I wished I could fly like them.

Someone scrambled up the rocks to join me. No, I wanted to be alone.

I didn't. The climber's face was Rose's.

"This is Maine," she said. She wore slacks and shirt similar to the ones I wore. "Acadia National Park. I'm eager to show it to you."

"It's beautiful." I wanted to say something less predictable. "'Inebriate of air am I, debauchee of dew.' That's one of my favorite lines from Emily Dickinson."

Rose's face shone with delight. "'Inebriate of air, debauchee of dew.' I'm inebriated with you."

She pulled me to her and kissed me. It had been so long since we had embraced. We kissed softly, then gradually built up the intensity of our kisses.

We found a smooth rock to lie on.

I took off her shirt and stroked her breasts. She slipped off mine and the air touched them. Then Rose's tongue did. I moaned with delight.

We held each other close, pressing our bodies together.

Before I entered the convent, I had read of a way to love that I longed to do with her.

I undid her slacks and slipped them off, using them as a blanket for her to lie on. I parted her legs and touched her softest parts. I touched her with my hands, then with my tongue.

Her exclamations drove me wild. I became a debauchee of her dew.

When she had come, we both cried with delight. I don't know who was more thrilled.

Then she drank from me. There was no sensation like it in the world.

"Please rose me. Rose me and rose me and rose me," I murmured.

"Please Mattie me, Mattie me, and Mattie me," she murmured back.

We were fused. I held onto her as tightly as I could. I wished we would never leave this world.

But we did.

Lying alone in my narrow bed, I wept at parting from her. Holding her hand under the curtain seemed so inadequate.

AFTER SUCH BLISS, HOW could our distant relationship in the convent ever be enough?

I dreamed of walking with Rose and talking whenever we chose, of telling each other everything. Almost everything. I dreamed of taking long vacations with her. And yes, I dreamed of living with her in a home of our own. I had never wanted my own house or apartment before. I had thought focusing on such material things was insipid. But now I could picture cooking with her in a small kitchen, eating our meals together at a small table where we could talk freely, and studying together, exclaiming over the most interesting passages in our books.

These thoughts interrupted my prayers and added color to our silent meals and subdued recreation hours. They soothed me when I tried to get to sleep.

When Rose held my hand under the curtain, I imagined sleeping beside her.

Her smiles warmed me more than ever. A Rosy light bathed the convent.

I strained to pick out her voice when we sang our hymns. I strove not to stare at her, but to hold her face always in my heart, the way I had tried to hold Jesus and Mary forever in my heart when I was little. Keeping Rose in my heart was far easier.

A consciousness of Rose's presence made my heart dance. The music of Rose's voice floated through my mind.

I lived in a state of joy. Was that how the most pious nuns felt about God?

I longed for more time travel lovemaking. Yet delight so filled me that I could be content without it until Rose chose a time.

Rose and I were finally assigned to work in the garden at the same time again. I watched her plant tulip and daffodil bulbs in preparation for the spring. I brought her cardboard boxes of bulbs while she dug holes in the soft soil, and I handed her the bulbs one by one. A white butterfly, late for the season, flew over her head.

The mockingbird made a racket from a nearby tree, though most other birds had fallen silent this late in the year.

"Have you ever thought of having a garden of our own?" My voice shook at my audacity.

Rose dropped her trowel. "What do you mean?" She didn't look at me.

"I want us to leave here and live alone together in a home of our own. We could still go to Mass every day if you want and work in groups that help other people."

"Oh, Mattie," she choked. "I didn't know you were dreaming of that. I can't leave the convent. I love it here."

My heart sank, but I tried to rally. "I know you do. There are many good things here. But as soon as we take our vows, Reverend Mother could assign us to live in different places. Even if we're allowed to go to graduate school in the same place, we would most likely be assigned to teach in different schools afterwards. That would be terrible."

Rose raised her head and looked into my eyes. "I know. I worry about that too. It would be awful to be assigned to different places. But we probably could still meet in time travels."

Rocks piled on my chest. "You would let them part us? How often would we be able to time travel? Time travels aren't enough." Maybe time travel is an escape that becomes an addiction, I thought but didn't say.

Rose bit her lip. "It's different for you. You don't really want to be a nun. But I do. This is my vocation. Living in the convent gives me peace."

"Going to live with me would shatter your peace?"

"Yes." Rose took a deep breath. "I want to live inside a life of prayer. If you felt the same, you would understand."

For the first time, I felt I hated the religion. "Don't you think some people outside the convent live a life of prayer?"

"Yes, but it would be much harder." She stood. "I do love you more than anyone else, but I love our community here too. This is my home, and these women are my family. If our love makes you discontented, perhaps we should end our relationship now."

"Rose! You really mean that." I trembled. I had gambled that she loved me more than the convent, and I had lost. "I don't want to take you away from the place you love. We can leave things as they are. Please don't stop loving me or meeting with me. I couldn't bear it if you avoided me."

"I don't want to avoid you, but it might be best." Rose twisted her hands in the black rosary beads that hung from her belt.

"No, it wouldn't. I'll cope with being sent to different places, but I can't stop loving you."

"I didn't say that I don't love you. I just don't want to hurt you. I don't want to lead you to believe that I'll leave the convent."

"If you're so happy with your life here, why do you need time travel to escape it?" Shocked at my own daring, I moved my hand to my mouth. Would Rose hate me for saying those words?

She jerked back and stared at me. "That's the thanks I get for introducing you to time traveling?"

"I'm sooo sorry," I stammered. "I shouldn't have said that."

Rose sighed. "I see you're in pain. I don't want to hurt you any more than I already have."

"I understand." I shivered.

"Perhaps if you left the convent you could find a woman who would live with you the way you want."

I let out a strangled cry. "No. I don't want any other woman. I don't want anyone but you." With great effort, I held back tears. "I can't keep on planting bulbs as if nothing had happened. I need to walk across the garden."

"Please do whatever will make you feel better. I'll finish the planting." Rose resumed squatting, picked up a bulb, and put it in a hole she had dug.

The mockingbird still sang. I wanted it to shut up.

ROSE ACTED NOTICEABLY LESS warm after that dreadful conversation. She still spoke to me sometimes, but only a few mundane words and her eyes didn't flash with love. I did not try to have personal conversations with her.

I walked like a robot. I could scarcely eat. The world had lost its flavor.

I hoped Rose would someday show a little more warmth to me.

Possible God, I begged, help me to be a woman that Rose could love at least as a friend. Help me to grow in grace so that I can love the convent even when she does not want to be with me. But I knew my words were futile because I didn't believe even in Possible God.

MY DREAMS WERE DESCENTS into hell. At least they wavered so much that I knew they were dreams, not time travel.

I saw Mary Louise, still sixteen years old, looming up in the cloister.

Mary Louise shrieked like a banshee. "I'll get you, Polka Dot Pimples! I'll drive you crazy. Nobody ever loved you. Nobody ever could love an insect like you."

"Go haunt whoever really killed you," I choked.

She lunged at me. "You! You killed me!"

I stumbled backwards and fell. "No, no, I didn't."

Mary Louise vanished, but Rose appeared in her place.

"I can't love a killer," she moaned. "Stay away from me."

"Rose! I'm not a killer! Please stay."

Rose faded.

I woke in tears.

Night after night, the dream returned, with only minor variations.

"You're a nun!" Mary Louise would scream. "What a joke! A murderer is a nun."

I was almost ready to tell my confessor, but not quite.

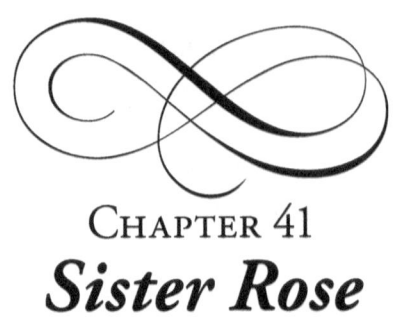

CHAPTER 41

Sister Rose

ROSE FORCED HERSELF TO maintain a calm countenance though she ached as if she had cut off an arm. *How selfish I have been to let Mattie love me so much*, she told herself. No, she should think of Mattie as "Sister Matthew" as a way of giving up their relationship.

Rose had known that Sister Matthew was unhappy with many aspects of convent life. Now she realized Sister Matthew stayed there only because of their love.

Yet Sister Matthew might find that she loved the convent for itself, not just because of her. A woman who cared so much about Emily Dickinson's work must have a spirituality of her own, even if it was an unorthodox one.

Being cooler to the woman she loved pained Rose, especially because she knew it hurt Sister Matthew even more. But perhaps it was better to wound her now than after they had taken vows and were sent to different convents. Perhaps it had been wrong to let Sister Matthew fall so deeply in love with her that living apart would be excruciating.

She must not gloss over the fact that she had injured Sister Matthew badly. Was she selfish for loving the convent more than she loved Sister Matthew? Why had she let herself make love with Sister Matthew without thinking more about the possibility of hurting her?

Rose prayed for guidance.

Was it true that time traveling, which had begun as an escape from her mother, had become an escape from the convent? Did it add to her life as a religious, or detract from it?

Maybe loving Sister Matthew might be an escape from the convent.

Rose thought of her mother crashing into a lamppost. Her mother had been so alone. Why hadn't she done more for her mother? She didn't deserve Mat...Sister Matthew's love.

The memory of her mother made Rose withdraw into herself. Had she escaped one woman who wanted to keep her all to herself to fall in love with another woman who asked her to give up everything?

The thought of never seeing the other sisters again brought tears to her eyes. The thought of never praying again in the convent's chapel made her catch her breath. The worst thought was having to get some dull job among people who talked about trivia and living in a world where she was expected to be attracted to men. And what if Mattie ever left her? Then she would be stranded alone in that world.

The sacrifice that Sister Matthew asked of her was too great. No matter what Sister Matthew said, she would always want them to leave, especially if they were assigned to teach in different schools.

How friendly should she be to Sister Matthew? Rose feared to smile too much. If she smiled, that might encourage Sister Matthew in false hopes.

Rose wept into her pillow at night. She vowed never to break anyone else's heart. She must never love anyone else the way she had loved Sister Matthew. Being a celibate nun had to be enough for her. It was enough for most of her sisters, so why not for her?

She must steel herself against the pain of seeing Sister Matthew. She must try not to look at Sister Matthew.

But she hoped Sister Matthew would stay in the convent. Perhaps they could be friends someday, at least when they were old nuns. Perhaps then they would no longer burn with desire as she still burned.

She longed to kiss Sister Matthew's lips, and her breasts, and to feel her tongue...she must stop thinking about their lovemaking.

Many nuns through the ages must have had similar troubles. Many nuns must have learned not to desire another woman and to hold back their love for another woman.

If the Church reformed, would it be possible for nuns to love one another without making it such a secret? For any women to love each other openly? At least, could future nuns have particular friends? Rose prayed for that kind of reform.

That faint hope did not help her now. Rose groaned to herself again and again. *How could she ask me to leave the convent? I miss her so.*

One day when Sister Matthew passed her in the cloister, she pressed a note into Rose's hand.

Rose frowned. She resented being handed a message. Sending a note was such a risk.

She didn't open the scrap of paper until she went to her alcove at night.

"Words by Emily Dickinson," Sister Matthew had scrawled.

"'Nature and God—I neither knew
Yet Both so well knew me...'"
But, Dickinson wrote, both kept her secret secure.

The words jolted Rose, as so many of Emily's poems did. Nature and God—her passions. Were they the same?

God and Nature—but the poem said Nature and God, why in that order?—her Two (or One) inspiration(s). Would pursuing Nature be pursuing God? Yes, They knew and would keep her secret. So would Sister Matthew. But writing a note was too indiscreet. Rose decided not to acknowledge receiving it.

Rose memorized the words of the note, then ate it. She wondered whether that might be a kind of communion.

After several nights, she heard a rustle and knew Sister Matthew had summoned up the courage to reach under the curtain for her.

Tears formed in Rose's eyes, but she did not reach down to hold Sister Matthew's hand.

CHAPTER 42

Sister Matthew

THE DARK NIGHT OF the soul descended on me. Nothing could bring back Rose.

Possible God, what can I do? I'm stumbling through the day. Every minute feels like an hour, a miserable hour.

I need someone to confide in, at least about my nightmares. I don't much want to talk to Father Nolan, but he's the only one who is required to keep whatever I say secret.

I knelt in the pew for my weekly Confession. My eyes were fixed on the altar ahead. No other novices had the dilemmas I faced. I watched their innocent forms enter and leave the confessional one by one.

When it was my turn, I walked into the confessional and closed my eyes. Even the darkened confessional box did not feel dark enough for me. "Bless me, father, for I have sinned. When I was in high school, I was so angry at another girl who was mean to me that I thought I wanted her to die." I stammered. "Then she was murdered. The memory still haunts me, especially at night."

"Have you never confessed this sin before?"

"Yes, I have."

"Then you have had absolution. You should not brood on the past."

"But I have nightmares about it. She screams at me and accuses me of murdering her."

"Pray before you go to bed and ask Our Lord to help you to resist these nightmares. Don't believe in them. You have a morbid fascination with this poor girl's death. Pray to put it aside and think of Our Lord and the saints."

"Thank you, father." Trembling, I plunged on. "But there's more. The police never solved the murder. I wonder whether I really might have killed her, though I don't remember it."

His voice harshened. "Stop this nonsense right now, sister. The police investigated this killing. They would have arrested you if you were guilty. It's incredible that a high school girl would commit a murder. These thoughts are a kind of sickness. Don't indulge in them. You must be neglecting your prayers or not praying deeply enough. Your life is supposed to be dedicated to God, not ugly fantasies."

"Yes, father." What else could I say? I couldn't bring myself to tell him that Sister Veronica had accused me of murdering Mary Louise.

"For your penance, meditate on the joyous occasions in the life of the Blessed Virgin Mary. Recite the Magnificat. Force yourself to concentrate on the goodness in life and reject the evil and ugly."

"Yes, father. Thank you, father." I never realized he could be so profound. I chided myself for underestimating him. But I couldn't tell him I had lost the best thing in my life. I loved another sister and she had rejected me.

He would have scolded me far more harshly. And I didn't trust the seal of the confessional that much. Would he drop some hint to Reverend Mother? Or would he demand that I confess to her and refuse to give me absolution for my sins—which to my mind didn't include loving Rose—unless I confessed to my convent superiors? I refused to give him that much power over me.

As I left the confessional, I prayed the Magnificat, supposedly Mary's prayer after the Angel Gabriel had appeared to her. "My soul magnifies the Lord and my spirit rejoices in God my Savior, because he hath regarded the lowliness of his handmaiden...." No, I was not worthy to pray those words. Perhaps Rose would be.

I wanted a punishment, not a blessing.

THERE WAS ONE CERTAIN place I could go for punishment.

In the next chapter meeting, I knelt before my sisters and said, "Dear Reverend Mother, Mistress of Novices, and my dear sisters, I have been brooding about a dreadful incident that happened when I was in high school. I have nightmares about it and wake to worry about it. I am not sure how much I sinned then. I think about that when I should be praying."

Reverend Mother frowned. Mean Mother Michael frowned deeper.

"You are living in the convent in a state of grace," Reverend Mother admonished me. "You have put aside your past life. You must put it aside completely. Hanging on to bad memories is just as much a rejection of God's grace as hanging on to pleasant memories. No matter what you dream, you must not dwell on the past in your conscious life. For your penance, reread the *Lives of the Saints* and think about them, not your own life."

I kissed the floor. Was I worthy to kiss the convent's floor?

Later that day, the Mistress of Novices drew me aside. "What a self-indulgent supposed confession." She looked at me as if I were a bug on the path. "Don't confess your dreams again."

"Yes, Mother Michael. I won't."

Had I hoped for her punishment?

THAT NIGHT IN MY *dreams, Mary Louise screeched at me. "Stupid Dot! Stupid Blot! Murderer! Pretend confessions won't save you. You hated me and I hate you. The stain will never leave your soul. I'll haunt you forever!"*

I shrank into a ball. "I didn't do it," I whimpered.

Sister Veronica loomed behind her. "I know you did it. I won't keep silent forever. When you least expect it, your murder will be revealed."

SWEET MOTHER GABRIEL APPROACHED me as I walked to the parlor for recreation.

"You look troubled, Sister Matthew. Would you like to pray with me in the chapel?"

Tears formed in my eyes. "Yes, thank you, Mother Gabriel." I wished she were the Mistress of Novices as well as the Mistress of Postulants. At least there was one nun in the convent who reached out to help me, though she was no longer my superior and didn't ask me what troubled me.

I didn't want to tell her anyway.

We went to the chapel, knelt beside each other, and prayed. At least Mother Gabriel must have prayed. I'm not sure my thoughts could be described as prayer. Her presence comforted me for half an hour and almost made me believe in Possible God. She would have prayed beside me even if she knew I were a murderer.

IN TIME TRAVELS, I searched for Rose. The thing with feathers still perched in my soul.

The mountains where we first kissed were filled with wildflowers but empty of Rose. I found no joy there.

My old bedroom looked the same as usual, but there was no Rose. I threw myself on the bed and wept. At least I could sob louder there than I could in my convent bed.

I found myself back on the Maine coast, where we had made love. I waited there. Perhaps Rose would come to be with me, at least to talk. The ocean's salty smell reminded me of our lovemaking. Even that remembered scent hurt me.

The wind howled like a hundred wolves. The waves thrashed as if they longed to devour the land. The rocks jutted like the walls of hell.

"Rose! Rose!" I cried into the wind. The wind swallowed my words.

Then the wind ceased, and the ocean calmed. Sunlight illuminated the land.

I waited. There was still no Rose. Being alone in the tranquil beauty tormented me even more than the storm had.

"Rose! Rose!" I called, again and again.

Alone. I was alone.

BACK IN THE CONVENT, I tried not to look at Rose. But it was so hard not to attempt a glimpse at chapel, in the hall, in the cloister, in the refectory, in the parlor. I couldn't stop watching her, much more than I had when we were together. Why be cautious? She didn't return my looks, so they couldn't compromise her. I didn't speak to her, and she didn't speak to me but stolen looks at her warmed my heart. And wore it raw.

I TRIED TO TAKE refuge in prayer. I prayed to understand at a deeper level that I was only one sad person in a universe of people who faced greater suffering than mine. People imprisoned for their religious or political beliefs, starving people, parents whose children had died, people who were denied the right to vote in my own country.

If I were a truly spiritual person—let's face it, a truly good person—I wouldn't think so much about my own pain.

Maybe if I were out in the world, doing more to help people, I would be better able to live with pain than I am while staying in the convent and spending so much time in silence.

But I didn't want to leave. The thought of never seeing Rose again was more than I could face.

I DREAMED I KNELT in a chapter meeting, but I didn't remember walking in.

"Dear Reverend Mother, Mistress of Nov—"

"Stop this charade," Mean Mother Michael demanded, glaring at me.

Sister Veronica loomed beside her. "Murderer!" She shrieked. "You murdered a sixteen-year-old girl, your classmate. You don't deserve to wear a habit."

"No! I didn't!" I cried.

"Murderer!" Sister Veronica advanced on me.

Sister Thomas moved behind her. "You injured our school, and now you pollute this order."

Detective Johnson and Officer Moriarty appeared behind her. "Arrest her!" Moriarty produced handcuffs.

"Wait," Reverend Mother commanded. "You must not arrest a sister of our order."

Would she rescue me?

She pointed at me. "You are expelled from our order."

"No, no, please listen to me," I begged.

"Take off your habit," Mean Mother Michael yelled. She stormed down and began to tear off my clothes. Sister Veronica joined her, slashing me with her fingernails as she tore.

I woke. Shaking, I wept. Would this nightmare come to pass?

Maybe I should kill myself.

I heard Possible God saying, "Don't even think of that. Don't be an idiot." Her voice sounded like my mother's.

CHAPTER 43

Sister Thomas

S ISTER THOMAS THE INQUISITOR went again to visit the convent adjacent to St. Agatha's High School. The drive from the order's Mother House near Baltimore where she now lived took less than an hour.

She made no appointments in advance. Before evening prayers, she called aside Sister Ignatius, a stern-faced nun in her forties who taught algebra and geometry.

"Please come to the parlor and speak with me," Sister Thomas said, trying to sound as casual as it was possible for the Reverend Mother's deputy to sound.

Sister Ignatius seldom smiled, and she didn't smile now. Her face was a perpetual map of resignation. If she had mysteries, they weren't joyful.

Since it wasn't time for recreation, no one would be in the parlor. Sister Thomas had never liked the room because little light managed to get through its narrow window. She sat in a straight chair, leaving the sofa for Sister Ignatius. That unsmiling nun took the other straight chair.

"How are your classes going this year, Sister Ignatius?" Sister Thomas tried to make the question sound like normal conversation, but since she almost never conversed with Sister Ignatius, it didn't.

"Not well. There should be more emphasis on mathematics. The girls are incompetent at it. One year of algebra and another of geometry are not enough to prepare them for college. Too few of them take advanced math." She seemed to be reproaching her superior.

"I'll ask Reverend Mother Cecilia to consider that." Sister Thomas tried to sound agreeable. "I want to discuss the murder of Mary Louise McKenna."

"Why? She's been buried a long time. What good can that do?" Since Sister Ignatius was never particularly gracious, the answer did not seem as jarring as it would have if another nun had said it.

"I have been thinking about it." She asked about what Sister Ignatius had done on that day. There was nothing unusual about her list of actions.

Sister Thomas found it difficult not to be as bored as she usually was when she spoke with Sister Ignatius.

"When you said what you did that day, you don't mention praying with your class. Did ask your class to pray for Mary Louise's soul?"

Sister Ignatius frowned. "Why should we say prayers during algebra class? If the girls had any sense, they would have prayed silently by themselves."

That bald statement was so true to Sister Ignatius's character that Sister Thomas decided it wasn't suspicious, so she put it aside to consider further at a later time.

After evening prayers, she asked Sister Veronica to come to the parlor. That nun smiled as if Sister Thomas were honoring her by speaking with her. Sister Veronica probably knew her smile increased her prettiness.

They walked in silence to the gloomy parlor. Sister Thomas sat and gestured for Sister Veronica to do the same.

"How are your English classes going, Sister Veronica?" Sister Thomas tried to make her voice cheerful.

"They are going very well, Sister Thomas," the pretty nun announced in a tone evincing a permissible degree of pride. "You know that most of the girls like the subject. The juniors are now reading *The Scarlet Letter*. That's a good lesson for them."

Since it was unlikely that any girls in Montgomery County, Maryland, in 1963 risked having scarlet letters pinned on them for sins of the flesh, Sister Thomas was not sure the lesson would be especially helpful. However, it might make them wary of clergymen, which unfortunately could be a wise precaution. "I'm glad your classes are going well. I knew they would be. I wanted to ask you a question about something in the past." She decided not to request a detailed recitation of Sister Veronica's day but simply to ask the question that puzzled her. "I have been thinking about the killing of Mary Louise McKenna."

Sister Veronica gasped. "That poor girl. I can't bear to think of it. What a tragedy."

Sister Thomas nodded. "Indeed. I am sure it injured all the girls in her class. When I was going over my old notes, I saw you didn't mention asking your class to pray together for the repose of her soul. Did you not remember to tell me that or was there some reason that you didn't pray with them?"

Sister Veronica drew away. An angry look shot into her eyes. "There was evil in that classroom. It didn't feel like a place for prayer."

Sister Thomas's heart thudded. She stared at Sister Veronica. "Evil?"

Sister Veronica nodded. "I was reluctant to tell anyone. The sin was too terrible. I couldn't force myself to make an accusation. But I had suspicions." Her voice sounded proud, almost gleeful. Her eyes gleamed.

"Why on earth wouldn't you tell me your suspicions? Finding out who did it was incredibly important."

"I thought no one would believe me. But I knew that one of the girls hated Mary Louise. I could feel the hatred emanating from her. When I hinted that she might be responsible for Mary Louise's death, she acted shifty. But I was afraid to accuse her. I didn't want to make a mistake that could ruin her life if I were wrong. Besides, her parents might sue the school if we accused her."

Sister Thomas had long since lost her patience. "Which girl? Having said this much, you must tell me her name."

Sister Veronica sighed as if she were reluctant, but she clearly enjoyed her pronouncement. "Maureen Collins."

"Maureen Collins?" The accusation made Sister Thomas feel as if she were going to vomit. "But she was distressed for the rest of the year."

"Yes. Because she was guilty. Instead of acting brazen, she hid behind a mask of sorrow. That disgusted me." Sister Veronica's voice showed her distaste.

Sister Thomas also felt distaste, but not for Maureen. "I need to think about this. Thank you for telling me." She gave Sister Veronica a nod of dismissal.

"It is a shock." Sister Veronica's voice oozed sympathy.

After the pretty nun left, Sister Thomas closed her eyes. She sat in silence. She flattered herself that she knew many of the girls, and she could not believe that Maureen could possibly be a murderer. *"If Maureen Collins is a killer, I'm Elizabeth Taylor,"* she told herself.

Instead, her suspicions turned elsewhere. After sitting alone for a long time, she decided to get a glass of the wine that the convent kept for holidays, something she had never done before.

AFTER A FEW DAYS of pondering, Sister Thomas prepared to amaze her superior. She entered Reverend Mother Cecilia's office. A reproduction of a painting of St. Cecilia by Tiepolo replaced an image by Caravaggio of St. Sebastian dying from arrows, greatly improving the atmosphere of the office. St. Cecilia was also a martyr, but fortunately she was generally not depicted in her martyrdom but as the patron saint of music. When St. Cecilia was forced to marry a pagan man, she sang to God in her heart during the ceremony. She then demanded that her husband allow her to remain a virgin, and after converting and seeing a vision, he did. Sister Thomas doubted that story.

Reverend Mother Cecilia had always been short and stocky, and now she could be described as squat. Her brain and decisiveness made her the lioness who led her pride.

Reverend Mother Cecilia would not appreciate tentative preludes.

Trying to sound her most authoritative, Sister Thomas said, "Reverend Mother, I want to talk about the murder of Mary Louise McKenna."

"You have discovered something? Please inform me." A tremor shook Mother Cecilia's usually calm voice.

"I have no proof, but I believe that Sister Veronica killed her."

Reverend Mother closed her eyes and sat silent for a moment. "Sister Veronica? Why do you believe she did something so horrible?"

"When I discussed the killing with her, she tried to pin the blame on one of her students, a girl I know fairly well. I found the accusation incredible and can think of only one reason why she would make it. I recently spoke with the girl she accused, who is now a novice with the Euphrosnyes. When I asked her about the day of the murder, she was still so frightened that I thought she might faint."

Reverend Mother Cecilia paused so long that Sister Thomas found the wait almost unbearable.

"And you are sure that the girl is innocent?"

"Almost as certain of her innocence as of my own."

"Not very doubting of you, Sister Thomas. I accept that you feel certain." Reverend Mother sighed. "What a coincidence that you mentioned Sister Veronica. I asked her to come to the Mother House, and she is here now. Yesterday I received a report from her doctor saying that she has pancreatic cancer and will not live long."

Sister Thomas gasped. "She's so young! Barely forty."

"Yes, I have been sad about her illness. But if you are certain she did this terrible deed, this is the time to confront her and ask for a confession. She must have confessed to a priest, but she should confess to us also. She should die with as clean a conscience as possible."

"I agree." Sister Thomas tried not to show her surprise at Reverend Mother's plan. Reverend Mother Cecilia had never been one to put off unpleasant matters.

"This is not a subject for a chapter meeting. Sister Veronica has been in the chapel praying about her cancer. I shall summon her here right now. You may stay here, but I shall be the one to ask her whether she did it." She picked up the phone and asked someone to tell Sister Veronica to come to her office.

Sister Thomas nodded, not showing her amazement at how quickly Reverend Mother responded.

When Sister Veronica entered, she bowed to Reverend Mother. The pretty nun's whole face sagged, and her eyes were red as blood. When she said, "Good day, Reverend Mother, good day, Sister Thomas," her voice broke.

"I hope your prayers are helping you with your sad news, Sister Veronica," Reverend Mother said, looking into her eyes. "You are about to face another difficulty. I think you may have caused Mary Louise McKenna's death. Is that true?"

Sister Veronica glared at Sister Thomas. "I know who suggested that."

"Consider that you do not have long to live, Sister Veronica." Reverend Mother's voice was the voice of Solomon.

Sister Veronica began to cry. "Mary Louise was an awful girl. She saw me kiss Alfredo."

Sister Thomas stared at her. Alfredo the wonderful gardener?

"The brat tried to blackmail me, Reverend Mother," Sister Veronica whined. "She wanted me to promise to give her As, no matter how bad her work was. She even demanded money. When I said I had none, she suggested that I steal some from the order. What could I do? I didn't want to be expelled. Alfredo wouldn't have left his wife for me."

Sister Thomas's anger overcame her. "You tried to put the blame on an innocent girl. Are you the one who made Maureen so distressed?"

"Did Maureen tell you that? What does her suffering matter compared to what I suffered?"

Sister Thomas thought it was a good thing she was a nun, or she would have struck Sister Veronica. Or perhaps throttled her.

"You should have heard the names Mary Louise called me," Sister Veronica whined. "I told her I'd meet her in the auditorium. I implied I would have the money, but of course I didn't take any. I chose that day because Alfredo and William would both be away. I didn't want either of them sent to prison for what I had done."

"How thoughtful," Sister Thomas couldn't refrain from saying. How premeditated, she thought.

Reverend Mother Cecilia shook her head at Sister Thomas, then directed her gaze at Sister Veronica.

"The order could have forgiven you for a sin of desire, but not for cold-blooded murder. The murder of one of your students. And compounding your crime by pretending another student was guilty of the murder."

Sister Veronica shook. "I repent, Reverend Mother. Please, please forgive me. I love the order."

"You have a strange way of showing it. You have damaged all of us." Reverend Mother paused. "There is one thing I must charge you to do to keep me from expelling you. You must make this known publicly."

Sister Veronica trembled. She gasped. "No, please, Reverend Mother. What about the order's reputation? What about my family?"

"What about Mary Louise's family?" Reverend Mother Cecilia said what Sister Thomas wanted to say. "They have the right to know.

Having an unsolved murder at one of our schools hasn't helped the order. How many people are haunted by the memory, not least the girl you blamed? This is the time to render unto Caesar what is Caesar's. I suspect that, given your condition, the secular authorities will let you stay in a convent until you die. They won't want to put a dying nun on trial. I shall do all I can to persuade them that is the best solution. And you should know that if you don't consent to making this matter public, I shall call the police anyway."

"Mercy," sobbed Sister Veronica.

"That is a virtue you should contemplate," Reverend Mother Cecilia said.

Sister Thomas tried to still her anger by praying for Mary Louise. She did not pray for Sister Veronica.

"Will you do what I ordered you to do?" Reverend Mother demanded.

"Yes, Reverend Mother," Sister Veronica choked in a voice that was barely audible. Tears streamed down her cheeks.

After Sister Veronica had finally stopped crying, Reverend Mother sent her to rest in the guest room where she was staying.

"You won't let her stay here, will you, Reverend Mother?" Sister Thomas did not try to conceal a note of anxiety in her voice.

"To make bids for sympathy to the other sisters? Certainly not. Please call St. Jude's Home for Ailing Religious and find out how soon they can take care of her. I shall call the press. I want her to go as soon as the news is released."

Sister Thomas would have made the same decision. "Will the cardinal let you make this public, Reverend Mother?" she asked.

"You know the answer to that." Reverend Mother smiled in a world-weary manner. "I won't tell him first."

Sister Thomas doubted many things, but she didn't doubt Reverend Mother Cecilia.

Chapter 44
Sister Rose

S
ISTER MATTHEW KEPT LOOKING at her with Oliver Twist eyes. Rose tried to ignore her. Didn't Sister Matthew understand that this kind of staring could jeopardize them both?

Rose attempted to lock her heart in a vault. She wanted to escape from feeling. Why did God let her love another person so much when she was supposed to give all her energy to worship? Why must she keep focusing on one person instead of the community? She needed to grow beyond her passion. How could she escape from it?

Rose longed to hear a loon. She must find a way to feel a connection with birds even in the convent. She needed to escape confinement during the day, when she lacked the time and private space to time travel.

While cleaning the parlor, she imagined that her arms were wings. Black and white feathers sprouted from them. Water, her only home other than the air, surrounded her. She dove, propelled down by her wings and her webbed feet. She needed fish, but diving felt more like a joy than a chore. With ease, she caught a small fish and swam underwater towards her nest among the reeds. She greeted her mate and fed bits of regurgitated fish to her two downy little ones. Her babies climbed on her back—how soft they felt. She swam along the edge of the lake.

A canoe drifted towards her. Her mate called a warning. She felt a call swell out of her throat. How good it felt. How much more powerful her call sounded than the twitters of small flitting birds and the quacks of ducks.

She swam away, towards the reeds.

Rose knew she could not become a loon but meditating on the life of the Virgin Mary and the sufferings of Christ had taught her how to envision the specifics of another being's life.

Reverend Mother Robert Bellarmine would not be happy at this use of meditation skills, Rose thought, but that seemed to be the only thing that could keep her from thinking about Sister Matthew. When Rose couldn't time travel, she could dive underwater.

Once she had discovered the underwater world, she spent more time there while she did her chores. And sometimes even in chapel.

ONE MORNING AFTER CHAPEL, Reverend Mother Robert Bellarmine stopped beside Rose and told her, "Please come to my office after breakfast, Sister Rose."

Rose's heart hammered. Had she done something wrong? She could hardly taste her oatmeal at breakfast.

She tried not to walk with unseemly haste to her superior's office.

Rose entered and strove to keep her face from showing her anxiety.

"Please be seated, Sister Rose." Reverend Mother's expression was neutral. "Is there anything you would like to discuss with me?"

"No, Reverend Mother."

"Is anything troubling you?"

Rose detected a note of concern in the older nun's voice.

"No, Reverend Mother." She had never lied to Reverend Mother before. The deceit shamed her.

Reverend Mother scrutinized her face. "Are you preparing for your first vows?"

"Yes, Reverend Mother. I think about them every day." Rose smiled, pleased at being able to tell the truth. Perhaps no other questions would require a lie.

"I have not discussed them with you for quite a while. Perhaps I have neglected you?" Reverend Mother gave her a quizzical look.

Rose gasped in astonishment. "Oh no, Reverend Mother. I don't think so."

"Is there any one of the vows that concerns you especially?"

Rose blushed. "Obedience, Reverend Mother. I try to obey all the rules joyfully, but I wish to spend more time outdoors. I try not to think about that, but sometimes I do."

Reverend Mother nodded. "We all have difficulty with obedience. We all have small areas in which we would like to be willful. We need to strive constantly. Perfect obedience is almost more than any human being can achieve. But I want to remind you about another rule." Her eyes narrowed. "Remember that particular friendships are not allowed. Do you have any difficulty with that rule?"

Rose struggled to keep from showing any emotion. "I don't have any particular friend, Reverend Mother." Now that she had broken up with Sister Matthew, that was not a lie. Maybe.

"I am glad to hear that, Sister Rose." Reverend Mother's facial muscles relaxed. "Is there anything else regarding the vows that you would like to ask me?"

"No, thank you, Reverend Mother."

"Please let me know if there is. You are a promising novice and I hope you will take your vows. You may go off to your duties now, Sister Rose."

"Thank you, Reverend Mother."

Rose walked away wondering what she would have said if she hadn't broken up with Sister Matthew. She supposed she would have lied. Thank goodness she could keep outright lies to a minimum.

Pain stabbed her heart. Her gut twisted. She shouldn't be smug about not directly lying. She had betrayed Sister Matthew. Rose bit her lip. She had betrayed her own love.

Rose told herself she could accomplish so much if she stayed in the convent. Perhaps she would become Mistress of Postulants or Novices someday. Then she would be able to help other young women and perhaps ease the rules on particular friendships. Was it too much to imagine she might someday be elected to head the order and really change the rules?

PERHAPS TIME TRAVELING WOULD help her feel better. Rose tried.

She stood high in mountains that were different from any she had seen. They looked almost flat, and their tops were fan-shaped, with bands of rock striping their sides and patches of snow near the base. But that description did not do them justice. They had such a mystical feel that Native Americans must travel to them for vision quests.

A trail began at her feet. She ascended through acres of wildflowers of every color, flowers she had never seen before. A marmot standing on alert whistled its alarm call. A bird hid among the flowers—a ptarmigan, in its summer mostly brown plumage. A few stunted conifers grew to the side of the trail, showing she must be situated at the tree line, the place where trees gave way to smaller vegetation.

She wished Sister Matthew were with her. Would they ever walk together again?

Rose dismissed the thought. No, she must thank God for this opportunity and experience it to the full, not wish for anything else. She might have been able to summon Sister Matthew to share this time travel, as she had done before, but she had given up that pleasure. She must continue to keep her distance, or risk resuming their love and hurting Mat…Sister Matthew—more than ever.

So many beauties dazzled Rose's eyes that she hardly knew where to look. The mountain on her left drew her amazement, but the mountain ahead of her also compelled her gaze. More and more varieties of wild-flowers spread before her.

She came to the top of a rise and saw below her a valley mostly covered by a long, narrow, dark-blue lake. She paused, stunned by the beauty.

Near the lake, white creatures ran across a field. Mountain goats! She had never seen any before. Why were they running?

To the left of the mountain goats, she saw a brown shape. A bear with a hump. A grizzly! The grizzly didn't pursue the goats but rather dug in the ground.

A grizzly. Her wish had been granted.

Rose found herself back in her convent bed. Tears pooled in her eyes. They weren't tears of joy. Seeing a grizzly through time travel was a poor substitute for seeing one in the world. In time travel, she had only a glimpse. There was no context. She wanted to watch the grizzly again and again, to learn more about grizzlies, to see what other animals lived nearby. What was the grizzly digging to find? An animal? Roots? She wanted to photograph grizzlies. She longed to learn where she had been, probably an American or Canadian national park, and go there. She wanted to climb that trail in the tangible world, again and again.

Her ingratitude shamed her.

What was the matter with her that time travel almost always took her to places of pleasure rather than places where she might do some good?

Rose prayed to become a better person, a better nun. Why did she keep seeking something other than God? She should empty her mind, but when she tried to, nature and Sister Matthew remained in it.

She heard Sister Matthew moan in her sleep. Rose's heart nearly broke through her rib cage. She longed to put her arms around Sister Matthew, but she must be strong.

CHAPTER 45
Sister Matthew

MEAN MOTHER MICHAEL APPROACHED me after our evening prayer. "You are summoned to Reverend Mother's office, Sister Matthew." Her eyes narrowed as if she were angry, yet her mouth smirked.

It was an unusual time for an audience with Reverend Mother Robert Bellarmine. Perhaps the visit would go just as well as my previous conversations with her, except for the one about my stolen reading of Shakespeare. I hadn't done anything like that recently. I had scrupulously adhered to the rules. Why did Mother Michael have that strange expression on her face?

I entered. "Good evening, Reverend Mother."

She did not smile. "Good evening, Sister Matthew. Please be seated."

I sat and waited for her to say more.

Her face was expressionless. "Sister Matthew, I think you are unsuited to remain in our order."

I felt as if I had been struck in the chest. "You don't think I should take my vows, Reverend Mother?" My voice faltered.

"You should leave tonight."

"Tonight, Reverend Mother?" I squeaked.

"Tonight." Her voice sounded as stern as if she believed I had murdered Mary Louise all those years ago. Had the Agatha Christies told her that?

"It has come to my attention that you have unnatural attractions to other sisters. You need to pack your things and leave."

I almost fell out of the chair. I must defend myself. "This is a mistake, Reverend Mother."

"I am not mistaken, Maureen. You are not fit to be called Sister Matthew." She hadn't used my original name since I was a postulant.

Whatever I do, I must protect Rose. She must be able to stay here. I must not mention her name. "I do not have impure thoughts about other women, Reverend Mother." I didn't say I don't love a woman or define impurity. Remembering making love with Rose was not impure. There was nothing salacious about it. "Did Mother Michael accuse me?"

Reverend Mother frowned, not showing any hint of forgiveness. "Whether your tendencies are conscious or unconscious, I have noticed them. I, not Mother Michael, am the one who realized your nature. For weeks you have been stealing glances at Sister Rose de Lima, staring at her, and trying to attract her attention, but she has ignored you. You looked at her as if you wanted to devour her. I am appalled that you obviously had impure thoughts about that sweet, pure novice. There is no point in continuing this conversation. We are returning to you the dowry your family gave us when you entered. I wish you well."

"No, you don't." I shook. Tears formed in my eyes. "Sending me off after almost two years because of some suspicion. Not giving me a chance to defend myself."

In her most regal manner, Reverend Mother rose from her chair. "The subject is closed. You do not belong in our order. Control yourself and go get your things. Do not speak to anyone else before you leave." She handed me a cheque and some cash, as well as my old driver's license for identification.

I took it without reading the amount on the cheque. What else could I do?

"Do you want any of your relatives to pick you up. Or should I call for a taxi?"

"Please call for a cab. I can be ready quickly. I hope you show other sisters more charity than you have shown me." I left her office and closed the door behind me.

Reverend Mother Robert Bellarmine cared nothing about me. That knowledge was added to the pain of the expulsion. She could be liberal about many things, but not about women like me.

My staring at Rose had betrayed me.

I would never see her again.

Packing didn't take long. Someone, probably Mother Michael, had put the suit I had worn when I entered the convent on my bed. It still was wearable. I took off my habit for the last time and folded it like a good sister.

The suit felt loose, but not impossibly so. My hair was unfashionably short, but I'd go to a hairdresser soon and ask her to cut it like Shirley MacLaine's.

I pulled up my mattress and took the volume of Emily Dickinson's poetry. I thought Mother Gabriel wouldn't mind my keeping it.

I wouldn't talk to anyone, especially not to Rose. I feared she would be stigmatized if I said goodbye. Walking past her curtains hurt.

When I passed Sister Agnes's curtains, I remembered how we had underestimated her staying power. She would probably spend the rest of her life devoutly confessing her faults and kissing the floor.

I walked past Sister Ursula's alcove and thought she would also stay in the convent, perhaps happily.

By the time I reached the front door, a cab waited in the circular driveway.

I bade farewell only to the statute of the Virgin Mary in the hall.

I hadn't said a single prayer since Mother Robert dismissed me. I didn't know whether I ever would again.

Chapter 46
Maureen

ALTIMORE WAS MUCH CLOSER than my parents' home in Chevy Chase, and I was far from ready to see them. I told the cab driver to take me to the Baltimore Best Western. I knew that was a clean and reasonably comfortable motel chain. I booked a room under my old name, Maureen Collins. My old driver's license had been placed on my bed next to my secular clothes.

I didn't cry until I entered the mercifully anonymous motel room and locked the door. I flung myself on the bed and sobbed.

I would never see Rose again.

My identity had been shattered. My name, my clothes, my home, my chapel, my community, all were gone, stripped from me.

I had lost faith, hope, and love.

At least I no longer had to pray aloud words I didn't believe. I could choose whether to pray to Possible God.

There was no one to help me fight off despair.

I couldn't tell anyone I had been expelled. I would say that after a great deal of reflection, I had decided not to take the vows.

What would I do? Teach, probably. Early November was the wrong time of year to look for a teaching job. Could I afford to go to graduate school?

Rose. My heart ached, my head ached, my arms ached, my belly ached. I wanted to scream. Rose.

I howled but tried to stop myself so the motel staff wouldn't think someone was being murdered.

Rose of my heart.

Possible God, protect her. Mary, mother of God or not, comfort her.

I didn't even have a photo of Rose. We weren't supposed to take photos of each other.

I thought of the other sisters I would miss, like Sister Ursula and Sister Catherine the infirmarian, and especially Mother Gabriel, but the loss of Rose blotted out the loss of others.

An hour or so later, I tried to think of the positive. I could see my family. Could I keep up the pretense that I had left of my own volition?

Although it was nearly midnight, I phoned my mother.

Hearing her voice saying hello made me want to sob on her shoulder and on the other hand to hide my shame from her.

"Hello, Mom. It's Maureen. I'm sorry if I woke you." I hoped she didn't discern how false my cheery tone was.

"Maureen! You must know I'd be glad for you to call me anytime. What a surprise! They're letting you phone us now? And letting you use your name with us? How are you?"

I couldn't say I felt fine. "After a great deal of reflection, I decided to leave the convent today. I'm at a motel in Baltimore."

I heard a gasp. Please, let her not be angry.

"That's wonderful! I'm so glad you made that decision. I was hoping against hope that you would."

"You're glad?"

"Yes, dear." Her voice trilled. "I prayed you would leave and lead a normal life. I always wanted you to get married and have children. But it was useless to argue with you. You've always been so strong-minded."

I sat down on the bed. "I'm not thinking of marriage."

"You've just left the convent. There's plenty of time for you to meet men. You're only twenty-three. Oh Maureen, you've made me so happy. Come home right away so I can hug you."

I tried to hide my shock. "I need a little time to collect myself first."

"But you'll come home soon, I hope. What a celebration! I'll cook all your favorite dishes."

"Um, yes, I guess I'll be there in a few days."

"I can't wait to tell your father. He'll be so happy."

"He will? He seemed so glad when I entered the convent. Won't he be disappointed?"

"Oh, honey, he put on a brave face." I could picture her shaking her head. "He knew I'd try to talk you out of it. I've always had to be the one to say the tough things to you." Her voice held a note of resentment. "He's missed you. He always grumbled about how short and stiff our visits were the whole time we drove back from the convent. We knew you had to put on an act about how great everything was there."

"Really? I'm not surprised that you didn't like the visits, but I thought he wanted me to stay."

"For someone so smart, you can be dense. Don't you remember how furious he was that you didn't know about the March on Washington? He complained about it for days. We've been so worried that you wouldn't be able to live up to your full potential. We knew you wanted to go to graduate school and were afraid they wouldn't send you. We'll be happy to help you go."

I began to cry. "Oh, Mom, I'd love that. Thank you so much. I'm longing to go back to studying English literature. I think the order would have sent me, but I couldn't be sure."

"Thank goodness you're leaving. Of course we hated nuns after we learned what happened at St. Agatha's."

The words slapped me in the face. "What happened at St. Agatha's?"

"Your nuns kept the news from you? It's been in all the papers and on the local TV news. Such a horrible thing, and it happened when you were there."

"What?" I shouted.

"One of your teachers, Sister Veronica, finally confessed to killing your classmate Mary Louise. What a horrible woman."

I almost fell over. "No! She couldn't have!"

"She did. Some nun! The newspaper said she confessed that Mary Louise caught her breaking some rule and threatened to expose her. Now Sister Veronica has cancer, so she wanted to save her soul before she died. All I could think was, thank God you weren't her victim."

I burst into sobs. I was her victim. Sister Veronica had tried to push me into feeling guilty and confessing to save herself, or at least to act so guilty that the police would suspect me. Mary Louise. The poor stupid little creep. She had tried to blackmail the wrong person.

I wondered what Mary Louise could have found out about Sister Veronica. Speculation was useless. I would never know.

Sister Thomas hadn't been questioning me because she believed I was guilty. What a relief.

"Oh dear, the shock may be too much for you." My tears had upset my mother. "I shouldn't have told you. But maybe that's better than seeing it in the news."

I managed to choke out a few words. "Thank you for telling me. That was the right thing to do." I realized that trying to absolve myself for the sin of at least hating Mary Louise—and maybe worse—was another reason I had gone into the convent. And the reason why I had never considered joining the Agatha Christies and risking spending any more time around Sister Veronica.

"Please come home as soon as possible so we can see you and hug you without having a nun standing over us. I'll cook lamb chops every night."

I closed my eyes. Things were happening too fast. "I'm still over-whelmed by my decision. I need to just sit and think for a while, but I'll come home sometime soon."

"Of course, darling. I can't wait to see you, but I understand you need to ruminate a little. Goodnight."

"Goodnight, Mom."

I went to the sink and got a drink of water. I wished it were some-thing stronger. I had never tasted alcohol, but drinking it sounded like a good idea.

I was relieved that my mother sounded pleased, yet her wish that I marry worried me. A normal life? I am not what she means by normal.

Rose. The absence of Rose felt like a presence, an empty place by my side.

I wished I could tell her about Sister Veronica. I would never be able to tell her anything again.

Rose would miss me, but she would be fine. The sacraments would console her.

I cried.

I even cried for Mary Louise. She should have had a chance to grow up. Maybe she would have become a nicer person. I wasn't Catholic enough to believe that she would go to hell because she died in the mortal sin of committing extortion.

But Mother Veronica probably would have believed that she had sent Mary Louise to hell. Had Mary Louise haunted Sister Veronica's dreams?

I had met many nuns who annoyed or saddened me but realizing I had known an evil nun shocked me.

Visiting *Macbeth* should have enlightened me. Macbeth and Lady Macbeth blamed their murder on guards whom they had killed. Did my unconscious understand that when it took me there? Did I simply not allow myself to guess that Sister Veronica was the killer? Did my mind become blank at a crucial time because I had seen Sister Veronica behind Mary Louise, but my mind rejected the knowledge?

I wanted to visit Sister Thomas and thank her. She must have been the one who solved the mystery and confronted Sister Veronica. Dear Sister Doubting Thomas had kept searching for the murderer. She wouldn't refuse to see me because I had left another order.

After two years of the convent's beds, the hotel bed felt too soft. The silence in the room, the absence of the sounds of other sisters' sleeping, made me feel as if I were alone on an island. If only I could hear Rose's nighttime breathing.

It was almost morning when I fell asleep. There would be no need to rise for early prayers. Or perhaps ever to pray again.

CHAPTER 47

Sister Rose

R OSE WOKE AND, ON impulse, reached her hand under the curtain. No hand reached out to clasp hers.

Let Sister Matthew sleep late. Or was she too hurt to accept Rose's overture?

It was Rose's turn to ring the bell. She enjoyed the reverberating sound.

When she returned to the dormitory, she heard the muffled noises of novices dressing. One by one, they emerged from their curtains.

Sister Matthew didn't appear.

Rose opened the curtains to Sister Matthew's alcove. Sister Matthew was gone, and so were her few possessions. Her habit laid folded on the bed.

If Mattie had decided to leave, she would have said something. She must have been expelled.

Rage exploded inside Rose. She had never known rage before. Her Mattie had been dealt a terrible blow and was suffering alone.

What would she do about it? Rose thought about her life in the convent. She loved so many things, the communal prayers, the other nuns, the...Mattie. Mattie must have been forced out. Rose weighed the Congregation of St. Euphrosnye versus Mattie.

Had she been called to the religious life? Or had she been called to love Mattie? Perhaps that was why she had found her way to St. Euphrosnye's. Loving another person could also be a calling. Maybe her path was vowing to love a woman. This woman. Why would God have let them develop a deep love if they were supposed to stifle it?

Maybe she hadn't been "called" at all. God wasn't a matchmaker. Maybe she and Mattie had just found each other. That was fine. That was more than fine.

Dear God, give me the strength to choose Mattie, she prayed. Her decision was clear.

Rose darted out of the dormitory and ran down the stairs.

"You're going to be late for chapel. But you must not run." Mother Michael stood smirking at the bottom of the staircase.

Rose spoke loudly, not in a nun's modulated tones. "Sister Matthew is missing."

"She has left. We must not speak about her."

Rose trembled with anger. "Oh yes, we must. Did you send her away?"

"You are not allowed to ask about that. You must go to the chapel right now."

"No."

Reverend Mother Robert Bellarmine walked down the cloister towards the chapel door.

Rose hurried after her. "I must speak with you immediately." Rose glared at her superior.

"How dare you address Reverend Mother in that fashion!" Mother Michael glowered.

Sister Agnes, who had been walking properly down the cloister, stared at Rose and scurried to the chapel as if Rose had turned into Satan.

"Peace, Mother Michael. I shall speak with Sister Rose." Reverend Mother took command of the situation. "Come to my office, Sister Rose."

Not sparing another glance at Mother Michael, Rose followed Reverend Mother.

The moment they entered the superior's office, Rose demanded, "Sister Matthew is gone. Why is that, Reverend Mother?" Scorning to sit, she remained standing.

Reverend Mother sat at her desk and spoke in her most imperial tone. "You know you are not supposed to ask that question, Sister Rose, but I shall answer you anyway. I hope that will end your burst of temper. I asked Sister Matthew to leave because she has tendencies to improper attractions. It was necessary for her to leave."

Rose shook with fury. The truth burst out of her. "Then it is necessary for me to leave, too. I love her. I want to be with her forever."

Reverend Mother's eyes widened to saucer-like proportions. "Then you lied to me about not having a particular friend. You lied grievously."

"Yes, I lied." Rose felt not the slightest particle of guilt.

"I could see that Sister Matthew looked at you with unnatural longing, but I didn't know that she had dared to approach you."

"I am the one who approached her! I first kissed her many months ago."

Reverend Mother pulled back. "Have you taken leave of your senses, Sister Rose? How can you make such a proclamation? Do you have a fever?"

Rose tried to rein in her anger. "No," she said in a more even tone. "This convent is not the place for me. I simply love Sister Matthew. Where she goes, I shall go too."

Reverend Mother sucked in her breath. "I believed you were steadier than this, more devoted to God. Sister Rose, I shall forgive this outburst if you go to Confession and resolve to forget this attraction. I thought you were one of our most promising novices."

"You didn't give Sister Matthew that chance, did you?" Anger surged through Rose's veins again. "I'll bet she would have taken it. I don't want any more favoritism."

Reverend Mother glared at her. "How dare you question my judgment."

Rose decided to use her ultimate weapon—her knowledge. "Why don't you care about our order's history? The women who founded the Congregation of St. Euphrosnye were lesbians. Mother Nora Shaughnessy was a lesbian. You're such a scholar that I'll bet you've found that out."

Reverend Mother jerked back in her chair. Rose had never seen her so nonplussed.

"Where did you ever get such a shocking idea? Don't make up slanders about our beloved founder."

Rose pounced on her verbally. "You've done the research. I know you have. I can see it in your eyes. You have no right to exclude women with lesbian tendencies."

Reverend Mother shook with anger. "Stop telling this disgusting lie. Don't you dare ever speak of it again. Do you want to destroy our order's reputation? Do you want the Vatican to investigate us?"

"You can't tell the truth, not even to one novice. May the spirit of Mother Nora Shaughnessy haunt you forever." Rose moved towards the door. "Do you know where Sister Matthew went?"

"No. I ordered a taxi for her. She might have gone to her parents' home."

"Goodbye, Reverend Mother. You can call a taxi for me too."

Rose stormed upstairs to get her things. She imagined Mattie packing as quietly as possible. How could Mattie not have told her what happened? Rose blamed herself for her coolness to Mattie. Breaking up with her had been cruel and insane. But dear Mattie would forgive her.

A frowning Mother Michael brought some money, a check, and the clothes Rose had worn when she entered the convent. "Sister Rose, let me try to dissuade you from this precipitous—"

"No." Rose grabbed the clothes from her and turned her back.

The Mistress of Novices had no choice but to withdraw.

On her way out, Rose saw no beauty in the statues in the hallway. Instead, she pictured Mattie walking miserably out of the door.

The cloisters no longer looked beautiful. The garden, faded this late in the year, looked like a withered Eden. Let Archangel Michael tend it.

Mother Michael, who had never liked Mattie, had her way after all.

ROSE OPENED THE TAXI door and climbed in the yellow coach to another world. She asked the driver, a white man with gray hair, "Did you pick up a woman who left here last night?"

He didn't turn around, but she could see his widened eyes through the rearview mirror. "No. I just started my shift."

"Would that driver still be on duty?"

"No."

"Your company must have a record of where he took her. Could you please find that out for me?"

"Hmpf. I can't ask, and they won't tell."

Anxiety surged through Rose. "Please try. She is a friend of mine. We both decided to leave the convent. We're going to take a trip together. But she forgot to tell me where she was going last night. I need to find her," Rose pleaded. Lying didn't worry her. "Please, sir."

The driver sighed. "I guess it wouldn't do any harm to ask. My dispatcher might think that I'm crazy, or you are." He picked up his handset. "Calling dispatch. Number 32 calling dispatch."

"What is it, Number 32?" The voice sounded weary.

"This is a little strange, but I just picked up a woman at St. Euphrosnye's Convent—no, she isn't a nun. I would have said 'nun' if she was a nun—and she says another woman left the convent in one of our cabs last night. She wants to know where the driver took that woman. Can you tell me? No, I don't think there's anything fishy about it. They both used to be nuns. Can you find the record?" He paused and kept driving. After a few minutes, a sound came from the handset. "Okay, thanks, Harry."

The driver turned his head. "You're in luck. Our records say she went to the Baltimore Best Western."

Rose sighed with relief. "Thank you so much. Please drive me there. I'll give you an extra tip for your trouble."

"Okay. I like to make customers happy."

Rose veered between feeling delight at the prospect of seeing Mattie and shame over breaking up with her. She tried to find the words to apologize.

As the taxi bore Rose past wooded areas and fields, the world opened to her. She would walk again through forests and beside rivers. She would climb mountains and see crashing ocean waves. She would hear loons again and maybe even see a grizzly bear. She would visit the Rocky Mountains and the Pacific Northwest.

She would meet people, many people, not just people to pass by in stores but people to know. She might never be as brave as the Freedom Riders, but she could march in protests. That would be a prayer.

Her idea of prayer expanded. Living was a prayer.

Why had she imagined leaving the convent meant being trapped in a house with one other person? Love did not have to be a trap.

Mattie had opened the world for her. She was riding to Mattie. She was riding to the world.

Chapter 48
Maureen

WHEN I WOKE, DAYLIGHT illuminated the motel's white walls and bedspreads.

The absence of Rose, the impossibility of seeing Rose, dimmed the light.

Ex-nuns don't commit suicide, do they?

I chided myself. There was still a world out there, and I had an obligation to do a little bit of good in it, even if I were miserable. My parents would be unbearably hurt if I did myself in. I didn't need a priest to tell me that.

I wasn't hungry, but I thought I should eat. A card on the nightstand said the motel provided breakfast. I went downstairs and found the area where food was laid out. I took a sweet roll, a banana, and cereal and returned to my room.

I forced myself to eat and tried to plot my next moves.

I should buy toiletries and a few more clothes. Secular clothes seemed ridiculous. What on earth should I buy? It was autumn, so I needed something warm. A couple of sweaters and a coat. An umbrella. I made a list.

No, I probably didn't need that much. I had asked my parents to give away my clothes, but if my mother had hoped I would return, she may have kept some of them.

Was it late enough in the morning to call Sister Thomas? I might as well try.

I called directory assistance and got the number of St. Agatha's Mother House. I dialed.

A sweet-voiced nun answered the phone.

"Could I please speak to Sister Thomas? This is Maureen Collins."

"Just a moment."

Almost immediately, a familiar voice came on the line. "Maureen! Sister Matthew! I'm so glad you called. I was going to call you."

I summoned up my courage to mention my departure, but my voice choked. "I left the order yesterday."

"I'm sure you considered it seriously and did the right thing, Maureen. The convent isn't for everyone."

Tears of gratitude formed in my eyes. "My mother told me the news."

"Yes, we were unknowingly harboring a murderer." Anger pulsed through the phone lines. "I hope she didn't hurt you."

My tears began to flow. "She accused me of killing Mary Louise. She kept at it."

"That wretched woman! How could she? I was afraid something like that had happened. You were so frightened when I saw you at St. Euphrosnye's."

"I thought you were investigating me."

"I would never have imagined you could be a murderer. That woman suggested it to me. That's what made me guess she had done it. I'm so sorry she persecuted you at our school. I wish you had come to me then, but I can understand that you were too intimidated."

"Thank you, thank you, for finding out the truth, Sister Thomas. I can never thank you enough."

"It was my duty. I'm sorry it was so long delayed. I hope you will come to see me. I probably understand what happened to you better than anyone else could."

"You do. Thank you, Sister Thomas. I'll come soon."

"Please do."

I felt too overcome with emotion to talk any longer. "I shall. I need to cry a little now. Thank you again."

"You do have a great deal to think about. There is a life after the convent. Have a good day, Maureen."

"Good day, Sister Thomas."

I sank onto the bed. Sister Doubting Thomas was now my patron saint. I would tell her how I had blacked out the memory of whatever happened when Mary Louise was murdered. I think I would even tell her that Sister Veronica's taunting made me wonder whether I really had killed Mary Louise.

After dwelling on Sister Thomas and the dreadful Sister Veronica, my thoughts turned back to Rose, and I cried for another reason.

Could I see Rose in time travels? It had happened before. I mustn't count on that. She hadn't time traveled to see me since she broke up with me. She couldn't love me as much as I love her.

I need to go to a bank and deposit the cheque from the convent. No, I had closed my account before I entered the convent. I would have to open a new one.

I shouldn't be so angry at Reverend Mother Robert Bellarmine. She was following the rules. Although she might not have been charitable to me, I should be charitable to her. The rules dictated that women who loved women must leave the order, but she lacked absolute proof that I was one. Why was it so difficult to be liberal about women like me? Or even compassionate?

I tried to push myself to go out and buy supplies, but I wanted to get under the covers and sleep forever.

A while later, I heard a knock at the door.

"I don't need the room cleaned." My voice faltered.

The knocks continued.

I forced myself up out of the chair and opened the door.

Rose.

I swayed.

She took me in her arms, propelled me back into the room, and sat me on the bed. She plopped down next to me.

"I should have called first," she said. "The shock was too much."

"Rose," I whispered.

She wore secular clothes, a gray suit.

Her sweet, short, dark brown hair, so long covered, awakened my desire to stroke it.

"You're not wearing your habit. You didn't leave, did you?"

She looked into my eyes. "I left as soon as I heard what happened to you. How could you imagine I would stay?"

"Oh Rose, you shouldn't have. You love the convent so much."

"Not as much as I love you, Mattie." She smoothed my hair.

"I'm just sorry you had to go away alone. I thought you probably were in a motel or hotel, but I had to persuade the taxi company to tell me which one."

I held back from touching Rose. Her words seemed too good to be true. "I'm afraid you'll be unhappy out in the world. You can go back to the convent."

"No, I can't, and I don't want to." She held me tight. "I told Mother Robert that I loved you and had to be with you."

"Rose!" I sobbed on her shoulder.

"We'll always be together, Mattie."

"Thank you, thank you." I clung to her.

She loved me. She had come to be with me. We could make love in the real world. We could sleep together.

"I can't believe you're really here," I told her.

"Let me show you that I am." Rose kissed me even more fervently than she ever had before.

The taste of her skin, the taste of her tongue thrilled me. I had never thought to taste her again, to rub my face in her hair, to smell the sweet back of her neck.

Her breasts! I uncovered them and pressed my face into them. She kissed the top of my head.

Then she slipped off my clothes and kissed me, from my head to my feet. She stroked me until my skin thrilled so much that I thought I would float away.

My senses were even sharper than they had been when we made love during time travels. Every touch overwhelmed me.

Rose parted my legs and touched me softly, then slipped her tongue into me. I cried with delight because she had returned.

She moved her tongue gently, then more urgently. I flowed to meet her.

Then she rested on me, giving my already heated body even greater warmth.

"Thank you, thank you for wanting to be with me," I sobbed.

"I am so glad I'm here," she said, kissing me with a mouth still full of me.

I moved to my side and began joyfully to make love to her.

Each touch thrilled me more. She blended into me and let me taste her dew.

My life would now be filled with joy.

After a few hours, I said, "We'll need food sometime."

Rose groaned. "I don't want to go out."

I smiled at her. "We don't have to. There's an ad on the desk for a pizza place. We can call to order a delivery. What do you like on your pizza?"

"Whatever you want. There wasn't enough pizza in the convent."

After eating and more lovemaking, finally we decided it was time to try to sleep.

I could scarcely believe the miracle of sleeping next to Rose. I nuzzled her shoulder and kept my head there. She would not disappear. I wanted to stay awake all night just to experience lying in bed with her, hearing and feeling her sleep. But I must have drifted off.

CHAPTER 49
Rose

ORGIVEN. ROSE REJOICED THAT Mattie had forgiven her. She snuggled tighter to Mattie. How could she have imagined living without ever experiencing the pleasure of sleeping beside Mattie?

Rose felt no need to time travel. Far from it. She felt perfectly content.

But she found herself in a large crowd of women. They were marching on a city street in the dark. How strange. Whoever heard of a nighttime march? Signs said, "Women Unite! Take Back the Night." The marchers chanted, "Women, united, will never be defeated!" "Mujeres, unidas, jamas sera vencidas!"

The other women were wearing pants, and so was she.

Mattie marched next to her. There were lines in her face, her hair had turned gray, and she had put on a little weight. She took hold of Rose's hand, right out in public.

Mattie would be in her future life. Rose sighed with relief. Somehow things would turn out well. They would even find a community of women. Someday, somehow.

She heard a loon calling in the distance.

CHAPTER 50

Maureen

THE NEXT MORNING, I woke beside Rose. In a bed. After sleeping together the whole night. It was a miracle. I drank in her scent.

Could life possibly continue to be this good?

Rose had chosen me.

Thank you, Possible God. You didn't really believe in all those regulations anyway, did you? You didn't care about having all those virgin brides.

She stirred beside me. I touched her arm.

"Mattie?" She opened her eyes. "Mattie!" She kissed me.

I still worried. "I hope you won't regret leaving the convent."

She shook her head. "No. I think you're the one who had a vocation, not me."

I stared at her. "A vocation? When I don't even believe in anything the Church teaches?"

"But you were seeking. I was just escaping from life."

"You broke off from me so I wouldn't distract you from being a good novice."

Rose shook her head. "So I wouldn't distract you also."

"Really? Is that possible?"

"Do you think I would lie to you?"

"Of course not."

"I've discovered many things about myself." She spoke shyly. "I want to learn how to be a park ranger or something like that."

"A park ranger?" I was afraid I used too high a pitch. "That's a big change from being a nun. But you'd be great at it."

"I hope so. I know you want to teach English. Do you care very much where you go to graduate school?"

"Yes. I want to go exactly where you want to be, in a place where you can do what you want to do. Maybe the University of Montana?"

"Oh, Mattie. We'll find a place that's right for both of us."

Rose kissed me deeply.

"We don't need the convent. The path to the spiritual is in nature for me, as it is in literature for you."

I gasped with delight. "Yes, it is!" I mulled those words. Literature is the path for me. That's true.

I snuggled up to her. "There's so much I have to tell you. But not right now." At last I could mention Mary Louise's death. That still would be difficult. How do you tell the woman you love that you had thought you might have murdered another girl?

"I have so much to tell you too. I learned incredible things about the founding of the Euphrosnyes. Mother Nora Shaughnessy and the other founders were lesbians!"

I almost fell off the bed. "You're kidding."

"No, they were. I met them in time travels. I don't know whether they were still sexually involved after they started the order, but they definitely saw themselves as lesbians. They would never have instituted the nonsense about particular friendships. I confronted Reverend Mother with that knowledge. She denied it vehemently, but I believe she had learned or suspected that they were."

I shook my head in wonder. "You're even more amazing than I knew. What an incredible time travel."

"I wanted to learn about the beginning of the order, and I certainly did." Rose paused. "Maybe I won't need to time travel any more now that we can be together."

My heart soared. Being with her in the real world was far better than time travel.

"The world outside the convent won't be mundane now that I'm with you," I said, stroking her cheek. "I'll buy a cookbook and learn to cook. I want to cook for you."

"You certainly know how to cook me." Rose gave me a wicked look and kissed my nose. "Our life will be an adventure. I can't wait to take walks with you, not just in the woods, but everywhere. Doing things with you will make them special." She sounded genuinely happy at the prospect.

"We have years to learn to know each other better and better." I kissed her and looked into her dear blue eyes. "Do you have relatives or friends you want to tell about leaving the convent?" I hated to ask because I thought she didn't, but I had to.

"No, I don't." She kept her voice brave. "My ultra-pious Uncle Tim will be annoyed that I've left the convent. He'll say something sarcastic. I can wait to tell him. I just want to be with you."

I put my arm around her and held her tight.

She didn't say the Euphrosnyes had been her family, but we both knew it. She loved them so much more than I did. Yes, I admit I had loved them—some of them. I would miss Mother Gabriel the most. And Reverend Mother Robert Bellarmine, however unrequited my caring for her had been.

"Do you know what I thought about when I was afraid I was dying of pneumonia last winter?" she asked. "Besides longing to be with you. I wanted to see a grizzly in the wild."

I had expected her to say something about God. "You thought of grizzlies when you believed you might be dying?"

Rose nodded. "I think I knew then that meant I wanted to leave the convent. That's probably why I resisted so much when you suggested it."

"I'd like to see a grizzly too. We'll travel to the national parks." The prospect delighted me. "You can teach me all about birds."

"We'll see the world. It's not morally wrong to want to see the world." Rose beamed.

My parents won't be thrilled if I move away from Maryland, but at least I'll be more authentic with them than when I was in the convent. At some point I'll break it to them that marriage and children still aren't in the cards. They will become fond of Rose, after they get used to the idea that she and I will live together. I hope that will be soon. I'll have to call her my friend, at least at first. But we'll be together.

THE END

If you enjoyed this book, please review it so other readers can know about it. That would help me out a lot.

Find me on Goodreads

https://www.goodreads.com/author/show/206327.Carol_Anne_Douglas

Amazon Author Page

https://www.amazon.com/Carol-Anne-Douglas/e/B001KCRC3K

Acknowledgments

I WANT TO PARTICULARLY thank Nancy Manahan, co-editor of the ground-breaking anthology *Lesbian Nuns: Breaking Silence*, which first brought forth the stories of lesbians in the convent. Nancy's personal story, though not depicted here, was an inspiration for this book.

I thank my friends who have lived in convents for helping me with many details about convent life: My cousin, Daniele Flannery, and my friends Nancy Manahan, Jamie Malagrino, Sharon Rodgers, and Luanne Schinzel.

My editor, Laura Ownbey, provided a great deal of guidance in developing the book. I appreciate her help.

I am very grateful to my beta readers, Becky Bohan, Nancy Manahan, Elena Graf, Sara Fleming, Linda North, Anne Benedicte Damon, Ruth Baetz, and Marian Grace. I am also grateful to Liz Quinn for proofreading these pages.

Many thanks to Sara Yager for making a beautiful trailer for this book.

I thank Terry Roy for designing the cover and laying out the print and e-books. Terry's endless patience is just as great as her skill.

My life is enriched by many friends. I am grateful for their constant support of my life and my writing, especially Virginia Cerello, Tacie Dejanikus, my cousin Daniele Flannery, Vickie Leonard, Tricia Lootens, my cousin Colise Medved, Liz Quinn, and Betty Jean Steinshouer.

Books by Carol Anne Douglas

Novels
Lancelot: Her Story
Lancelot and Guinevere

For Young Adults
THE MERLIN'S SHAKESPEARE SERIES
Merlin's Shakespeare
The Mercutio Problem

Nonfiction
Love and Politics: Radical Feminist and Lesbian Theories

About the Author

CAROL ANNE DOUGLAS IS a long-time feminist. She worked on the feminist news journal *off our backs* for 35 years. Carol Anne taught free classes in Feminist Theory for several years through the Washington Area Women's Center and taught Feminist Theory for a decade at George Washington University. She is an active member of Old Lesbians Organizing for Change (OLOC). She has written several novels: *Lancelot: Her Story, Lancelot and Guinevere, Merlin's Shakespeare,* and *The Mercutio Problem,* and a feminist theory book, *Love and Politics: Radical Feminist and Lesbian Theories.* An avid birder, she spends as much time as she can in nature. She lives in the District of Columbia (and supports statehood) and winters at Carefree Community in Florida.

Visit me online!

Website
http://www.carolannedouglas.com/

Goodreads
https://www.goodreads.com/author/show/206327.Carol_Anne_Douglas

Amazon Author Page
https://www.amazon.com/Carol-Anne-Douglas/e/B001KCRC3K

Facebook
https://www.facebook.com/carolanne.douglas.946

Twitter
https://twitter.com/CarolAnneDougl1

www.ingramcontent.com/pod-product-compliance
Lightning Source LLC
Chambersburg PA
CBHW021320250626

47155CB00002B/559